Eat, Pray, Hex

CRESCENT MOON MYSTERY #1

TARA LUSH

COVER DESIGN BY

LOU HARPER / COVER AFFAIRS

EDITOR

THE AUTHOR BUDDY

To all the women in midlife out there…
You are magic.

Chapter One

In the days before my wedding, my mother bestowed on me a nugget of her wisdom. Now two decades later, I repeated her words like a mantra as I climbed out of the car.

"Sweetie," she purred, holding her martini like it was a holy chalice, "when it comes to love and real estate, remember the golden rule: don't settle for a fixer-upper unless he's got a personal renovation crew and six-pack abs."

Back then, I promptly ignored her advice.

Here's how that went: after twenty years of marriage, the alleged love of my life screwed his secretary. Who was also my secretary, since Chad and I owned the business together. I tossed his beloved $360 Eton twill button-down shirts into the pool, then our marriage sputtered to an end with a lengthy court battle over alimony and our business. That was a few years, and many tears ago.

As I walked up the steps of the Crescent Moon Inn, I vowed not to ignore Mom's advice a second time. Why would I ever want to own anything here, in Florida? This place was definitely a fixer upper, I didn't see anyone with six-pack abs around, and I was absolutely selling this dump the second I got the chance.

Hopefully, that would happen by sundown. Or sooner. Then I could blow this pop stand and head somewhere interesting. Like four hours south to a spa resort in Miami Beach. Or a hotel on Sanibel. Margaritas, the ocean, and the blissful sound of silence awaited.

But first, this mess. And boy, was it ever a mess. I averted my eyes from the peeling paint.

With careful movement, I set my backpack down on the porch and adjusted the fanny pack I'd slung around my waist. Would my suitcase be okay in the car? A plaintive meow wafted from the backpack. It was one of those specialized cat carrier packs, with a bubble-like, half-sphere so the cat could see out. There was a commotion inside the bag and a rustling, then a feline face popped into the plastic window.

I kneeled before him, as if he was a small, trapped king. The hem of my knee-length cotton dress skimmed the faded, painted blue wood porch. "You okay, Freddie?"

He meowed again, which made me want to grin. Whenever Freddie was in the backpack and stared out the little bubble, he looked like a furry orange astronaut. He hated the thing, but there was no way I was leaving him at home in California with a cat sitter. I'd done that when moving my daughter into college and he hadn't eaten for a week afterwards.

"I'll let you out soon. Promise," I said, jamming a finger through one of the several small holes in the plastic bubble. Freddie responded by rubbing his nose against my fingertip.

"Hang tight, buddy."

Straightening my spine, I glanced at the old, wooden door, unsure if I should open it or if there was a buzzer. The place was an imposing, three-story Victorian, with faded dark yellow paint that was more Addams Family than quaint historic relic.

As I was about to touch the knob, the door swung open. I stepped back, surprised.

"Well, hey there, darlin'!"

I didn't say a word. Couldn't. Because I was taking in the tall man standing before me. He was clad in faded jean shorts, a Hawaiian shirt that clashed with his neon green flip-flops, and a royal blue trucker cap that declared "Gator Country." Both his long, reddish-gray hair and salt-and-pepper beard were as wild as the Florida Everglades, and I thought I spied a pukka shell necklace around his neck. His skin had the hue and texture of someone who hadn't developed a sunscreen habit.

"I'm Amelia Matthews," I blurted. "Hi."

He beamed. I thought he might be missing a tooth somewhere on the side of his mouth, but it was hard to tell, and impolite to stare. Making this more awkward, the intense September sunshine was beating down on me. I was horrified to realize a trickle of sweat was running down my bare leg.

I was used to dry heat, not this. It felt like I had stepped into the inside of someone's mouth.

"Amelia! That's a nice name. I'm Jimbo. The day manager here at the hotel. Real glad you're finally here. Come on inside. Wait, what am I doing, inviting you in? You own this dang place. Get over here, girl."

He held his arms out, as if expecting a hug.

I do not hug strange men. Or men at all.

Not wanting to offend a guy who was technically my employee, I extended my hand. "It's so good to meet you, Jimbo."

My worries about offending him were unfounded because he grabbed me and shook vigorously while beaming. He patted my hand with his free one, and now I was trapped in his sweaty grasp. "My deepest condolences about your aunt, Miss Matthews. Sorry we're meeting under these circumstances."

"Thank you. I appreciate that." I tried to pull my hand away, and he clasped it for another beat. Finally, he let go.

"She sure loved this old place. I visited her here as a kid."

At least, that's what my family had told me over the years. I didn't remember squat.

"Well, come on in and take a walk down memory lane." Jimbo stepped aside to allow me to walk through.

As I picked up the backpack and stepped over the threshold, my cat decided now was the time to let out a long, plaintive wail. His face was pressed against the plastic, making his head look enormous. I stifled a giggle as I set the pack on an old chair swaddled in red velvet.

"I didn't realize you had an animal with you," Jimbo said.

My hands flew to my cheeks. "I'm so sorry, I thought I mentioned that in my emails. It's been so hectic since finding out Aunt Shirley passed. If it's a problem, I can stay somewhere else."

Somewhere that didn't smell like mold and dust and the faint hint of creepy secrets lingering in the air.

A quick sweep around the lobby — I used that term loosely, since this was more of a showroom for oddities — revealed a collection of peculiar artifacts adorning dusty shelves and crowded display cases. I mopped the sweat off my forehead with my palm. It was also a bit stuffy inside, as if the humidity was seeping through the walls.

Old hardcover books, unidentified things in jars, a painting of a long-dead, stern-faced man…

A brief thought hit me: the dude in the painting was someone's long-lost relative. I blinked several times, trying to adjust my eyes to the low light after being in the Florida sunshine. Was the guy in the painting holding a … skull?

I leaned in, momentarily mesmerized. Yep, that was a skull, all right. I steadied myself on the back of the velvet chair and immediately felt a static shock. Yow.

"It's not a problem at all. We allow pets here. But we can waive the cleaning fee for the hotel's owner." Jimbo's friendly southern drawl ripped me away from the strange painting. "Come on over to the front desk. I've got a buncha stuff to give you."

Still dazed, I shuffled over. It was an actual roll-top desk, and Jimbo sucked his teeth while he flipped the pages in a book. There was a thick electronic device on the desk that looked more like an eighties word processor than a laptop. Apparently, the inn's check-in system hadn't been brought into this century. Or into the last one, either.

"I've got a whole dang packet for you. Where is it?" He muttered for a while as I inspected a bell jar on a shelf. Inside the glass was a giant insect that spanned the length of my palm.

"Is this from around here?" Jimbo looked up and I pointed.

"Sure is. We have cockroaches as big as Buicks."

He stopped chuckling when he saw the horror on my face. "But we have an exterminator come every month. Your aunt, Miss Shirley, she insisted on it."

"Thank goodness for that," I murmured, then scanned a

bookshelf. All seemed normal there, with a few Jane Austen novels sprinkled amongst the Dorothy L. Sayers hardcovers.

"Aha, here we go. Sorry about all the confusion."

He handed me a thick manila envelope. When I took it, another shock zapped my hand. What was up with this place? On the envelope's front was a post-it note with my name in blocky cursive. My aunt's handwriting. A pang of sadness shot through me, mostly because I wished I'd gotten to know her better.

I knew she'd owned the place for decades. Since I didn't recall my earlier visit as a kid — Mom had said I was about six — I hadn't put much thought into it. Little did I know she was the owner of a spooky inn that would make Tim Burton jealous.

Jimbo grinned at me, hands on hips. I wasn't entirely sure what I should do with this packet here in the lobby and wanted to wash the grime of air travel off me. Freddie was probably antsy to explore — or use his litter box.

"Is it possible to get a key? I know it's early." I smiled, hoping I didn't sound too demanding.

He clapped his hands. "How could I forget? Of course! We've set aside the prettiest room for you. Has its own bathroom and everything. Wouldn't want the owner to have to share the john with anyone else."

Inside, I winced at the thought. Then again, it didn't seem like there were many guests here. The entire place had an empty, almost forlorn feeling. Back in its heyday, the Crescent Moon Inn must've been something grand, though.

While Jimbo rifled through papers and a cardboard box, a shrill ring cut through the silence.

"Sorry," he muttered. "Gotta grab this."

He picked up the receiver of an old, black phone. The

kind with a dial. I didn't think anyone still had landlines, but here, it made sense. I pretended to study the painting of the dude with the skull so I could eavesdrop on Jimbo's conversation.

"Crescent Moon Inn, this is the one and only Jimbo… oh, hey, Liz. What's shakin', bacon? Yeah, she's here. Just arrived. Yeah, I'll send her your way. Oh. You coming here? When? Half hour?" He shifted the receiver away from his mouth. "Miss Amelia, you free in about thirty minutes? Someone wants to meet you."

I turned to fully face him. "Um, sure. I need to get my cat settled, though. Who is it?"

"Someone you're guaranteed to love." He spoke into the phone again. "Come on by, Liz. Okay. Yes, yes. Later."

He placed the handset on the cradle again. "Liz Lopez. She's the owner of a new age store here in town and was a friend of your aunt's. She wants to meet you and welcome you to Cypress Grove."

Although I preferred the welcome wagon stop by another day, I smiled tightly. Saying no was difficult for me.

"Sounds wonderful. I guess I'd better freshen up then and let Freddie out of his carrier. Can I get into the room now?"

"Sure can. Here, let me show you. Follow me."

I scooped up the backpack with the meowing Freddie and followed after Jimbo. We scaled a creaky wooden staircase that still retained its grandeur.

"I'll give you the two-cent tour," he said when we were halfway up the stairs. He immediately launched into a monologue about the year the inn was built (1895), the type of trees on the property (camphor), and how many blocks it was to Main Street (six).

While he talked, I ran my free hand over the worn, wood

banister. A tingle shot up my arm, and a memory flashed in my mind, as vivid as if it had happened moments ago.

I was six and running up these very stairs. My legs pumped fast as I chased my brother, who was two years older.

"Mike. Mikeeeeeee," I hollered.

"Volume, Amelia. Indoor voice," my mother's bored-yet-firm voice called out.

I grimaced and began to tiptoe up the stairs in an exaggerated manner. This place was fun!

"Oh, it's no problem, Linda. The guests won't mind. It feels good to have a child's laughter in this old place."

At the top of the stairs, I stopped and did a half spin around the banister.

"Amelia!" My mother's voice was sharp. "If you're going to act like an animal, we'll put you outside in a barn!"

I was now at the top of the stairs, gripping that same banister so hard my hand felt hot. My feet had stopped moving. Jimbo was still talking as he walked down the hall. He soon realized I wasn't behind him.

"Ma'am? You okay? You look like you've seen a ghost."

Chapter Two

I couldn't tell Jimbo that I'd had the most vivid memory of my childhood I'd ever experienced. One that was so sharp and clear that it left my legs rubbery.

A wan smile spread on my face. So did cold, clammy sweat. Stupid perimenopause. "Everything's fine. And I'm sure there are no ghosts here."

His face crumpled for a split second. He recovered quickly, but the brief flicker of emotion made me wonder what was behind his expression. "The room's this way, ma'am."

We walked down the hall, and I strained my mind to recall more of my previous visit here. But all I could remember was the staircase. The sound of my sandals slapping against wood. The acrid smell of lemon cleaning products mixed with the comforting scent of bread. Still, it was more than I'd recalled in years. My childhood memory was so notoriously terrible that it had become something of a family joke.

"And here's your room, Ma'am." He stopped at a door.

We were at the far end of the second-story hallway. The light was wan and similar to downstairs, slightly creepy.

"Please, call me Amelia," I said. Not being a southerner, I was a little uncomfortable being called ma'am. But I was forty-seven, so maybe it was time.

"Okey-dokey, smokey." He pushed open the door. "I think you're going to love this. All of our guests do."

I was skeptical that my tastes aligned with Jimbo's and worried the room was going to be dank and heavy like the rest of the place.

But I couldn't help but let out a little squeal of surprise when I saw the room. It was an enormous space, with room for a bed and a sitting area with a golden loveseat and matching chair. Everything was decorated in feminine, soft colors of lilac, gold, and cream.

Columns of sunlight streamed through two open windows. As dark as it was in the hall and the reception, this bedroom was awash in welcoming sunshine. It was also about ten degrees cooler, probably because of the small, white window unit A/C that chugged along for dear life.

"We call this the Lavender and Lace Room. It's one of two that has an attached bath and a balcony." His voice was filled with pride, as if he decorated it himself. I mean, maybe he did, since I didn't remember anything from my childhood.

I set the backpack on a low-slung, polished mahogany coffee table. "It's lovely," I said while unzipping the back-pack. Freddie was yowling his head off.

"Sorry, I need to get him out of this bag. He's been cooped up for the flight and the ride here."

"I'll leave you two alone. Do you have any other bags? I can bring them up."

"Oh! Yes. That would be wonderful. Thank you. There's a

suitcase in the trunk." I handed him the keys.

"I'll get that right up. Remember, Liz will be by in about a half hour. I think you'll want to get to know her. She probably knew your aunt better than most."

Freddie leaped out of the open backpack and onto the gold and cream-colored rug, looking like the gentle giant he was. I straightened to stand. "Thanks. I'm looking forward to that."

Jimbo looked down at the cat. "Freddie, huh? He's a big one."

"His full name is Freddie Purrcury."

Jimbo chuckled, a deep, rich sound. "Love it. You take care, Amelia."

As I walked him to the door, he broke out in a verse of *We Are the Champions*. He sang it all the way down the hall, and I shut the door. Jimbo didn't have a half-bad voice. Meanwhile, Freddie was sprinting around the room.

First, I set up the cat food, water, and bathroom areas, keeping an eye on Freddie. He was tearing around, jumping from the bed to the floor, to the loveseat, to the back of the chair. Around and around.

"Get out all that energy, little man," I murmured.

It didn't take long to explore the spacious room and attached bath. I paused in front of the mirror above the sink. My reddish-brown hair was flat and the wrinkles around my eyes seemed overly pronounced.

There had been a time in my life where I could travel all day and arrive at my destination fresh. That time had obviously passed.

Padding out of the bathroom, I sank onto the loveseat, and Freddie dashed over my lap, punching my abdomen with his paw.

"Oof."

He barreled onto the next cushion, stepping on my aunt's manila envelope in the process. Sighing, I moved it to an end table. Probably I should see what was inside, but I had to check messages and make sure my child and my home were still standing.

The home was, but there were no offers on the listing. Bummer.

I tapped on my messages and found one from my daughter Jenny. She was in her junior year in college in Arizona and sent a photo of her standing near a palm tree in a bright yellow T-shirt.

How is Florida? Do you love it? Are you going to move there to run the inn and wear muumuus 24-7? Maybe a golf cart?

This brought a grin to my face. That was one of the few details I knew about Aunt Shirley, probably because my mother had taken thirty seconds out of her busy schedule to unload her memories of her former sister-in-law. According to Mom, Shirley's muumuus billowed around her like vibrant, technicolor sails catching the jaunty breeze of life.

"It seemed as though she carried an entire island vacation in the very fabric of her outfits, each one adorned with hibiscus flowers and palm trees swaying in harmony," Mom, ever the dramatic storyteller, said. Shirley had been my father's sister. She'd even smelled of coconut and vanilla, Mom added in our most recent conversation.

Quite an aesthetic difference from this old hotel.

I'm not quite at that point yet. Call you tonight. Love you. Be safe.

Jenny texted back a heart and a kissy face emoji.

I then tapped over to the contacts and pulled up my brother Mike's number. He was on a similar adventure as me this week, only in South Carolina. In her will, Shirley had left him a property as well, and I could only imagine it was equally as weird as the Crescent Moon. At least I hoped so.

"Ammy," he answered, calling me by my childhood nickname.

"How's it going on Sullivan's Island? Is it strange?" My eyes followed Freddie while I talked. He was poking his head under the bed, and now only his twitching tail was visible.

"Strange? No, it's incredible. I'm thinking we'll spend every summer here. The kids are going to love it. Maybe retire here in a decade or so. It's a beachfront condo, kinda small, but with gorgeous ocean views and almost brand-new furniture. How's it in Florida?"

"Hold on. You mean to tell me that Aunt Shirley left you a condo with beach views and I'm left with an Addams Family lookalike hotel in a Florida swamp, of all places?" I closed my eyes and allowed my head to tip back in exasperation.

Mike guffawed. "I thought it was near Orlando. That's not a swamp."

"All of Florida's a swamp, Mike."

My brother chortled, which annoyed me. "I'm sure it's not all that bad. I mean, is it clean? Are there bedbugs?"

I glanced over at the bed. It looked incredibly inviting, especially after a red-eye flight from the west coast. "No, I don't think there are bedbugs. My room is quite nice. Clean and well decorated. It's…"

"It's what, sis?"

"I dunno. It's weird. The downstairs is creepy. There's a painting of a dude with a skull. It's really odd and dark for Florida. Well, the room isn't. The rest is. Everyone, well, the one guy who works here, is pleasant. But it's definitely not a place I want to stay for too long. Do you remember visiting when we were young? Mom told me we visited, and today I had a memory."

"You had a childhood memory? No way."

"Yeah. We were running up the stairs. It was the strangest thing, as if it happened yesterday." Prickles of awareness flowed through me. "I remembered us running up the stairs and Mom scolding me. Did that happen?"

"Totally. And we went to that alligator park. It was heckin' amazing. Don't you remember that?"

Alligator park? One would think I'd remember a momentous occasion such as that, but my brain was empty. "Nope. Not at all. I mean, why did Shirley even give this to me? Why did you get the condo? I'm so confused, Mike."

Now that I thought about it, I should've gotten the condo. Mike was handy. He was a building contractor. He could've rehabbed this place in no time. Made a mint flipping it, even. I pictured Freddie and me lounging on an oceanfront balcony at sunset.

"Oh, one more question. Why didn't Shirley ever visit us?"

The sound of a car honking wafted into my ear. "I dunno. Dad told me before he died that they had some sort of falling out. But he didn't explain more. Did Mom say anything?"

"You know Mom. She's too busy shopping for golf clothes and holding court at the martini bar."

"Yeah, she's living the high life in Arizona. Listen, have you met any psychics while in Cypress Grove?" His voice took on a familiar teasing tone, one that every sibling in the world knows.

I let out a snort. "Oh, Mike, come on. That's some fake

news on the internet. Pfft. No one's talked about psychics."

"I dunno, entire books have been written about that area. Cypress Grove, Mount Dora, Cassadaga. I'm sure Aunt Shirley was drawn to all that woo-woo stuff. Dad did say she was into the new age lifestyle. Sounds like it, if the hotel is odd."

"There are no psychics here. Listen, I need to freshen up. I'm meeting a friend of Shirley's soon."

"Okay, keep me posted. Let me know if you participate in any séances. Maybe you'll become a witch. Join a coven. Dance under the full moon." He chortled.

My eyes rolled back in my head so hard I could see brain matter. "Enjoy your beach condo, dude. Bye."

I tossed the phone on the cushion next to me. Exhaustion tugged at my eyelids, probably because I didn't get a wink of sleep on the plane. I never could. But my mind was wide awake, going over all the possible things that could go wrong here. Or at home, where I was trying to sell our home. My home, since I was the only one living there.

Gah. Whenever I was tired, doubt and insecurities crept in. It was precisely the time I ruminated and wondered if I'd made a wrong turn or three in life. But I couldn't get caught up in that, not now.

Still, I wished I hadn't promised this Liz person I'd meet with her. I could take a nice, hot shower then draw the curtains and slip into that gorgeous bed…

No. I needed to talk to Liz. She should be able to explain my aunt's final years and possibly shed light on some crucial details.

Like why Shirley left me — a divorced mom and the former owner of a California cookie delivery service — a hotel in the middle of steaming hot Florida.

Chapter Three

Since I was a little early for my meeting with Liz, I took my time and familiarized myself with the hotel's second floor. I peeked in one room because the door was cracked, and it was every bit as lovely as my own. It was decorated in a white and light blue color scheme, and the windows looked out on a beautiful tropical garden in the backyard.

How odd. The lobby was dark and foreboding, but the five rooms were sunny, elegant, and inviting. Did the lobby and hallway need renovating before I sold the place? For the millionth time, I wished my brother was here. He knew all this stuff, whereas I knew my way around a cookie recipe and not much else.

I paused to inspect the framed photos on the walls in the hallway. I yawned a couple of times, still thinking about that large, inviting bed. That red-eye flight from the west coast had been rough.

Several of the pictures were standard inn fare: faded black and white photos of Main Street, a painting of the hotel in its better days, a collection of kitschy Florida postcards from the sixties. It was a cool time capsule, and the collection gave the place a unique, vintage feel.

Maybe with a bit of sprucing up, this place could be a moneymaker. As it was, I didn't think it had a bright future. How many guests were even staying here now? I hadn't seen evidence of any.

I paused at a framed portrait. It was of a young man, a picture that looked as though it might have been a school photo from an era gone by. It was in color, but the muted hues and the old-fashioned, pompadour hairstyle screamed 1950s. There was a brass plate underneath, and I turned on my cell phone flashlight to see better in the low light.

Leaning in and squinting — I probably needed readers, but I wasn't ready to fully accept that fact yet — I whispered the words aloud.

William "Billy" Jenkins 1938-1956

A devoted son, brother, and hotel employee

Rest in Peace

Hunh. That was weird. Why would the hotel keep a framed tribute to an eighteen-year-old who died decades ago? Yet another puzzling detail about this place, and probably one I wouldn't have time to sort out.

I shut off my flashlight and made my way down the staircase. My earlier memory came to mind, and I strained to recall more details. But, nothing.

When I was halfway down, I heard a woman shouting.

"Marvin, I did not kill that man! Did. Not. Is that what you think of me?"

Horrified, I picked up the pace and ran into the lobby.

"Wh…what's going on? Is everyone okay?" By now, I'd worked up a sweat.

A woman with the most glorious head of frosted salt-and-pepper curls and wearing a flowy caftan whirled to face me and took a dramatic curtsy. A grin spread on her face. She had a beautiful complexion, with a tawny tone and practically zero wrinkles even though I suspected she was close to my age.

The woman giggled. “Don’t panic! Everything is peachy. I’m rehearsing my lines and using Jimbo as my audience.”

I stopped next to a large, taxidermied alligator. It stood on its hind legs, its stubby forearms extended as though it was reaching for a drink.

How had I missed that when I first arrived? My head swiveled from Jimbo to the woman, then to the gator. I edged away and forced a smile. “Oh. That’s wonderful.”

“Miss Amelia, this is Liz, the lady who wanted to meet you. She got a speaking part in a local dinner theater. Isn’t that cool?”

I glanced at Liz, pasting on a smile. “Why, yes, it is.”

She approached with her hand extended. “The look on your face! I’m sorry. Didn’t mean to alarm you. It’s wonderful to finally meet you. Shirley mentioned you a lot.”

I shook her hand, my brow knitting together. “She did?”

Liz reached with her free hand to squeeze my shoulder. “I’m so sorry for your loss. It was so sudden. One minute she was having lunch downtown, the next minute she was in the hospital. Listen, let’s grab some food. I’ll give you a tour of downtown on the way. There’s a great café that has the most delicious coffee and sandwiches, yes, yes!”

“That sounds perfect.” Caffeine would give me the will to power through the rest of the afternoon. “I’m one of those people who are unusually affected by jet lag, and I’m trying to resist sleeping until later tonight. Coffee is essential.”

“Do you mind walking?”

In this heat? I wanted to ask. But didn’t, because it would

be nice to see the town on foot. I was wearing a dress and comfy sandals — an outfit that always kept me cool in the hot, dry northern California summers. Surely, I could handle walking a few blocks here in Florida.

"That's perfect, let's do it."

We said goodbye to Jimbo, who declared that he was "holding down the fort." He also added that someone was coming to take a look at the air conditioner and he hoped that was okay with me.

"More than okay." I couldn't wait to sit properly and enjoy a meal. "I'm not sure it's good for guests to walk into a warm reception area."

"We'll snip that problem in the butt, Miss Amelia. I mean, ma'am. Amelia."

I paused, then realized he was trying to say, "nipped in the bud."

Outside, it was approximately the temperature of Satan's sauna. I should've applied more sunscreen on my pale skin. We strolled down the street, which was dotted with other grand old homes and towering live oak trees. Everywhere I looked was verdant and lush. The tropical foliage seemed to be thriving in this humidity.

I was glad something was.

"It's a lovely town," I remarked, even though I had only seen a few streets so far. "Is it… always this hot at this time of the year?"

Liz hooted loudly. She had the kind of laugh that made you want to laugh as well. "Oh, honey. Is this your first time in Florida?"

"No, I've been here before. When I was young, we visited my aunt and the hotel. And I've been to Panama City Beach." I paused. "During Spring Break back in '93."

"Eep," Liz squealed. "MTV-era Spring Break! Impressive."

"There was nothing impressive about it." I snickered. "Can you imagine if we'd had social media back in those days?"

She stuck her tongue out in a mock gag. "Seriously. The heat will take some getting used to, until your blood thins out."

"Oh, I'm not staying in Cypress Grove. No, no. I'm here to assess the situation and talk to a real estate agent. In fact, if you have any recommendations, I'm all ears."

"Of course, I know tons of folks. When we get to the café, I'll give you a list of some locals. In the meantime, if you don't mind, I'd love to show you around a little bit along the way."

"I'd like that." Liz seemed genuinely thrilled to be strolling along the sidewalk with me, as if she didn't have anything else to do on a workday. Perhaps her shop was closed on Mondays.

As we walked, she explained the history of the town, starting with the Seneca Indians and ending with the reputation of "psychic capital of the world."

"So that *is* true," I mused aloud.

"Oh, yes. You didn't think it was?"

"I wasn't sure. Are you a psychic?" I immediately felt bad for asking such a blunt question. Was there an etiquette about this kind of thing? If there was, I didn't know it.

"Hee! Absolutely not. I come from a long line of psychics, but I don't have the gift. That's why I opened my store. I'm the supplier, the support system. I sell tarot cards, candles, crystals, and stuff to all the mediums in town. Although, I am taking grimoire classes."

I wasn't sure what that was, or whether I should ask. Liz continued to talk in an excited tone.

"Oh, here's something I want to show you before we get to Main Street. You're going to love this, being a cookie entrepreneur and all. C'mon, we have to cross the street."

She darted across two lanes, her muumuu flapping in the wind. There was no traffic, thank goodness, and I followed. All the while, I wondered how she knew I had a cookie business. Probably my aunt told her.

For a second, I thought she was leading me into a vacant lot, but then I spotted her pointing up at the gothic script of an arched iron sign.

"Enchanted Eternity Park," I read aloud. The gate was open. From the sidewalk, it looked like a tropical botanical garden, but now that I studied a little harder, I realized there were gravestones within. "This is pretty. For a cemetery."

I wasn't sure why Liz would choose to stop first at a graveyard, but I guess it made sense in the psychic capital of the world. Yeesh, this place was odd. Liz seemed to be a genuinely fun human, though, so I wanted to humor her.

"You've got to see this. It's the most unique cemetery in the world."

"That's a serious claim to fame."

She grinned as we walked through the iron gates. I swiped a hand over my sticky neck, thinking a bug's gossamer wings had grazed my skin. A slight chill went down my spine, and I wasn't sure if I should welcome that sensation given the temperature — or be wary of it. Jeez, this jetlag was doing a number on my body and mind.

We walked down a main road for a bit, taking in all the pretty, moss-draped oaks.

"It's a shame your aunt didn't want to be buried here," Liz

said. “But she was adamant about her plans. I even tried to talk her out of it.”

“What were her plans, anyway? I only found out that she passed because a lawyer called about the will last week. Shirley was my father’s sister, and he died ten years ago.”

Liz stopped. She stood in front of me and grabbed my hands. “Did you get her letters to you? I know she was working on them while she was in hospice.”

Letters? Must be in that envelope. I shook my head. “She wasn’t close to my mom, or to me and my brother. It’s weird, I get the feeling there was a falling out between her and my parents, but I never got the full story.”

She squeezed my hands. “I know. She talked about it a few times. I think you should begin to look for answers in the letters she wrote to you.”

I shifted away, out of her grip. We began to walk further into the cemetery. “Where is she buried, anyway?”

“She’s not. She donated her body to science. A body farm kind of thing, a new one in Pasco County.”

Liz must’ve noticed my look of confusion because she quickly added, “That’s here in Florida, a couple of hours away.”

“I see.”

Liz was picking up speed as she turned off the main road into the cemetery and led me down a dirt path. The place was surprisingly large, a fact I’d have never guessed from the street. We walked in silence for a few minutes.

“What’s the deal here?” I scurried to keep up with her. “Why is it so special? Is this where all the famous psychics are buried?”

I racked my brain, trying to recall the name of one famous psychic, but could only come up with a woman who did TV infomercials then was indicted for fraud. Come to think of it, I think she was from Florida. Probably not the best example to mention.

"No, it's not related to that at all. This wing of the cemetery," Liz stopped and opened her arms wide, "is for the recipes."

I pressed my palm to my chest, unsure of what she was showing me. "Pardon?"

Horror must have been obvious on my face because Liz chuckled again. "All of the folks buried here decided to put recipes on their headstones. Look."

"Recipes?" I asked, confused. "For what?"

She pointed at an average-sized, gray marble headstone. LOPEZ, it said on the front. There were two names, Jose and Rosalia. Next to the woman's name were the dates 1889-1987.

Liz pointed. "This is my grandmother. Now come around to the back."

I stepped around the grave, making sure I didn't step anywhere I shouldn't. Liz was squatting on the backside of the headstone, and I stared down and read the first line engraved in the stone.

"MANGO COBBLER." Underneath those words was an actual recipe carved into the rock. "Mix the first three ingredients together. Melt butter in a baking dish. Pour mix into the pan. Spoon mango evenly on top, then bake at 350 for 30 minutes until done. Wow. That's… something."

I had read thousands of recipes over the years, and I always appreciated the simple ones. Never had I read one on a headstone before.

"Her cobbler was so delicious, I can't even put it into words." Liz softly stroked the grave marker. "She'd make it for every summer get-together, and we never let a crumb go to waste."

"I'd love to try the recipe."

"It's to die for." She beamed at me and I snickered.

"I've had blueberry and apple cobbler, and of course, peach. But never mango."

"She was from Cuba, so she used mango in a lot of recipes."

Liz and I strolled through a row of graves. Each contained a recipe, and I was surprised to see that some were quite involved. Clearly a lot of thought had been put into not only the recipes, but the displays on the granite. Many were ornately carved. Works of art, even.

"All of the headstones in this section have recipes. It's become kind of a town competition. Many in town strategize for years about which recipe to engrave. It all started with the original owner of the Haunted Hearth bakery. When Edna Simmons put her recipe up for banana bread, everyone got kinda competitive. Some people are more under-the-radar and don't tell anyone, leaving that final surprise for their funeral. Oh, here's Edna."

I squinted at the tombstone as I read, then shook my head. "I think that's a lot of sugar for banana bread. And I wouldn't personally use lard."

"She died in 1959, so her recipe is a little dated. But that's the fascinating thing about this place. All of the recipes are time capsules." The excitement on her face was palpable. "Of course, everyone wants a unique recipe. There was one year, oh, about five years ago, when two people died around the same time, and they'd picked out a near-identical recipe. Total scandal."

"What were the recipes?"

"Key lime pie." She clicked her tongue against the roof of her mouth. "It's always better to pick something more obscure."

"That's quite cool. What a gem to have in the community."

I wondered what it would be like to have such tightly woven threads in a town. Although I'd lived in Sonoma for the entirety of my marriage — and had run my popular cookie delivery business there — I never felt as though I truly belonged. As a kid, Dad had moved around for his job as a salesman, and we'd tagged along. No place ever felt like home.

I inspected a few other headstone recipes. Janice Dover's snickerdoodles with a twist. Charlie Ward's bean dip. Tess Thomas's apricot ice cream.

"Wow," I muttered, more to myself. That snickerdoodle recipe looked truly delicious. I snapped a few pictures. If I still had my business, I'd add it into rotation. A twinge of annoyance came over me, because I missed my career. I needed to shove those thoughts aside this week.

"Liz, do you have a recipe in mind for your headstone? Or, is that an inappropriate question? Sorry. You're way too young to be thinking of your funeral."

Laughing, she brushed a few dried leaves off the top of Charlie's headstone. "I'm probably five years older than you."

"Forty-seven." I pointed to myself.

"Fifty. And it's never inappropriate in this town to talk about death. I have a few recipe ideas in mind but haven't decided. I'm hoping I still have a bit of time to think about it."

She winked at me, and I laughed. "Thanks for bringing me here. Truly. It's really special."

We wandered the rows of graves, with me taking photos

and her telling me the backstory of the town's departed residents.

"Here we go. This is Cheesy Louisie's grave." We stopped at a large headstone. It was a solid, tall block of near-black granite. Louise Kendall died only a year ago, according to the dates on the front of the headstone. The top was carved into a triangular wedge of marble cheese.

"Everyone in town thinks she has the worst recipe in the cemetery."

I gaped at the instructions, then recoiled in horror. "Flayed Man Cheese Ball?"

"It is the most disgusting thing. It's a cheese ball in the shape of a human face. It uses prosciutto for skin and olives for eyes."

I couldn't help but giggle. This was not happening. I did not hear that right. Or did I? "You're joking," I said as I read the recipe aloud. "Wait, you're not joking. Lightly coat a face mask with cooking spray? Then lay the prosciutto in strips to form the muscle tissue. No way..."

It was too much, or maybe I was too tired. Or heatstroke was setting in. But I dissolved into laughter, which was probably terribly rude. I doubled over, unable to contain myself.

I tried to stop, but Liz was also laughing, telling me that Louise used to bring her signature, Silence of the Lambs-like cheese ball dish to book club. "She'd arrange various crackers and fruit around it. One time she used grapes as a hairstyle. It looked like a bad rendition of a Greek god," she deadpanned.

By now, I was snort-laughing. I waved my hand in the air.

"One time, George Watson popped out an eyeball! He demonstrated how to attack someone with two fingers, some sort of martial arts move. He reached in and grabbed the olive.

But that doesn't compare to the time Louise overdid the lips, and she looked like Khloe Kardashian."

I leaned against a headstone, tears running down my face. "Stop. I'm gasping. Can't breathe. Crying!"

I hadn't laughed this long or this hard in years. When Liz suggested we take this party to the café for some sweet tea and a sandwich, I wholeheartedly agreed — but I was a little sad to leave this weird graveyard and all its wacky culinary secrets.

Perhaps, if I had time, I'd come back.

Chapter Four

The Haunted Hearth Bakery had more charm than a southern belle at a debutante ball. I walked into the free-standing, flat-roofed building, sandwiched between Liz's new age shop and a candy store on the town's main drag.

The restaurant was something else. It was painted grass-green on the outside with pink-trimmed windows, giving it a tropical vibe. And inside? It was a riot of bright colors that immediately boosted my mood—which was already pretty uplifted because of all the laughing in the cemetery.

The walls were the palest of pink hues, and the tables and chairs were all whitewashed wood. A cozy stone fireplace was in the corner, and I wondered if it ever got cold enough here in Central Florida to use it. I couldn't help but notice the colorful art prints hanging on the walls, all tropical-themed palm trees and birds.

Those prints would look pretty in my sunroom. Then I remembered I soon wouldn't have a sunroom because my house was on the market. It was another fallout from my divorce. So many changes in such a short time — and more to come, since I had no earthly idea where I'd live once the home sold.

But that wasn't my concern now. I was famished.

The Haunted Hearth was packed, and I figured we'd be stuck waiting for ages to snag a table. But Liz had connections. She knew most of the staff and half the diners, it seemed. So, we were whisked to a window-side table within minutes.

Thank goodness for the café's powerful air conditioner because Florida's heat was no joke. Liz suggested the peach sweet tea.

As we settled in, I looked around, taking in the pretty, relaxed vibe. "I expected something spookier, you know? Something with a little more dark and eerie vibes, like the inn's lobby."

Liz placed her menu in front of her. "Oh, they used to be all about the psychic-haunted theme, but they did a total makeover and went all Palm Beach on us. Better for the tourists, they said. Not really my thing, but hey, it's always busy in here. Can't believe we got a table so quickly."

Curiosity gnawed at me as I glanced over the menu. "So, what's good here?"

Her eyes lit up, "The chicken salad. Seriously, it's the tastiest I've ever had. When I was going through my divorce, I'd come here, order a quart, and devour it all by myself. It was my celebration meal for not having to share food ever again."

I smirked, "Oh, I know that feeling all too well."

She arched an eyebrow. "You divorced too?"

"Separated three years ago, the divorce was final eight months ago. And you?"

"Two years ago."

"Sorry to hear that." Her sad smile tugged at my heart-strings. "Got kids?"

"Two. My son is in college, the other's doing her own thing in Tampa. How 'bout you?"

"I've got a daughter. She's a junior at Arizona State. My marriage hit the rocks around the same time she left for college."

"A common trend. Your aunt didn't spill too many beans about your marriage, though. Interesting, huh? Considering how much she liked to talk."

I took a sip of the tea and relished the sweetness. Yep, I was in the south. "My mother mentioned that Aunt Shirley tended to spin long, elaborate tales without much point to them."

"She talked about your baking business. Cookie delivery, right? My memory's been foggy since I stumbled into peri-menopause like a gator on meth."

I chuckled. "That's a perfect analogy. Yeah, I used to own a cookie delivery business in Sonoma. Started small with catering to tourists then expanded across three counties in California."

Liz's eyes sparkled, "That's an incredible idea! Why not expand it here?"

I sighed. "Well, my husband was awarded our business. The cookie company was my idea in the early days of our marriage, and we ran it together for years. I was the baker, he was the business guy. When we divorced, he had the capital and a friendly judge who was in the same frat at Stanford."

Although maybe I could do something similar in a different state…no, what was I thinking? I had a return ticket back to California and intended to use it.

Liz's expression turned to disgust, “Ugh, men. Can't live with 'em.”

“Can't dump their bodies in a deep lake either.”

Liz burst into laughter. “Amen to that! You know what my ex is up to now?”

I tapped my finger against my chin. “Let me guess, he's off frolicking with a woman half his age? New family? Sports car?”

“Surprisingly, no.” She took a quick sip and swallowed. “He’s on a round-the-world sailboat trip. Alone. He needed to ‘be free.’ Said he wanted to, and I quote, ‘be one with the ocean.’ He posted a photo to Facebook the other day and he looked like Tom Hanks in Castaway. He’s an explorer. That’s what he calls himself. An explorer. He used to be an accountant, now he’s Christopher freaking Columbus. Which is appropriate because he’s from Spain.”

We couldn't hold back our laughter at the absurdity of it all. “Men are ridiculous,” I declared with a shake of my head.

We chatted a bit about motherhood, divorce, and living alone for the first time in decades. I was delighted to discover that she also loved cats, and we shared photos of each other’s fur babies from our phones.

Soon after, a waitress delivered our food, and my mouth watered when I saw the small mountain of chicken salad atop a bed of crisp lettuce.

“I don’t think I’ve ever had it with apples and grapes. Or pecans. And the texture! I can taste everything. It’s not mushy,” I said between mouthfuls.

Liz, who had ordered a fried chicken sandwich and fries, swallowed. “It’s the owner’s family recipe. Handed down over generations. It’s a very southern take on chicken salad.”

“Whatever it is, I’m eating every bit of it.”

Between bites, Liz told me more about the town. It was mostly the type of advice one would give a tourist. Where to find coffee, who made the tastiest key lime pie, the best place for a stroll on the shores of Lake Cypress.

"Of course, if you want a psychic reading, that's a little more difficult. So many people to choose from."

I pushed a pecan around on my plate with my fork. "I don't know if I believe in that kind of thing. I think it's wonderful that others do, but I'm not certain it would work for me. Or if I need it."

I chewed on the inside of my cheek, hoping I wasn't coming off as mean or arrogant.

Liz smiled. "I understand. I wanted you to know it's available."

"Thanks. I appreciate that and want to thank you for bringing me around town. Shedding some light on my aunt and all." Even though she'd told me only the scantest of details about Shirley. "Come to think of it, I wanted to ask. Why did she leave the hotel to me? Do you have any insight? My brother is a building contractor. He'd be a much better fit for that hotel. She left him a condo in South Carolina, though."

She nodded, as if she expected this question. Then she paused for a few beats. I'm not a fan of long, drawn-out silence in conversation, so it was difficult for me not to chime in.

Finally, she opened her mouth. "Your aunt said you have a gift."

"A gift? With what?"

"I'm sure it's in her letters. She simply said you had a true gift; she saw it when you were small, and that it was needed at the hotel. Said she'd tried to get you to come to Florida."

I frowned and stared at my plate. "About five years ago, I got a Christmas card from Shirley. It was odd, since I never gave her my address and it was the first contact I'd had with her in my adult life. But my daughter was in high school and we were busy with sports so I didn't question it. I sent one back, in fact. We sent cards back and forth, and come to think of it, in last year's card she said she wanted to talk to me about Florida."

Liz lifted her shoulders. "I'm sure you'll figure it out while you're here. Shirley was a wise woman. She had a reason for choosing you over your brother. Say, let's pay and I'll take you next door to my shop."

Nodding, I took my wallet out of my purse. Liz waved me off. "My treat. You get the next lunch."

"You sure?"

She grinned. "Absolutely."

"Okay, next time, then." Despite all of the odd things I'd learned over the last couple of hours, I knew I'd love to hang out with Liz again. From her easy laughter to her gentle demeanor, I knew this was someone I could be friends with.

We had paid and were about to leave when a trim Black woman approached our table. "Liz, hey! How was everything?"

Liz rose to fold the woman into an enormous hug. "Shawnda, it was delicious, as always. I want to introduce you to someone."

I also stood and extended my hand.

"This is Amelia Matthews. Shirley Hall's niece. You know, the one who inherited the Crescent Moon Inn. Amelia, this is Shawnda Hersey. She's the owner of this café and the mastermind behind that chicken salad recipe."

"Thank you for coming to our little restaurant," Shawnda said, giving my hand a firm shake.

"I'm honored to meet you, because that was awesome chicken salad. I haven't had any that good, ever."

"Well, thank you, honey. You staying in town for a while?"

"I don't think so. A week or so. It was kind of a shock to discover that I own an inn in Florida."

The two women nodded and beamed.

"And I'm from California." I nodded along with them. No one said anything for a beat, which made me feel awkward. It was as if they were waiting for me to come to some obvious conclusion. "But I'll be here for a while trying to get everything in order, so I'm sure I'll be back here."

Shawnda gently squeezed my arm. "I'm so sorry about Shirley. She was the best. We're all glad she didn't linger long in her state."

"Thanks. I appreciate that. I'm glad to see she had such great friends here in town."

"She did. And for your planning purposes, we make extra chicken salad on the weekends. That's when people buy it in bulk, for picnics and parties." Shawnda winked.

"Get here early," Liz chimed in.

We waved bye to Shawnda, with me promising to return for the Friday fish fry. Liz and I walked next door to her store. As I suspected, it was closed on Mondays.

"Welcome to the Astral Attic," she said while unlocking the glass door.

We stepped inside, and she turned on the main light. "Hang on, I want you to get the full effect. Let me turn on the music and the fairy lights, too."

The sound of the *snap-snap-snap* of switches being turned on filled the store.

Soft, warm light twinkled from the ceiling, casting a gentle glow over the shop. The air carried a soothing scent of sandalwood and lavender.

"It's so pretty," I squealed. I'd been in many new age shops in my decades in California, but this was the most gorgeous one I'd seen so far.

The walls were adorned with tapestries depicting mystical scenes of cosmic journeys and celestial wonders, handcrafted by local artists. Shelves lined with an assortment of crystals in every hue imaginable shimmered with a subtle energy. Amethyst, rose quartz, and citrine stood beside lesser-known stones like labradorite and moonstone.

Liz led me further into the shop, the wooden floorboards creaking softly under our steps. A cozy reading nook beckoned with velvet, hunter green cushions and an inviting armchair nestled between towering bookshelves filled to the brim with volumes on tarot, astrology, and dream interpretation. Leather-bound grimoires shared space with contemporary self-help books.

The Astral Attic had it all. Gentle wind chimes. Delicate dream catchers. A hand-carved wooden table showcased a collection of intricate pendulums. Beside the table stood a glass display case, housing an assortment of carefully selected talismans and amulets.

"Protection, luck, love. What do you need? I've probably got it," Liz quipped.

"I'll take a heavy dose of all three," I joked. "Well, maybe not love. I'm not prepared for that yet."

With the chilled-out, ambient music playing in the background, I poked around the store. Liz went behind the counter and began opening a stack of mail. After several minutes, I approached her.

"Love your store. I'm going to return when I have more time. I probably should get back because of Freddie. He's been in the hotel room alone for a couple of hours."

"I completely understand. We'll see each other again, I'm certain of it."

"Thanks for all of your hospitality and for lunch." I paused, wondering if I should ask her a question that's been on my mind since earlier in the hotel hallway. "Since you grew up here, I'm curious about something at the Crescent Moon."

Something that had lingered at the recesses of my brain since we left the inn.

"I can try to help, although history isn't my strong point. I'm much more interested in," she waved her hand around the store, "a different kind of universe."

"Of course. I saw something there at the inn. A framed photo of a young man who died several decades ago, with an engraved brass plaque underneath. I found it odd that he'd be memorialized like that. William Jenkins. Billy. Does that ring a bell?"

Liz beamed. "You're learning a lot about the town."

I didn't say anything for a second. "What happened to Billy?"

Liz shrugged, her eyes flickering with a mix of mystery and mischief. "Well, hun, here's the kicker – no one knows. It's unsolved, has been for decades."

"Great," I muttered, feeling the hairs on my neck prickle. "So, what's the story?"

Liz leaned in closer, draping her arms over the wooden

counter. Her voice dropped to a conspiratorial whisper. “His body was found in the attic of the hotel.”

“And no one thought to tell me this?” I exclaimed, trying to keep the panic from seeping into my voice.

“It happened way before I was born,” Liz said. “The killer was never found, and the whole thing's been gathering dust in the annals of local lore.”

I tried to take a deep breath to steady myself, but the words that came out were more like a string of nervous babble. “Yikes, yikes, yikes. I didn't sign up for this.”

Liz's eyes sparkled with mischief, but she quickly turned serious. “Your aunt bought the place long after the whole shebang. But hey, she did have the hotel smudged every year with sage to ward off any malevolent spirits.”

“Sage for the hotel? Seriously?” I raised an eyebrow.

Liz nodded with a grin. “Absolutely. I'm telling you; this town's got a colorful history. But don't let that spook you. The inn’s got potential, and with the right owner – like you – it could be the gem of this town. Your aunt, well, she wanted you to ease into the ownership. That’s why she wrote you a bunch of letters, and why she made me promise to spend time with you, to slowly acquaint you with the town, the hotel, and all the local quirks.”

I couldn't help but chuckle at her enthusiasm. “Gem of the town, huh? Me? That's about as likely as me winning the lottery. Or marrying a hot, younger Italian male model and moving to St. Barth’s. Or marrying any man at all.”

Liz's laughter filled the store, vibrant and infectious. “Oh, sweetie, you never know what surprises life has in store for you. Hopefully you'll stumble upon some juicy clues about the cold case while sprucing up the place.”

“Yeah, right. I'll add amateur sleuthing to my long list of

nonexistent skills. I'm a cookie chick, not a paranormal hotelier."

"Hey, you never know what might come in handy," Liz winked, her eyes twinkling again. "And if you ever need some psychic guidance or a little spiritual intervention, you know where to find me. Seriously, take my cell number down. I have a feeling we'll be seeing a lot of each other."

She handed me a card, then came around the counter. We hugged briefly, and she asked if I knew how to get back to the hotel. I said yes, even though I wasn't entirely sure.

I wanted to be alone with my thoughts, and all this new information.

It took me an hour to get back to the hotel, mostly because I stopped in a few cute shops on Main Street. I wasn't immune to the lure of retail therapy, and this seemed like as good a time as any to spend away my worries.

Even though I had more worries than cash.

I did, however, score an elegant handknit shawl for me and a T-shirt printed with a witch's hat for Jenny. I couldn't wait to tell her that I'd found one of her beloved "hipster Ts" here in Florida.

Then it was so hot that I stopped for a spell at Ice Ice Baby, a coffee shop specializing in only cold drinks. It was one of the places Liz had suggested. I ordered a lavender honey iced coffee, and holy wow, it was tasty. I also bought something called a "bruffin," or a brownie muffin.

I bit into it and groaned aloud because it was so delicious. A man at the next table glanced at me.

"Sorry," I whispered with a little wave. It was difficult to contain myself when excellent baked goods were in my mouth. This was way better than thinking about the weird inn

I'd inherited, the cold case murder in the attic, and my aunt claiming I had "a gift."

Me? A gift? Yeah, right. I was about as ordinary of a human as could be. I was the slightly overweight queen of mom jeans and sensible shoes. I own, and carry, a fanny pack (hey, it was called a "belt bag" in the store). My idea of a wild night was a book, a glass of wine, and a snuggle with Freddie.

My only gift was making large, delicious batches of cookies, and even that was gone now. I sighed. This entire trip only reinforced my mediocrity, it seemed.

I sat at a table and scanned *The Messenger*, the local paper, in an attempt to forget about my malaise.

Of course, I expected the woo-woo news items about the town's psychic side, things like "Astral Planes and You" and "Summer Movie Night: The Life and Times of an Indian Yogi." Even the town's politicians were getting in on the paranormal act.

Mayor Larry Norton was one of three dozen attendees at the monthly tea leaf readings at town hall...

I squinted at the photo, which showed a thin man in his seventies — maybe older — staring into a teacup. I took a sip of coffee. I'd thought my small city in Northern California was weird. There, though, yuppies and tech bros partied with wine snobs, and everyone tried to outdo each other.

Here, it seemed, no one was trying to one-up anyone. They let their freak flags fly. I turned the page of the paper and my eyes nearly popped out at one headline.

Nude Bicycle Ride Set For Sunday in Pioneer Park

Yikes. I wondered what the town's founding fathers would think of that.

Even the paper's crime blotter was unusual. The place

seemed to have a robust and wacky criminal element, which was surprising considering how adorable it was.

Local Man Throws Gator Into Drive-Thru Window

Florida Man Attacked By Squirrel While Taking Selfie

Area Woman Charged With Drugs Wears T-Shirt To Court That Said 'Seriously, I Have Drugs'

"What the what?" I whispered to myself. This whole place was so … odd. I laughed softly as I read the squirrel story. Apparently, the man tried to physically force the squirrel into the photo with him, so perhaps he deserved the attack. I was a firm believer that wild animals should remain wild.

Reminding myself to stay away from restaurant drive-thru windows and local squirrels, I finished my coffee and made my way back. It seemed to be at least twenty degrees hotter, and by the time I reached the hotel, I felt like I was melting faster than a popsicle at a nude beach.

I found Jimbo sitting in a rocking chair on the porch. Something was lodged in the corner of his cheek. Chewing tobacco.

"Miss Amelia, you're back," he cried while standing up. "I was worried you'd gotten lost out there."

Would I ever get used to this Miss Amelia stuff? It seemed so foreign, so southern. Yet Jimbo had a certain charm to him.

"Almost got lost but didn't. Liz showed me around. Saw the cemetery and the gravestone recipes."

"Cool beans!" He gave a little fist pump.

"It's a cute downtown. Also had a delicious lunch at The Haunted Hearth."

"I take it you had the chicken salad."

"That I did. How's it going here?"

He hitched up his jeans. "You know, slow. This is our dead month."

I winced, thinking of poor Billy in the attic. "How many guests do we have here now, anyway? Guess I should've asked that earlier."

Jimbo sucked his teeth. "None."

"None?" That seemed difficult to believe, given how busy the town was. Tourists had been everywhere on Main Street, and I'd spotted license plates from at least ten different states.

"Not a one. Our last guest left a few days ago. This whole week is open." He sank back down into the weathered rocking chair.

I also took a seat on the porch swing. "Wow, okay. I thought this place was busy every day."

"I can take a hiatus from work if you don't want to pay me. I have a side hustle as a landscaper. It's no biggie…"

I jumped in, hoping he didn't think I was accusing him of shirking work. "No, no, not at all. You keep whatever schedule Shirley set, and I'll keep paying you."

The last thing I wanted was to be left totally alone with this place, with no idea how to run it.

"Aww, thanks. 'Preciate that. I usually work from seven to three. Miss Shirley often let me go home early so I could focus on my side hustle."

A quick glance at my watch showed that it was four-fifteen. "I'm sorry. Oh, you should go, I've kept you too long. Please. Don't worry about me. Is there anything I need to know?"

Jimbo said the main thing was the phone. "Instructions on how to forward to your cell are on the desk."

I nodded. Inexplicably, he launched into a listing of the nearby local watering holes, from a biker bar to a "swanky piano joint." Nearby restaurants included a Jamaican jerk chicken restaurant and a pizza place.

"Thanks," I said, knowing I wouldn't go anywhere tonight. As far as nightlife, I hadn't been out at a bar alone since, well, never. I wasn't hungry because of the chicken salad, the giant coffee, and the bruffin.

"There's always delivery if I get desperate," I said.

"Oh, and there's The Cauldron. You should definitely check that out. It's within walking distance. That's owned by Sheila and Pam. They're a lesbian couple, but it's not a lesbian bar."

I nodded, unsure of what he was getting at. "Got it."

"It's an everyone bar. They welcome anyone who walks in, unless they're being a jerk. Then they're not welcome. I'm sure you're used to inclusive stuff, being from California and all. It's not always the case in Florida, but we try here in this town to be accepting of everyone."

I was charmed by Jimbo's sweet declaration of inclusivity. "That sounds like a great place. I'll try to check it out."

"They have a real solid dart board setup there. They're also thinking of doing ax throwing events."

I'd never played darts in my life and no one deserved to be near a perimenopausal woman with an ax. "Maybe some other night. I'm a bit tired, so I'm headed upstairs to relax. I'll see you tomorrow?"

"Absolutely, ma'am."

He tipped his blue hat in my direction and walked off the porch and onto the sidewalk. I wondered if he owned a car. Then a thought hit me.

"Jimbo?" I ran down the steps as he turned in my direction. "What should I do if there's a problem at the inn?"

His face took on a shocked expression. "I totally forgot. I'm sorry. There's a list of emergency numbers by the phone, near the forwarding instructions. And I live a couple blocks away."

He pointed down the street. "My number's on that list, so call me anytime if you need anything. I'll be here in two shakes of a gator's tail."

Thanking him, I waved and watched him lope away. Then I looked up at the old, three-story building, and wondered if Freddie and I should go to a chain hotel for the night. It would be more comfortable, I rationalized. Safer. Without paintings of scary old men holding skulls.

Nonsense.

This was now my property, and my aunt had lived here alone for years. She'd probably entertained thousands of guests over the decades and had acquired half those odd treasures. I could spend one night alone — well, with Freddie — in the place.

I'd faced darker moments.

I marched into the building and up the stairs. As I walked down the hall, Freddie's plaintive meow echoed through the closed door.

When I got inside, he was sitting on top of the suitcase, waiting for me. Even though I'd only had him about a year, I knew when he was mad. And tonight, he was beside himself. He let out a loud, pitiful meow and jumped down. He wound himself around my legs.

"I was gone for a few hours. Don't panic." I scooped him up and took him onto the bed. He sprawled out, his front and back paws in opposite directions. "Let me see that belly."

He started purring immediately, and we spent the next fifteen minutes stretched out next to each other. I ran my hand through his soft fur and gently squeezed his ample belly.

"I'm going on a fact-finding mission, Fred. You coming along?"

He continued to purr and shut his eyes. With a little groan, I eased off the bed, feeling my joints creak like an old rocking chair that had seen better days. As I stood upright, I couldn't help but laugh at the sound that accompanied each movement.

It was as if my body had formed its own midlife percussion band, adding a symphony of snaps, crackles and pops to normal, everyday movements.

I surveyed my suitcase, which Jimbo had hauled up. I'd only brought one, figuring I wouldn't be here long. Probably I should unpack first. Then my gaze landed on the envelope that Jimbo had handed me earlier today. It was sitting on a dainty, white end table, right where I'd left it.

That already seemed like a lifetime ago. I padded over and scooped it up. It was a large manila envelope with obviously more than a few sheets of paper inside. I undid the clasp and pulled out the contents.

A handwritten note was paper clipped to a stapled stack of papers. I gasped, recognizing the handwriting immediately.

My Dearest Amelia,

I hope this letter finds you in excellent health and high spirits. As you read these words, I find myself drifting away into the ether of our family's long-standing connection to the paranormal world.

Our family's… what? This was the first I'd heard of it. My parents had divorced when I was nine. Dad died ten years ago and Mom… well, she'd recently remarried to a man with a Corvette and a cigar habit. They were happily playing house in a condo in Sun City, Arizona. No one had paranormal ability, as far as I knew.

An ability to drink, snark, and keep slightly toxic secrets? Yes.

Witchcraft and fortune telling? Definitely not.

Aunt Shirley had been a little batty, apparently. I began to read aloud.

It is with a mix of emotions, both excitement and trepidation, that I pen this letter to you in the winter of my life.

You see, my dear niece, life is often filled with surprises, and this one is no exception. Upon my passing, I have left you something truly extraordinary—the Crescent Moon Inn. I have always believed in your innate abilities, and I am certain that you have the gift of psychometry, which allows you to sense and experience the energies of objects and places.

"Okay, this isn't funny anymore. Psychometry? Shut the front door," I said aloud, skepticism dripping from my tone. This had to be a joke. Shaking my head, I read on. "What is psychometry, anyway?"

Freddie meowed in response.

"No more treats," I told him.

During one of your visits as a child, you stumbled upon an old money clip in the attic. You were five, maybe six at the time. You weren't entirely sure how to verbalize what you were seeing and feeling. All you said was that the steel clip was hot, and that you saw "bad people."

I didn't remember any of that. But why? Both my mother and father had near photographic memories, but all my life, I'd struggled with memorizing things. College had been difficult for that reason, and I was all too happy to graduate and begin work as a baker.

Unbeknownst to me at the time, that old money clip was decades old, and present during the murder of Billy Jenkins—the young man whose unsolved homicide here at the hotel still haunts the town to this day. Little did I realize then that the incident was your first encounter with psychometry. You were too young to understand the significance of what happened, and I didn't want to burden you with such knowledge at that tender age.

A day after you touched the clip, you had an encounter with another object, one that scared all of us. Your parents weren't happy about any of this, and they wanted to keep you from your latent ability. This is probably why you and your family never visited here again and why I had a falling out with your father.

Ugh. I'd always wondered why my father showed no interest in visiting his sister in Florida. Was I the root of the rift? It sure seemed that way. A pang of guilt hit me.

But now, it is time for you to embrace this gift and use it to unlock the secrets that lie within the hotel's walls.

I let out an undignified grunt. I didn't want to unlock anything. All I wanted was peace and maybe a skinny margarita. Still, I felt bad for young Billy. His story tugged at my heartstrings.

The hotel, though grand and full of history, hasn't been faring well lately. A restless spirit —his name is Billy — has become active, and he's causing quite a ruckus. I tried everything in my power to appease him, including seeking the services of exorcists, but the spectral occupants remained unyielding. This has obviously affected the hotel's bottom line, and I'm sorry to say we're nearing bankruptcy. I've run out of time to fix the problem.

I swore aloud while looking around the room. If spirits had taken up residence, were they here right now? Wouldn't Freddie sense something from another realm? What was going on?

He had jumped up on the bed and was busy making a nest by pawing at the duvet. "So adorable, yet so useless," I sighed, and continued reading. This was weirder than I expected.

For this, I apologize, Amelia. I never wanted to

burden you with this unusual responsibility, but fate has chosen you, just as it chose me. It is your destiny to carry on the legacy and find a way to bring peace to the wandering soul here. Once you do this, the hotel will thrive again. I am sure of it. If you sell the hotel without addressing the spirit, it will eventually take over the town, or worse.

"So this is MY problem now?" I yelped. This was beginning to make me nervous. "I don't want to save anything but my bank account."

I glanced over at Freddie, who was now in nap mode and glaring at me with one open eye. "Sorry to disturb, little meatball."

In your quest for unraveling the mysteries of the hotel, I suggest seeking out a man named Oliver Everhart, a local historian and college professor with a fascination for the paranormal. He holds valuable knowledge about the history of the town and might have some insights into the spirit that lingers within the hotel's walls.

Now, my dear, brace yourself for what might seem like a peculiar journey ahead, one which I assure you is absolutely essential. I have prepared a series of clues, scattered throughout the hotel, which will guide you in your efforts to understand and tame the restless spirits. It is my hope that these clues will help you fix the situation that plagues the hotel.

Oliver has already agreed to help. He is a kind man with a wealth of knowledge, and I believe he will be a valuable ally on your journey.

"Oh, great," I muttered. "Just peachy. A buddy."

Remember, Amelia, you possess a unique ability that connects you to the unseen world. Embrace it, for it will be your greatest asset on this endeavor and for your future. Trust your instincts and know that you are never alone—I will watch over you and lend you my strength when needed. Do not be afraid.

"Easy for her to say. She's dead." I paced the room for a few minutes, trying to absorb the cryptic letter. My neck was starting to sweat, a sure sign a hot flash was imminent. Gah. Did I want to stay here alone with a "restless spirit?" Panic ratcheted up.

Always remember, Amelia, that love and courage can transcend all realms. Embrace your gift, unlock the mysteries of the unsolved murder, and bring peace to the restless spirits within. Save the inn, and save yourself. I have faith in you, just as I have had since that winter day when your sweet, curious little self first arrived at this place.

With all my love and eternal support,
Aunt Shirley

Chapter Six

I didn't waste any time. I had to act before nightfall and scram.

Apologizing to a sleepy Freddie, I carefully shoved him into the carrier, then packed a quick overnight bag because I didn't want to haul around a suitcase. That could stay here with the ghosts or spirits or whatever. I had another disposable litter box in the car since I'd bought two when I arrived in Florida.

Small miracles. There was no need to flee from a malevolent spirit with a used kitty litter pan. Go me.

I stomped downstairs, hoping the noise would scare off any lingering undead beings. If my footsteps didn't, Freddie's yowls might. I'm sure he thought we were headed back into the giant torture tube that hurtled through the air. Which didn't seem like a terrible idea.

Trust me, leaving Florida was a viable and reasonable choice. My best option, now that I thought about it. Getting a last-minute flight back to California and forgetting this trip ever happened sounded like a grand idea. If I left now, I could be at the Orlando airport in an hour.

First, I grabbed the key to the front door, then the instructions for forwarding the phone, then the list of emergency contacts.

Once I was in the rental car, I cranked up the air conditioner and made sure the hotel's calls went to my cell. Then I sat for a while with my eyes closed. Was I being silly or smart by leaving? Aunt Shirley wanted me to deal with this. But did I owe her anything? A nagging part of me thought I did, although I wasn't entirely sure why.

I needed an outside opinion, stat.

I opened my eyes and scrolled through my contacts. Who should I call? I imagined explaining everything to Mom. She'd think I'd gone mad and suggest I pop a Xanax. I had some friends back in Sonoma, but they wouldn't understand, either. The women I hung out with in Sonoma were like me: overworked, overtired suburban moms. They dealt in the practical and sensible. Shoes, solutions, life paths.

I lived in a world of efficiency and simple explanations. Well, until I arrived in Florida.

Then I remembered: Liz. She'd understand. She also seemed like a woman who had out-of-the-box ideas. I fished out her business card and gave her a ring.

"Hey, you! I was thinking about you, wondering how you were getting on at the inn."

"Not well."

"Oh, no, really? What happened?"

"Things got weird."

There was a pause. Liz sounded like she was stifling a giggle. "Honey, I'm from Florida. Another word for weird is Tuesday. Or Wednesday. Or any day of the week."

"I read my aunt's letter. In it, she explained that I have the gift of psychometry, that there are restless spirits at the hotel, and that it's up to me to evict the spirits. Oh, and the spirits might somehow menace the town."

"Whoa," she whispered, then whistled a low tone. "That's a lot to take in."

"I did the only reasonable thing I could think of, which was to pack my cat into the rental car."

"Did you leave?" Liz yelped.

"Not yet. Well, sort of. I'm sitting in the car, on the street outside of the hotel." I glanced at the building, and it seemed to taunt me with its peeling yellow paint.

"Oh good."

"No, it's not good, because I have no idea what to do now. Where to go. I can't stay there, not with it being haunted or whatever." I let out a snort of exasperation. "Maybe this is all a joke. Am I being unreasonable?"

Liz cleared her throat. "It's difficult for me to say, since I'm not afraid of the undead."

I couldn't believe I was having this conversation. "My aunt suggested I talk with some guy in town. A historian."

"Oliver Everhart."

"That's him. I dunno what he'll do for me, but I should probably have a conversation with him before I split. What's he like?"

"He's a gem. Smart as the day is long. Do you know how to reach him?"

I reached for my aunt's letter and the paperwork. "No," I said while flipping through the pages. "She left me a deed to the house, the title, some insurance paperwork. Wait. The property insurance is six grand? A year? That's robbery."

This situation was getting more and more craptastic by the

minute. Freddie meowed loudly, his voice bouncing around the interior of the economy sized rental car.

"That's a Florida thing. Listen, let me text Oliver to find out if he's in town. He teaches at the University of Central Florida a few days a week. I'll call you right back."

She hung up. I cranked the A/C up to the max and tried to remain calm. To pass the time, I turned on the radio but shut it quickly off when the first bars of the Eagles' *Witchy Woman* came on.

I didn't want any more reminders of the paranormal happenings in this town. For a few minutes I tried to distract Freddie with some cat snacks, but he refused. Now the inside of the car smelled like a fish market.

Sighing, I twisted the rear-view mirror so I could inspect my face. I tilted my head and craned my neck, trying to get a clearer look at my chin.

Was that what I thought it was?

I scooted closer to the mirror, which wasn't easy because of the steering wheel. Crud, I still couldn't see. So I got out a compact mirror from my purse.

"No way," I muttered.

It was a chin hair. A long, black, bristly thing. I'd been getting them in recent months, another sign that the "change of life" was upon me. The only change I noticed is that I was growing a goatee.

I'd been trying to keep up with tweezing, waxing, and threading back home, but the stupid hairs seemed to grow in the span of hours. I swore this hair hadn't been there when I left California last night.

Perimenopause, as far as I was concerned, could suck a bushel of lemons.

I dug around in my purse for a pair of tweezers then realized they were upstairs in my suitcase.

"Mother ducker," I whispered. There was no way I was going back into a haunted hotel for tweezers. I wasn't *that* vain. Yet.

My phone buzzed and I snapped the compact shut. It was a text from Liz.

> Oliver's home and waiting for you. Good luck and let me know how it goes. xo

She included the man's address, and I tapped it into the car's GPS. Normally I wouldn't meet with someone face-to-face while sporting a chin hair that would make a billy goat jealous, but I had no other choice.

Plus, this Oliver guy had to be a million years old. Town historian? Professor? An old-fashioned name like Oliver? He had to be elderly. As I drove, I pictured him in a jacket with suede patches on the elbows. Gray hair. A pipe.

No, I didn't need to worry about my facial hair. The man probably wouldn't be able to see that level of detail because of his cataracts.

"Right, Freddie?" I asked aloud as I drove.

This time, he didn't meow.

Oliver Everhart lived in the cutest historic bungalow close to downtown and the inn. I probably could've walked here. It was pale blue, with white trim, and an inviting, wide porch. I shouldered Freddie's backpack, marched up to the front door, and knocked.

There were pots of pretty Bird of Paradise flowers

flanking the door. I imagined an elderly man and his equally old wife, lovingly tending to this entire property.

The door swung open to reveal a man about my age. The historian's son, I suspected. He had a mop of messy black hair with a few streaks of gray at the temples, black-framed hipster glasses, and a wicked grin. The guy wore a black T-shirt and jeans, both of which showed off his muscular physique.

A tattoo of — I think — a witch on a broom decorated his right bicep. Okay, whatever. I was here for a purpose, not to gawk at a hot silver fox. His skin was fair, but not as pale as mine.

"Hi, I'm here to see Mr. Oliver Everhart. Professor Everhart. The town historian. I'm Amelia Matthews."

He chuckled. "You've got him."

My jaw crept open. This was the town historian? A man who looked like he could star in a remake of Fifty Shades of Gray? I licked my lips and assessed my options. Oliver's gaze landed on the cat backpack.

As if on cue, Freddie mewled pathetically.

"Sorry, I can't leave my kitty in the car." I inwardly cringed at the double entendre.

"No problem at all," he said breezily, standing aside so I could enter. "I love cats. Come on in."

I entered, acutely aware that I was sporting the beginnings of a beard on my chin. My face wasn't just dewy from the humidity, it resembled an oil slick. And to top it off, I was carrying a backpack containing a chonky, irritable cat.

This day was getting worse by the second.

"I've been expecting you," he said. "Come on, let's sit in the dining room. I've gathered a bunch of articles and other material in anticipation of this."

I settled at a polished dining room table that held stacks of books, folders, and papers. I wasn't sure where to put Freddie, and Oliver's slightly formal demeanor left me uneasy about unleashing the cat on his house. On the floor or on a chair? Some folks didn't like animals on their furniture, so I set the pack on the floor.

Oliver remained in the doorway. "Do you want to let your cat out? I don't have any pets at the moment, and there's no way he can get outside."

It was a kind offer. "Sure. Let's do that."

I unzipped the carrier and Freddie hopped out. With his tail held high, he sauntered to a sunbeam and flopped down.

"That's Freddie Purrcury," I said, feeling more than a little ridiculous.

"Nice to meet you, Freddie." Oliver knelt and allowed the cat to sniff his hand. Before I could warn him, Oliver extended his hand. I braced for an attack, but to my surprise, Freddie allowed Oliver to stroke his tummy.

"Would you like coffee, iced tea, or something stronger?"

I looked into his eyes, which were deep and dark, like eighty percent cacao chocolate. "Definitely something stronger, thanks."

"Gin and tonic with top shelf liquor, wine, or beer?"

I pondered this for a second. "Gin and tonic sounds like heaven. Extra ice, please. This heat. I don't know how y'all do it." Wait. Why did I say *"y'all?"* I'd never used that word in my life. It was as if the southern-ness of the town was seeping into me.

He stood. "It's brutal. And always a bit shocking to newcomers, especially this time of year. I'll be right back with our drinks. We've got a lot to discuss."

When he left the room, I tried to forget about my chin whiskers and glanced at a folder on the table. There was a yellow sticky note on the front. JENKINS HOMICIDE, it read in blocky letters. My eyes roamed to another folder. PSYCHOMETRY INFO. A third had a note that said simply, SPELLS.

I inhaled sharply. This man was into that stuff too? He seemed so normal. And handsome.

I reached for the first folder.

The sound of footsteps on the polished wood floor made me snatch my hand away.

"I thought I'd bring your cat some water. I might have a can of tuna around here as well. Do you think he'd enjoy that?" Oliver squatted and placed a bowl a few feet from Freddie, who studied him with interest.

"Tuna's usually a special treat, but today's been pretty unusual so I guess it's okay."

Oliver stood, nodded, and walked out of the room. My fingers itched to open every folder, but I needed to dip into my nonexistent well of patience and wait.

After a few minutes, Oliver returned carrying a wooden tray. "A gin and tonic with lots of ice for you."

He set the drink in front of me. "And a small bowl of tuna for Mr. Purrcury."

Freddie was on his feet and at the bowl in a millisecond. We watched as he hoovered up the tuna, licked his chops, then stared at me.

"That's it," I said, grabbing my cocktail. "Now let the adults talk."

He meowed in protest, then flopped on the floor for another nap. Oliver sat in one of the chairs next to me and raised his glass. "Cheers."

We clinked glasses and I took a sip. The refreshing, ice-cold drink ran down my throat and instantly elevated my mood. No matter how weird and terrible the day had been, I had to admit I'd consumed some top-shelf food and drink.

It occurred to me that it probably wasn't even five o'clock yet. I suspected that in this town, those rules didn't apply to booze. Nor did I care, given the circumstances.

We sipped and made small talk. "You're a historian and a professor?"

He nodded. "I teach Florida history at UCF, University of Central Florida. And I'm writing a book about the town."

"Oh yeah? That's fascinating. What about?" I was normally a big reader, but since my divorce, I'd gotten out of the habit. I'd brought along a novel to read on this trip, hoping I'd have time to relax and curl up with a book by a pool.

Fat chance. I realized now that had been a naïve fantasy.

"The paranormal history of Cypress Grove, starting with the Spiritualists in the late 1800s and going right up until today."

I nodded slowly.

"You don't believe, do you?" His laugh was gentle and rich.

I shook my head. "No. Yes. I'm not sure. Yesterday I would've said no, but after the events of today, I don't know what's up or down. I was hoping you could shed some light on everything. Starting with my aunt."

"That's understandable. You've sure been thrown into the deep end. I'm real sorry about Shirley, she was one-in-a-million and her illness came as a shock."

I smiled, happy to know she was so loved by people in this community. "Did you know her well?"

"I was starting to, mostly because of the book. I'd done two lengthy interviews with her." Oliver set his glass down and stood. He flipped through several folders and selected one. "I transcribe all my interviews. These are hers. You're free to read them later, if you'd like. I made copies for you."

"Thanks." I accepted the folder and thumbed through. The transcript was at least twenty pages long, so I shut the cover and looked up at Oliver. "I wish she'd told me and my family that she was sick. Her death came as quite the surprise. Then again, we weren't close at all."

"Understandable. At one point my sister and I visited her — my sister knew her first — and we asked why she hadn't told you. She said she didn't want to burden you with her problems. Said she wanted you to discover your gift after she was gone."

I opened my mouth, then closed it, then opened it again. "About that gift. Psycho… psycho… I can't remember the word. Psycho's a perfect description of how I feel right now, though."

"Psychometry. Also known as token-object reading. It's a form of ESP, or extra sensory perception. People with the gift can sense the history of an item. Some can even sense sounds, smells, tastes, even emotion, from touching something."

My expression morphed into one of horror.

"It's definitely a lot to take in." He used a gentle tone, like the one I used when I took Freddie to the vet.

"Understatement of the year."

I grinned. He grinned. My face heated, and not hot-flash warm.

I cleared my throat. "I don't believe it, honestly. I think I'd have known if I possessed this gift, er, ability, before now? In fact, I have a terrible memory for childhood events. I'm a forty-seven-year-old woman. Unless this is something that happens during perimenopause. Could that be it? Like estrogen plummets and I gain the ability to scan objects like a checkout at Wal-Mart?"

Oliver laughed. "It doesn't work exactly like that."

"Whatever. I've never experienced anything like that in my life. I think you're wrong. I think my aunt's wrong. Why me? Why now?"

Oliver chuckled and shook his head. "It doesn't have to do with your age. You've always had this gift, but it only manifests when you're in this town. At least that's my theory. Possibly only when you're in the hotel. We'll have to find that out through testing, trial, and error. These sorts of abilities can sometimes come and go. There's no logical explanation, although they can be hereditary."

I thought back to my aunt's letter. "*...our family's long-standing connection to the paranormal world.*"

"I guess, but you're going to see that you're meowing up the wrong cat tree. I don't have a gift for..." my voice trailed off and I gasped.

"What?" Oliver said, leaning toward me. He was so close I could smell his spicy aftershave. But there were no thoughts of lust, because I was suddenly floored by a memory. Well, two memories. Of earlier, and of my childhood. Prickles of awareness flitted around my body like fireflies.

"The staircase," I whispered. "I sensed something at the inn today when I touched the staircase banister."

I told Oliver everything. Which, honestly, wasn't much.

When I finished, he nodded and stroked his chin. "You don't remember anything about your visit here when you were a child?"

"I didn't until today. Until I touched the banister."

He held up a finger, then rose. "I'll be right back. Hang on."

I sat and drank in silence until he returned. He was carrying an old, hardcover book and wore a determined expression. "I'd like you to hold this and tell me what you feel and think."

I hesitated, eyeing the old tome skeptically as he handed it to me. "It was your aunt's. I have a hunch you might sense something from it." His dark eyes glimmered.

I took the book gingerly in my hands, surprised by its weight. It was weathered, with an old, brown leather cover and a cracked spine. The cover felt rough under my fingertips, like it had been through decades of war, and the faded title only added to its mysterious aura. I studied the title, which was made up of gothic gold letters. I ran a fingertip over the words, tracing the embossed letters.

"The Shadows of Memory," I read aloud. "That's not creepy at all."

I carefully opened the book. The tattered and yellowed pages seemed to have experienced lifetimes of their own. A musty smell filled my nostrils. The handwritten text in an archaic script danced before my eyes, interspersed with peculiar symbols and illustrations. I expected to feel something profound, something weighty, as I skimmed the pages, but there was only a mild tingling sensation in my hands. Not exactly the otherworldly experience I expected to have.

"It's an old book," I said, my voice tinged with disappointment. "I don't feel anything significant. Like you know when you've been sleeping in a weird position after a few too many glasses of wine, then you wake up and your arm is on pins and needles? Like that."

He grinned, unfazed by my lack of excitement. "That's more than enough. You might not believe, but it's definitely something."

I raked my teeth over my bottom lip. I studied the book once more, this time with a newfound curiosity. I tried to focus on the tingling sensation in my fingertips as I turned the pages, hoping for some magical insight, but nothing came. It was a dusty old tome, worn with age and filled with mysterious tales. Like a million others.

With a shake of my head, I handed it back to Oliver. "Sorry."

Disappointment snaked through me. It was as if I'd failed some sort of test.

"Don't apologize, we have to start somewhere. I suspect that your powers are strongest at the inn."

"I don't think I can go back there tonight." I glanced at Freddie, who was on his back and showing off his expansive belly. "I'm hitting a wall."

He shook his head. "Only when you're well-rested. I don't know much about psychometry, but from what I've learned, it's best to be alert when you try to tap into the energy."

I blew out a breath. "I need to read up on this, I guess. It still seems impossible that I'm capable of sensing things from objects. I'm the most boring person alive."

Oliver studied me for a beat. "I find that difficult to believe."

The intensity of his gaze flustered me, and I flapped my hands in the air. "Really. I'm a divorced mom of a twenty-year-old college student. I used to bake cookies for a living. Everything about me is average."

At least that's what my ex-husband told me. Repeatedly.

"Nope. Not buying it." He cleared his throat and turned toward the table. "Do you want to know more about psychometry? I've prepared a dossier of sorts for you."

"Sure." I was glad we were off the topic of me. Plus, I was touched he took the time to compile research. He seemed to be taking my situation quite seriously, which I appreciated.

Oliver adjusted his glasses. "Psychometry is this fascinating paranormal ability that not many have," he began, his voice taking on a professorial tone. I imagined him at the front of a classroom, then noted that none of my professors ever looked like him. Maybe I'd have paid attention more in college if they had.

"Gotcha," I murmured.

"The term itself comes from the Greek words 'psyche,' which means soul or mind, and 'metron,' which means measure."

He flipped through the papers on the desk until he found what he was looking for, then continued. "Practitioners of psychometry, or psychometrists, are able to sense emotions, impressions, or even visions related to the history of an object. It's like reading the memories imprinted on the item itself."

I leaned forward, intrigued. "So, when I touched that old banister at the hotel, I somehow tapped into its history and experienced that moment from the past?"

"Exactly!" Oliver nodded enthusiastically. "You might have unknowingly connected with the energy of the banister and experienced a glimpse of its past, which happened to include you. The tingling sensation you felt while holding the book, even if faint, suggests that you do have some psychometric potential. Some people have a natural affinity for it, while others develop the skill over time with practice and training."

"But why me?" I asked, genuinely puzzled. "I mean, I've never had any paranormal experiences before. Unless you count that one time I went to a haunted house in high school and my brother hid behind a door and popped out to scare me. I punched him in the face and broke his nose. Not intentionally, though."

"That doesn't really count." Oliver stifled a laugh. "Psychometry can manifest in individuals who have a heightened sensitivity to energy and emotions. Being in this town could have awakened this latent ability within you. Sometimes, traumatic or emotionally charged events can trigger such powers. At least that's what I've read in my research over the years"

"So, what do I do now?"

"Well, first, we continue exploring and experimenting. The fact that you felt something from the banister and the book is promising. We can try different objects, and I'll guide you through the process. Or we could go to the hotel tomorrow and test various things. Have you been inside your aunt's place?"

I shook my head. Shirley had lived in a suite on the bottom floor of the hotel. "Not yet. Wasn't really looking forward to that part. Going through a dead woman's things isn't my idea of a fun time."

"It's essential to stay open and receptive to the energy around you. The more you practice, the stronger your abilities might become. Especially at the hotel. It might be the only place you can use your power. We'll have to find out."

I nodded, feeling a mix of excitement and trepidation. The idea of having a paranormal ability was both interesting and overwhelming. Okay, and scary as heck.

"Additionally," Oliver continued, "it might be helpful to research more about psychometry, as you mentioned earlier. I've gathered some resources and books that might give you a better understanding of the phenomenon. And, of course, we can delve deeper into the history of the hotel to see if we can find any clues that could help you hone your abilities."

"Wow. Okay." I didn't seem capable of offering any intelligent response after hearing all this.

"Good. We'll take it step by step. And remember, there's nothing 'average' about having psychometric abilities. Embracing your unique gifts can lead you down paths you never thought possible. A life you never imagined."

I'd lost my husband and my business. I also knew that selling my home in California was on the horizon, and I didn't have a job or much in the way of alimony to support the taxes and insurance. It was difficult to imagine anything for the future.

"Remember, Amelia, mysteries and secrets often lie hidden in the most unassuming places."

I flipped through the folder. It was filled with long paragraphs, printed copies of book pages, and diagrams. The letters seemed to swim before my eyes.

"I can't focus on this right now. I'm too exhausted and keyed up. Maybe you could tell me about Aunt Shirley. When she sent me that first Christmas card five years ago, I should've picked up the phone and called her. Gotten to know her. But I wasn't in a place at that time to take on anything emotional or new. Mostly because…" my voice faded, then I swallowed a lump in my throat. "My marriage was on the rocks back then. I went through a pretty nasty divorce. That's swallowed up a lot of my time. It happened right when our daughter was graduating from high school."

Now I felt awful for not keeping up with Shirley's life. So much had gone by the wayside during those difficult years. I glanced to Oliver.

There was no grin or hint of mirth in his expression. "I'm sorry. I've been there. Not with a kid, because I don't have any. But I went through a bad spell too in a relationship."

"Being an adult kinda sucks, doesn't it?"

"No one lets you in on that secret." His grin was back. "I'd love to tell you about Shirley. I met her at an event at the local bookstore. Which you should check out sometime, it's a neat place. That is, if you like to read."

"Love to read."

"Shirley was quite the character. Eccentric, witty, and always had a glint in her eye like she knew something no one else did. Which, I suppose, might have been true, given the goings-on at the hotel."

"Did she ever talk about anything paranormal or her

beliefs in spooky things?" I asked, hoping to gain some insight into my aunt's world.

Oliver chuckled. "Oh, definitely. Shirley was a firm believer. She loved to tell stories about the hotel's history, especially the ones involving mysterious occurrences. She rarely used the words 'ghost' or 'haunting' with new guests. But she was convinced the place was filled with spirits and residual energy. I remember her once regaling a group of locals with a tale about a mischievous ghost who rearranged furniture in the middle of the night."

I chewed on an ice cube while taking this in. "I didn't know any of this. We moved around a lot when I was a kid, and my father wasn't close to his sister at all."

"She loved to travel. Her last trip was to Romania on a Dracula tour. We went to lunch after she came back and she was so excited to show me her photos." He shook his head and laughed. "She had several pictures of a reenactment of a ritual killing of the living dead."

My lips pulled back into a grimace. "Really? My mom told me that when she first married my dad, they visited the hotel and that Shirley made delicious cinnamon rolls. I can't imagine her being interested in ritual killings. Yikes. She didn't say anything in her Christmas cards, either. I mean, that's not really Christmas card material. She also sent me a postcard, come to think of it."

"She loved sending postcards. I'd get one whenever she traveled." Oliver's smile was wistful. "I got one from Romania. I think that was her last travel postcard."

"I got that too. It was weird because it was the only non-holiday thing she'd ever sent." It was interesting how Oliver and I shared this invisible connection.

He talked for a bit about Shirley's deep love for the hotel, and how long she'd tried various things over the years to draw more guests. Themed mystery weekends, Valentine's Day events, special Florida resident packages. Some ideas worked, others didn't.

He shook his head. "Then she got sick about eight months ago. A few things started to break around the hotel. A bunch of us in town tried to help, but there were some big-ticket items, like the hot water heater. We assumed she'd bounce back, but her health took a real turn quickly at the end."

"The hot water heater? Jimbo only told me about the A/C. Someone's coming tomorrow."

Oliver winced. "That could be a pretty serious repair bill. I'm sorry to have to tell you that."

A chuckle slipped out of my mouth. "Somehow, that's not the most surprising or most troubling thing I've heard today."

"Really? Because in Florida, a broken A/C is about the worst news you can get."

I recalled how much I'd perspired today. "Understandable. But no, I'm not sure which is the worst news. That the A/C is out, that I own a haunted hotel, or that I have some nebulous sixth sense."

I took a sip. "Oh, and I forgot. The unsolved murder. There's that too. And the recipes."

"Recipes? Unsolved murder?" Oliver took off his glasses and frowned. Without them, he looked even more handsome. *Oh dear.*

"Yeah, the cemetery with the engraved headstones. Liz took me there. That was pretty cool. I spotted some interesting recipes."

"Of course. That's one of the main attractions in town. And the homicide? You're referring to Billy Jenkins, I assume?"

"Unless there are others?"

Oliver didn't say anything. He shifted in his seat.

"Are there others?" I asked.

"Other cold cases at the hotel? No, not that I know of. But the Jenkins cold case is the stuff of legend around town."

"Oh yeah?" I drained my glass. "Might as well lay it on me. It'll be like the cherry on top of a really weird day."

Oliver blew out a long breath. "It was August 8, 1956. Billy Jenkins asked a girl on a date. Her name was Annie Baer. It wasn't just any date, it was a trip to Orlando, which was a big deal back then. To see a sold-out show at the Municipal Auditorium. The singer was Elvis Presley."

He let that last detail hang in the air.

"Wow, I didn't know he even toured in 1956, but I'm not really up on my Elvis history. I'm more of a New Wave kinda girl myself."

He responded with a chuckle. "They attended the concert and then drove back to town in Billy's father's Ford Fairlane. According to the rumors, the couple went to the lake to make out at a popular lover's lane spot. However," Oliver clicked his tongue, "Billy was found dead in the attic of the hotel the next morning."

I rubbed the back of my neck. "Goodness. That's awful. Who found him?"

"His friend, seventeen-year-old Larry Norton."

My brows drew together, then I reminded myself not to frown because I couldn't afford Botox. "That name sounds familiar."

"He's the town's mayor."

"Oh! Yes, that's it. I saw him in the local paper today. He was at the monthly tea leaf reading. How awful for him, to find his friend dead. Such a young age."

"Apparently it was the scandal of the year. But no one was ever charged."

"And now Billy's haunting the hotel. Great."

We sat in silence for a few seconds. I snuck a glance at my watch. It was now eight at night, but it felt like three in the morning. I tried to calculate how long I'd been awake, but math and logic, combined with the cocktail, conspired against me.

"Would you like another drink? Or maybe a snack? I'm sorry, I'm a terrible host. I've been unloading all this information on you without feeding you." Oliver looked genuinely remorseful.

"No, no, it's fine. I'm beat. And I still need to find a hotel. Maybe I'm being a baby, but I don't want to sleep in the Crescent Moon tonight." I glanced at Freddie, who was out cold.

"You know…" Oliver stood up. "I have a rental property. An apartment above the garage. No one's in it. You probably didn't see it from the street, because it faces the backyard. I have two rentals here. One's the garage apartment and the other's a tiny house. My sister lives in there. You and Freddie are welcome to stay in the apartment."

"Oh, I wouldn't think of imposing."

"It's no bother, and it's free. You'd be close to town and the inn, and you wouldn't have to drive. Come on, let's grab your luggage and get you two settled in."

I hesitated. Was it safe to stay in a total stranger's apartment? Probably not, but I was bone-tired. I owed it to myself to check it out before I got behind the wheel in this condition.

"Thanks. Let me wrangle Freddie into his backpack."

To my surprise, he helped by unzipping the pack and holding it open while I poured my sleepy cat inside. Once the kitty was secured, Oliver handed me a few of the folders and we were off.

On our short walk out of the house, into the yard, and through a door in the free-standing garage, Oliver talked about the history of his house, and how long he'd lived there.

"First I did the landscaping, then built the tiny home and finally, fixed up the garage."

It was impressive that he'd done all this himself. Everything looked like it had been renovated by a pro. He opened a door at the top of a staircase. Inside was a spacious and clean studio apartment.

The soft glow of a shell-shaped lamp greeted me as I stepped into the space.

The wooden floor gave the place a warm feel, and I noticed a small, inviting seating area with plush coral-colored cushions arranged near the window. A gentle breeze wafted in, carrying the scent of night air, and I could hear the distant chirping of crickets outside.

The kitchenette stood to my left, boasting small versions of sleek, stainless-steel appliances and an expensive-looking espresso machine. So far, so good. To the right, a cozy queen bed beckoned, adorned with soft, inviting linens.

My gaze went to the front door. There were two locks, including a sliding chain latch. My muscles relaxed for the first time today.

Oliver leaned against the small kitchen counter. "You can stay for as long as you want, Amelia. Seriously. I'm in between renters and just had it cleaned. Haven't even put up the new listing yet."

"Of course, I'll pay you. But thanks. This is a huge lifesaver."

"I won't even think of taking payment. Give me your keys and I'll grab your luggage."

I winced. "I left it at the hotel. But I have an overnight bag, so I'm all set. Oh, and Freddie's litter box is in the trunk."

"I can grab that." He pointed with his thumb. "It's calm and peaceful back here. Uh…" he paused. "Can we exchange numbers? I'm leaving early tomorrow for school but I'd like you to have mine in case you have questions. I know this has been a lot of information today."

"Absolutely!" I scrambled to find my phone in my bag.

We swapped contact info and he went downstairs for the litter pan and brought it back up. As his footsteps faded on the stairs a second time, I made sure to lock everything, then put a chair next to the door, under the knob.

I couldn't be too cautious.

By now, Freddie was exploring his third new place of the day, and he jumped on the bed, uninterested.

"I'm right behind you, buddy," I said.

After showering quickly and donning a pair of pajamas I'd packed in the overnight bag, I shut out the lights and crawled into bed next to Freddie. He immediately curled into the crook of my leg.

I'd wanted to stay up and read my aunt's interview transcript, but I was simply too exhausted. With the sound of Freddie's purring, I fell into a deep, satisfying sleep.

Chapter Eight

The sound of birds chirping woke me from my slumber. Soft sunlight streamed into the room from the window. I turned my head toward the light and found Freddie perched on the windowsill, his tail swishing back and forth.

I stretched and smiled, reveling in the feel of the comfy bed. Already I knew I was in a far better, and clearer, state of mind than yesterday.

Freddie turned his head to look at me. He let out a loud meow and jumped to the bed, sailing through the air like a giant, orange panther. He landed next to me.

"Hey, buddy." I reached to scratch under his chin. "What do you think? See any birds outside?"

He let out a little *brrrrap* sound and butted my hand with his head.

"Oh, you want your second breakfast, don't you? Well, today, you're in luck." I always left Freddie dry kibble overnight but fed him wet food when I woke up.

After kissing Freddie on the top of his furry head, I flipped the duvet back and went to the small kitchenette. To my surprise, it was seven in the morning. Despite the three-hour time difference from California, I felt refreshed and ready to take on the day.

The first order of business, of course, was coffee.

It took me a few minutes to figure out the espresso machine, but after I did, the soothing aroma of fresh brew filled the air. While that was underway, I tore open a pouch of food for Freddie and put it in his bowl.

I watched him scarf it down while taking my first sip. Ahh. We were both happy now.

A small, white table and matching chair were in a corner, near another bank of windows. I sank into the seat and drank my coffee, musing about the events of yesterday.

It felt like I'd watched a long and confusing movie. Surely the situation here wasn't as weird as I remembered. Today would be a new day, and I'd tackle the air conditioner situation at the hotel first. Then I'd contact a few realtors.

The issues at the hotel —my aunt's pleas for help, the restless spirit that allegedly resided there, the unsolved, decades-old homicide — weren't my problem. Neither were the town's oddities. These folks could be strange until the end of time. Liz, Jimbo, even handsome Oliver.

Not my circus, not my monkeys. Those things could only affect me if I let them. I needed to be cold and calculating. A businesswoman. Let the next owner deal with the paranormal shenanigans. If they even existed. I needed to get this off my plate and get home to California, then decide what to do with the rest of my life.

Feeling resolute, I downed my coffee. I was pondering whether to brew another when I heard the distinct sound of a woman's voice coming from the direction of the backyard. She was singing a familiar tune from the…70s? 80s? The words were clear and distinct, and after a few lines, I recognized it.

It was *9 to 5*, by Dolly Parton. The singer couldn't hold a tune, but she was belting it out as if she was at Madison Square Garden.

I glanced to Freddie, but he seemed unbothered by the noise because he was licking his butt.

"What the duck?" I muttered while walking to the window.

A gauzy, almost see-through white curtain covered the window, and I pulled it aside.

There, on the lawn, was a woman assembling what looked like a gazebo made of sticks. She was singing at the top of her lungs, but that wasn't all. She wore a white cowboy hat, a white T-shirt, jean cutoffs, and hot pink cowboy boots.

I watched as she tied the sticks together with rope, singing as though she didn't have a care in the world. The song ended, and she immediately launched into another.

Wait. No. That was chanting. Like the kind they did at yoga classes.

"Ommmmmm," she said loudly, and terribly off-key. "Ommmmmm shanti!"

Who was this? Oliver's girlfriend? Wife? He hadn't mentioned whether he was single. Then I remembered: he said his sister lived in the backyard in a tiny house. I quickly checked the rest of the backyard, and indeed, there was a small building that looked like a garden shed, except it was painted in tie-dye colors.

How had I missed *that* last night? I let the curtain fall into place.

As she warbled through a long chant, I decided to shower, change, and begin the day. Amazingly, I unearthed an old pair of tweezers from the bottom of my bag — maybe the magic of this place was truly working, I thought wryly — and removed the chin hair. A second had joined it overnight, and I tried not to think about whether Oliver had seen it. Denial was appropriate in some cases.

Stuffing my feet into my sandals, I realized I had a mountain of stuff to do, and no food. Couldn't start the day on an empty stomach, and I was eager to return to Ice Ice Baby for another delicious coffee and a muffin.

Freddie would have to stay behind. He'd be safe here. Oliver repeatedly said last night that the cat could hang out while I went about my business. I didn't want to impose on him any more than I already had, so I planned to also look for a hotel.

"Be a good boy." I knelt and stroked Freddie's back.

On my way downstairs I tried to make as little noise as possible. I knew Oliver's sister — or whoever it was — was still outside, singing at the top of her lungs. She'd shifted into a modern country song, one I'd heard but didn't remember the name.

"Na na na na naaaaaaah!" she trilled.

I didn't feel like meeting a new person right now. Nor did I want to explain why I was staying here. And if I interrupted her, she'd probably be terribly embarrassed.

Once I was outside, I bent at the waist, so I could duck behind a hibiscus hedge. If I stayed behind this, maybe I wouldn't be detected.

I crept slowly in this position, acutely aware that the woman had stopped singing. The birds started up again, as did my perspiration. Crap. I took another step.

"Girl, you don't have to hide your walk of shame from

me. My brother's a single man, and I don't have any issues with consenting adults doing adult things."

I froze. And gasped. I also tried to stand up but that didn't go as well as planned because a sharp pain ripped through my back.

"Ow," I said, clutching my tailbone. I sucked in a breath and slowly moved out of the awkward position. The intense stab of discomfort took my mind off my embarrassment, at least. Once I had raised myself to my full height, the pain mostly disappeared.

"Hey there, pardner. I'm Sage. Sage Everhart." She took a toothpick out of her mouth and grinned, showing straight, white teeth. "Ollie's sister."

"Hi, I'm Amelia Matthews. I'm not with Ollie, uh, I'm staying in the apartment."

She had the same dark, friendly eyes as Oliver. Her hair was lighter, though, more of a chestnut color. It flowed in waves over her shoulders and perfectly matched her girlish freckles. She had the same skin tone as Oliver, and the same eyes, too. If I had to guess her age, I would've said early forties.

"Oh, you're a new tenant? Ollie didn't tell me he'd found someone."

I shook my head while rubbing my lower back. "I'm only here for the night. Maybe two."

"Right on. I hope my singing didn't disturb you. Just tryna get in the mood, you know? Man, I love to sing. Gets the creative juices flowing, you know? Kinda like riding a horse on the beach." She didn't seem embarrassed in the least.

"Not at all. Barely heard it." I pasted on a smile.

"Did you say you'd be staying tonight?" She tilted her

head and studied me. Sage had a thick accent that was more Texas than Deep South. Odd, since Oliver had no accent at all.

"Possibly, yes."

"I'm holding a full moon ritual tonight. That's what the canopy's for." She swept her hand in the air, in an arc shape. "Tonight's theme is going to be *letting go*. You have anything from your past you'd like to let go?"

I froze, my mouth hanging open. Did I ever. "Well, maybe? I'd have to think about it."

"Great. We'll be out here after dark. Bring your own booze. I provide the snacks. Dunno if I can talk Ollie into coming though. Maybe you can. He's been wrapped up in some project. Research about the Crescent Moon Inn. But he's always busy with something." She chuckled, then reached to tap me on the side of the arm. "Get that back taken care of, you hear? You need a recommendation for a reiki practitioner? I know an excellent one who also does aura massages."

I had no idea what an aura massage was and wasn't about to find out. "I'm fine, really. Feeling great. And thank you for the invite tonight. I'll see if I'm finished with my work. My business. My stuff. Lot to do." Now I was babbling.

"See ya round, cowpoke." She winked, put the toothpick back into her mouth, and strutted away.

I hurried to my car and let out a long breath once I was inside. Maybe it wouldn't be as easy as I thought to ignore all the weirdness here in Florida.

Chapter Nine

The coffee and cinnamon streusel muffin at Ice Ice Baby called my name the minute I strolled inside.

I refrained from asking for the muffin recipe, but just barely. The thing was almost the size of my head and probably contained a cup of sugar, but I didn't care.

Calories were meaningless in the face of what I was dealing with here in Florida. Okay, calories were meaningless on a regular day, too. That was another reason I didn't fit in where I lived in California. It seemed like every woman was watching her weight, whereas I figured if I was healthy according to my doctor, I was fine at my current size.

As I carried the plate to my seat, a thin, older man at a table looked at me and grinned. "All that for you?"

"You bet," I said briskly and powered past, in no mood for small talk from mansplainers.

"Better watch your waistline," he muttered.

I stopped, whirled, and shot him a cutting smirk. He was no looker, with his grayish pallor and cargo shorts hiked up to nearly his chest.

"Oh, don't you worry about me, dude. My waistline can handle all the fabulousness and cinnamon muffins it wants."

What a jerk. More than almost anything, I hated when people commented on women's bodies, especially in public like that. Part of me wanted to tell him about my recent, perfect physical. But that seemed like a very middle-aged thing to do, talk about my cholesterol and glucose levels.

Plus, I didn't need to justify myself to a human ingrown toenail.

I returned to my table a few feet away and sat with my back to the wall so I could keep an eye on that guy. You never knew with men.

My brief flash of annoyance subsided when I bit into the muffin. It was perfect. Almost cakelike, with plenty of streusel topping and cinnamon.

As I was polishing off the last crumbs, a woman approached the man who had verbally accosted me.

"Mayor, how wonderful to see you," she burbled.

The jerky guy was the mayor? Larry Norton? I pretended to study my cell while eavesdropping on their conversation. They chatted amiably about a zoning issue. Parking for a local business or something mundane.

He rose and walked out with the woman. Interesting. My brain kicked in — I wasn't too sharp in the mornings — and I remembered that he was the one who found Billy Jenkins dead all those years ago.

Hmm. It was an interesting detail to file away, and possibly something to mention to Oliver later. Come to think of it, I should probably text him. I pulled out my phone.

Morning! Thanks for letting me crash in your apartment! I slept so well. I really appreciate your hospitality.

His response came almost immediately.

I'm so glad! Feel free to stay as long as you'd like.

A goofy smile spread on my face as I read his text. I didn't want to impose, yet I also didn't want to waste time finding a decent hotel.

I might take you up on that, but please let me pay you.

I wouldn't think of it. Although, you said you were a cookie baker…

"Heh, heh, heh," I chortled aloud, then glanced up to see if anyone had heard me talking to myself. They hadn't. I'd spotted Oliver's kitchen in that gorgeous bungalow, and it seemed nicely appointed…

You give me access to your kitchen for an afternoon, and I'll make you the tastiest cookies of your life.

DEAL

A little surge of joy went through me. There was nothing that I loved more than baking for people. Since Jenny left for college — and since the divorce — I'd had no one to cook for.

I glanced at my watch. It was eight in the morning, and time to make my way to the Crescent Moon.

I left Ice Ice Baby with a to-go bag containing a second muffin, since I wanted to bring one to Jimbo. I sensed that he was a hard worker, and part of me worried about his future if I sold the inn. Maybe I could include some clause that required the new owner to keep him on for a period of time.

Once I was on the sidewalk, I glanced up and down the colorful, quaint main drag. The buildings were a mishmash of old brick and wood, and many had New Orleans-style balconies with intricate scrollwork. A few shop owners were setting out signs and rolling up cheerful striped awnings. I strolled for a while, window shopping.

It really was an adorable place. Had it been California, the muffin would've cost three times what I'd paid, and there would be crowds on the street at this hour.

Instead of going to my car, I figured I'd see if Liz was in her shop. It was only a couple of blocks away, so I strolled while carrying the muffin bag. Still, I didn't want to show up unannounced. People could be weird about that sort of thing. While sitting on a green bench near a post with hanging pots of beautiful geraniums, I texted her.

Good morning! I have a lot to tell you. Are you at the store today?

I am! Can't wait! Where did you sleep last night?

Oliver's.

Oh.

She added a winking emoji.

You know, he is widely considered the most eligible bachelor in town.

I snorted a laugh.

I'll be there in fifteen and I'll tell you all about it. I see a couple of stores that look interesting :)

Sounds good, make sure you check out the antique shop! It's called Timeless Treasures. Some real unique stuff. Cheap, too!

Unique and cheap are my middle names

I rose and perused a few stores. One was a vintage clothing place, with a Fleetwood Mac T-shirt from the 1970s that would look good on Jenny. It wasn't open yet. I'd have to come back.

The store next door was the antique shop, the one Liz had mentioned. when I peered through the glass, I let out a little cry of happiness.

There, in the window, was the perfect lamp. It looked like a Tiffany, or a replica. I'd coveted these lamps for years but could never find one that was affordable in California. The lamp's base was shaped like a graceful peacock, and the glass shade shone with the brilliance of the bird's colorful feathers.

I texted Liz quickly.

I might be longer than expected. I see a lamp that needs to come home with me.

I had to know the price, and by the time I pulled open the door I was already scheming how to ship the thing back home. Maybe I could fit it into a carry on somehow. But could

I wrangle a fragile lamp and an ornery, eighteen-pound cat onto a plane?

"Welcome to Timeless Treasures," a woman's voice called out.

I wound my way through stacks of furniture, inhaling the scent of dust and Lemon Pledge. "Good morning," I called out. "I wanted to ask about that beautiful lamp in the window."

"Of course, of course. I'd love to show it to you."

I was finally at the counter, where an older woman sat at a tall seat. I smiled. "Thanks. Is it real? A real Tiffany?"

"It sure is. Here, let's get it out for you."

With immense effort, she rose from her chair. "Sorry, I recently had knee surgery. This is my first week back."

I apologized for making her jump through hoops so early in the day, and she smiled. As she slowly made her way around the counter, I turned to check out something shiny that had caught my eye. It was a free-standing, oval mirror, with an ornate gold frame.

"Gosh, this is also gorgeous. But I don't think I can carry it on the plane."

She paused at the mirror. "That came out of a local hotel owned by an acquaintance of mine. She wanted me to have it, but I simply don't have any place for it in my home. It's quite old. That's actual gold leaf over iron."

"Oh, really?" I murmured and reached to touch the edge of the frame.

When my fingers hit the cool metal, it was as if I'd been shocked by a million volts. Suddenly, the world around me blurred, and I was transported to a different place. Was this another memory long forgotten? *What the duck...*

I was six years old, standing in a dimly lit hotel room. My parents were unpacking and Mike was making fart sounds with his armpit on the bed.

"You're gross," I said to him.

"You smell like a raccoon in the garbage," he retorted.

Furious, I wandered off to explore. The door was open to one of the other rooms in the hallway, and I stepped inside.

A large mirror stood there, reflecting my curious gaze. As I reached out and touched it with my tiny hand, a surge of energy coursed through me, and my surroundings twisted and contorted.

The mirror seemed to come alive, its golden frame pulsating with an eerie light. My young self stared wide-eyed as the glass rippled, revealing a dark, foreboding realm on the other side. Within that ominous reflection, I saw a demon. Its eyes glowed red with malice, fixated on me.

I tried to scream but couldn't.

Fear gripped my heart as I realized that the demon could see me too. It reached through the mirror, its clawed fingers stretching toward my trembling form. Panic surged through me, and I tried to pull away, but I felt rooted to the spot, trapped in the psychic connection between the mirror and me.

Between the demon and me.

"Amelia? Where are you?" My dad's annoyed grumble hit my ears, but I couldn't scream because the demon's hold was too strong.

Footsteps thundered. Within seconds, Dad was standing next to me. "Shirley, what in the world is happening to her? I thought we'd agreed never to discuss this." I'd never heard him shout so loud. I clapped my hands over my ears.

He grabbed my arm and pulled me out of the room.

But now I was in a different time. The present, but not exactly. A swirling, foggy, in-between state. I sensed the pres-

ence of something terrifying. The thing in the mirror. It was coming for me…

My mouth opened, but nothing came out.

I gasped and stumbled back, breaking the connection with the mirror. I cried out, loud. The vision faded, leaving me disoriented and overwhelmed. My heart pounded in my chest, and my breathing came in short, ragged breaths. The shop clerk's voice seemed distant, as if I were hearing her from far away.

I tried to speak, to tell her what I saw, but the words wouldn't come. When they did, they rasped out, garbled. *What the duck*, I attempted to say.

It came out as, "Blergh de blergyyyyy." Kind of like a muppet speaking an alien language.

The memory of that terrifying encounter with the demon had resurfaced, flooding me with emotions I thought I had buried long ago. What was going on?

As the world spun around me, my vision blurred, and everything went dark. My rubbery legs gave way, and I crumpled to the floor, hitting my head on a wicker plant stand and losing consciousness along the way.

Chapter Ten

A cacophony of voices seeped into my brain, small snippets of conversation that left me more confused than before. The words faded in and out. Who knew what was real and what was a dream?

"She looks like she's waking up. I still think we need to bring her to the hospital. Gosh, I love those chandelier earrings on her. So pretty."

"She touched that old mirror and went down. I hope that darned thing isn't possessed. I'll never be able to sell it."

"This little cowgirl will be fine with some vittles and water."

My eyes snapped open at the word *vittles*. Three women were crowded around me, peering into my face. The store clerk, Liz, and… Sage?

"Wh…what? Why? Why are you all here?" I croaked.

"There you are," Liz said with a soft smile. She placed her palm on my forehead. "Just a little banged up."

"Welcome back, pardner." Sage had the toothpick in her mouth.

The clerk was less kind. “Are you going to sue me?”

I shook my head and sat up. The sound of a paper bag crinkling made me look around.

“Oh, crap,” I said. I’d fallen on Jimbo’s muffin, and it was squashed.

Liz helped me to stand, and led me to a musty, overstuffed purple chair that looked like a small throne.

“What happened?” she asked, then turned to Sage and the clerk. “Let’s get her some water.”

“Comin’ right up,” Sage said, and strutted off, her boots striking against the linoleum floor.

I blinked several times. “How did you all get here?”

Liz pulled up a folding chair and plopped down. Today she was wearing a pale pink T-shirt dress, brown Birkenstocks, and a chunky quartz necklace. “When you didn’t come by the store, I decided to take a walk to find you. Figured you’d be here.”

“And Sage?”

Liz patted my arm. “I called Oliver when I realized you were unconscious. He asked his sister to come down since he’s at school.”

“How long have I been out?” I massaged the back of my neck with my fingers.

“About twenty minutes. Long enough for us all to get here. You had us worried.”

“You couldn’t have tripped on anything. I don’t understand what happened.” The store clerk was standing a few feet away, her arms folded and her lips twisted in a sour expression. She stooped to pick up the bag with the smooshed muffin, then straightened her spine. “I’m Midge, by the way. The owner.”

“I didn’t trip, Midge. And I’m Amelia. Nice to meet you.”

She blew a breath out of her nose and walked away. I turned to Liz and widened my eyes. "What's up with her?" I hissed.

She shook her head. "She's always prickly. Ignore her. So, what happened?"

The sound of a door opening hit my ears, then the clack of footsteps. Sage was back, carrying a bag.

"I grabbed a water and one of those blue frost Gatorades. Take your pick, buckaroo."

"Water. Thanks."

She reached in the bag and pulled out a giant bottle. "That's all they had. Y'know, you're probably dehydrated. You looked parched earlier today."

I accepted the bottle, took an enormous slug, then wiped my mouth with the back of my hand.

"I'm not dehydrated. I had a…" I swallowed. "I think I had a vision when I touched the mirror."

"Whoa, nelly," Sage whispered.

"Oh dear," Liz said while fiddling with the thick bracelet that wrapped around her wrist.

Midge wandered from behind a stack. "You didn't trip?"

"I can assure you; I didn't trip. I'm not suing you, or anyone."

"Then what happened?" Liz leaned in.

I explained exactly what transpired when I touched the mirror. Although I didn't want to, I also described the demon. I shivered when I was finished and stared at the three women's shocked faces.

"All my life, I've had a difficult time remembering things from my childhood. Anytime after about thirteen or fourteen, I can recall pretty well. But when I was a kid? Nothing. Until I came here." I paused for a beat. "I guess my aunt and Oliver might be right. That I have psychometric powers. Or however you say it." I wondered how much Sage knew about me. I didn't have the energy to ask.

"It's a gift," Liz said in a reverent tone.

Sage took off her hat, crouched and looked into my eyes. "You gotta learn to live with that, compadre. Take it out on the range and show it who's boss. It's an important ability, psychometry."

I squinted in Sage's direction. "Aren't you from Florida? Your brother said you were both natives. Why do you have a Texas accent, and what's with the cowboy schtick?"

It was probably rude to ask, but I figured if ever there was a time to give me a pass for being blunt, it would be following a psychic vision and collapse. I braced for Sage's ire.

To my surprise, she beamed. "I'm a cowgirl and a witch. You know, there are a lot of similarities between the two."

My gaze slid to Liz, who nodded earnestly. I shut my eyes. "Oh my word," I whispered. "Why is this place so weird?"

I opened my eyes to find the two women smiling at me. Behind them, Midge was inspecting the back of the mirror.

"I'm sorry. I don't mean to be so blunt. But ever since I arrived in town, things have been unusual. Like I'm in some sort of tropical Twilight Zone."

"It's okay, honey. We know this place can be a lot to take in sometimes." Liz patted my knee.

"The longer you stay, the more you'll get used to it," Sage chimed in. "Seriously, you okay? You want to see a doctor?"

I doubted whether I'd ever get used to it. But it didn't matter, because I wasn't staying. "No, I feel fine. There doesn't even seem to be a lump."

My hand went to my forehead and I felt around for anything amiss. There was nothing.

"When you hit the floor, you went face first into that stack of pillows," Midge said, sounding oddly disappointed.

"Well, then I better get going. I need to pick up the libations for this evening." Sage stood up and donned her hat. "I'll see you two little doggies tonight. Midge, I know you won't be there."

"I never drive after dark," the older woman groused. "But you kids have fun."

"See y'all later. I'll tell Ollie you're okay." Sage made the shape of a gun with her fingers and a little pew-pew noise before she wandered out.

"Why don't we go back to my store, and I'll make you a cup of tea?" Liz asked.

"That sounds okay." Better than staying here with Midge and her stink eye.

We left minutes later. Midge asked if I still wanted to buy the lamp, and I said I'd think about it and maybe return another day. In reality, I wanted nothing to do with that store. My insides were still shaking like the San Andreas fault after having the vision of that demon.

I was silent on the quick walk to Liz's shop. The sunshine was bright, so intense and white-hot that I had to scrunch my eyes shut a few times before my vision adjusted. That had never happened in California, where it was equally as sunny. Perhaps the vision in the mirror made something go haywire in my brain.

Exactly what I needed on top of perimenopause.

Once we got inside, verbal diarrhea took over. Everything I'd learned over the past day, from Oliver's research to the vivid memory at the mirror, poured out of my mouth. Chattering nonstop, I followed Liz into a back room as she made a pot of herbal tea. I was still talking when Liz gestured for me to take a chair.

"I don't even know why I'm telling you all this. I guess because you're the only person who seems normal here. Well, Oliver's normal, too. But…" I sighed, thinking about his handsome face and his muscular arms. I relaxed into the comfy seat.

"But he's a man." She shot me a knowing look.

"Exactly."

"Look, I won't lie to you. Things are strange here. And it's not uncommon for people to discover latent powers once they visit this town. But what you're experiencing seems extreme. Usually, folks see a ghost or come to a deep insight during a tarot reading. They almost never have vivid visions of the past. It sounds like your psychometric power is getting stronger the longer you stay. Your aunt and I thought this might happen, which is why we wanted to introduce you slowly to all the strangeness in town. We didn't want to overwhelm you."

"What does that even mean? What should I do?" I felt totally out of control.

The herbal tea was warm and comforting as Liz settled into an armchair across from me. She leaned forward, clasping her hands together, and wore a thoughtful expression on her face.

"Well, honey, it means you're becoming more attuned to the energy in this town. It's one of the most powerful spots for psychic energy in the United States. Sedona's the other place similar to here. You've got a gift, and it's starting to show itself in a big way," she explained. "But don't you worry, it's not a curse. You just need some guidance, and you'll learn to control it."

I let out a nervous laugh. "Guidance? Like, you're going to teach me to become a psychic superhero or something?"

"If by superhero, you mean, solve a decades-old cold case, then yes. That's what your aunt wanted. Well, I'm not going to teach you. But I can help. You might need several helpers."

"I still don't understand. Why me?"

"Why not you?" Liz sipped her tea and the question hung in the air. "Shirley said your father's side of the family — your father was her brother, correct? — had powers. She didn't elaborate, only said you carried on the line. So, I ask again. Why not you?"

I couldn't think of a pithy retort, so I silently drank my tea. Finally, I spoke up. "I don't know if I'm up for this. All I wanted was to sell the hotel. I need that money to live."

I didn't even want to think about the dismal financial situation I was in back in California. Selling my house would give me a little cushion, but not enough for more than a few months. Once again, I cursed my ex-husband for taking out a home equity loan.

"Understood. It might be difficult to do that, though. You'll need to disclose your knowledge of the paranormal, or extranormal, presence in the hotel."

I shook my head in disbelief. "What? You mean, I have to disclose it like I would a bad roof, or a…"

"A sinkhole, or a problem with the foundation, or some structural issue. Yes. It's a local ordinance. One must disclose hauntings or known spirits in real estate listings. Obviously, buyers don't want to take on restless undead when they buy a new place." Her curls bounced when she nodded.

It was as if this was the most reasonable and normal requirement in the world.

"This means I have to rid the place of spirits before I sell it. Okay, no problem," I said briskly. "Like getting new floors, or repainting. Cool, cool. Surely someone here in town can do that for me. A medium, or a psychic, or a priest to do an exorcism. It's about finding the right expert, no?"

Liz rubbed her lips together, then looked down at her teacup. "Your aunt tried that. Several times. I attended séances and other rituals there. Nothing worked. It seems like you're the only one who can fix this situation, from what she told me and from what you said about the letter. Start there, then we can talk."

Chapter Eleven

This was not welcome news.

Despite my surprise and overall skepticism about this situation, I managed to thank Liz for the tea, promise her I'd be at Sage's full moon gathering that evening, and buy a new muffin for Jimbo.

After all that, I went to the hotel. This time, I parked in the driveway instead of on the street. I marched up the walkway and pulled open the door, determined to take control of this situation. An electric current zapped me when I touched the knob. Gah. I yanked my hand back and shook it out.

Jimbo was inside, standing behind the reception desk and watching what looked to be a soap opera on a small television.

"Well good morning to you, Miss Amelia."

I gave him the muffin, and he was so appreciative you'd have thought I handed him gold. We made small talk about the weather while he wolfed it down. Once he'd licked all the sticky crumbs off his fingers, I got down to business.

"Can you please show me to my aunt's quarters? I need to look around for some paperwork and other stuff there."

"Absolutely, right this way." He wiped his hands on a napkin and I followed him through a door and into a library.

"I'm confused. This doesn't look like an apartment." My eyes scanned the tall stacks of books in the dim, gothic-tinged room. There was even a stone gargoyle perched atop a table. I patted him on the head, thinking it looked like Freddie when he was hungry. Another electric current crackled through me.

Was I going to have to watch what I touched? Should I wear gloves? What a hassle that would be.

"Check this out. This is how she got into her apartment." Jimbo reached for a book, an old, thick volume, and pulled it off the shelf. He stood back. A second later, the entire bookcase panel slowly slid to the side.

Delight spread across my face.

"A room hidden behind a bookcase? Whoa!" I was both impressed and confused. Although the latter emotion was becoming my default by now.

"Not just a room, but an entire apartment." Jimbo was tall and had to duck his head to slip inside.

I stepped past the bookcase and into the room. "Whoa, whoa, whoa. Look at this."

The room was a mix of old-fashioned charm and modern conveniences. It had a cozy living area with a worn-out yet comfortable-looking couch, a vintage coffee table in a sleek yet homey Scandinavian style, and a small, flat-screen TV. A fireplace adorned one wall. Ornate carvings and mystical symbols in frames were affixed to another.

On the other side of the room, there was a functional kitchenette, complete with a stove, a small fridge, and a well-stocked pantry. The shelves were filled with herbs, spices, and cookbooks with titles such as "Spells," and "Healing Fungi."

There was another book on the shelf, one that looked more like a journal. I pulled it out and nearly lost some of the papers crammed into the pages. I flipped through. It was a recipe book, and one tab caught my eye. Warm happiness spread through me even before I read the title.

Amelia's Cookies, it read.

She'd handwritten all of my recipes that I'd published in blogs over the years and collected all of them in this little book. I swallowed a lump in my throat. Aunt Shirley never mentioned in her Christmas cards that she'd seen even one recipe of mine, much less kept them in a book.

"Your aunt was a woman of many secrets," Jimbo said with a smile, almost as if he knew what I was thinking. "I'm going back to the front desk, so I'll leave you alone here. Holler if you need anything."

"Thanks. I will." I gave him a little wave and continued exploring the apartment.

In the corner, I found an old, roll top writing desk. The surface was cluttered with old letters, half-written-in note-books, and various knick-knacks. She seemed to collect miniature dolls. They were lined up on a shelf above the desk, and they stared at me with wide, uncanny eyes. I averted my gaze, not wanting to look or touch them.

If a mirror had made me see a scary being, what would a weird doll do? Best to steer clear.

Among the papers, I spotted an ornate envelope. My name was written on the front in my aunt's formal cursive. I picked it up, and another surge of energy passed through me. The sensation was becoming familiar by now.

"Here we go," I whispered, bracing myself for some

weirdness or vision. But nothing came, so I opened the envelope and pulled out a piece of stationary. At the top was a beautiful, embossed rose. It felt as though some invisible hand from the universe was guiding my aunt's words to me.

Weird, since I normally didn't believe in things like "the universe."

Dearest Amelia,

Congratulations on finding this second letter. I trust that you've spoken to Oliver by now and that he has given you some insight into the supernatural occurrences at Crescent Moon Inn. I know it must be overwhelming, but please believe that you have the strength and determination to face these challenges head-on.

I decided to break all this news to you in separate letters so you'd have time to get used to the information. Please forgive me.

As promised, I will guide you on how to banish the malevolent spirit that has taken residence at the hotel. The key to restoring peace lies in solving the murder of Billy Jenkins. His restless spirit is at the core of the haunting, and until his soul finds closure, the other spirits cannot move on.

Billy Jenkins was a kind and gentle soul, a young music lover and bellhop who used to play his guitar for guests under the old oak tree at the edge of the Crescent Moon Inn property. Everyone loved him and his music brought joy to all who heard it. But one fateful night, something terrible happened. His life was cut short, and his spirit has been trapped ever since.

To begin your quest, I advise you to seek out Martha Johnstone, the town's librarian, and a close friend of mine. She possesses a wealth of knowledge about the town's history and the secrets it holds. Ask her about Billy Jenkins and the events that transpired on that tragic night. Martha and her resources might provide you with a crucial clue to get started. She also has access to a vast archive of newspaper clippings in town.

But beware, Amelia. There are forces at play that would rather keep the truth buried. Not everyone in town will be forthcoming with information, and you must tread carefully. Trust your instincts and don't be afraid to dig deep into the past.

Now, for the location where you must go, I suggest visiting the abandoned icehouse near the lake. There's only one. It's a forgotten place, overgrown with kudzu and memories. This building holds a secret that might lead you to uncover the truth about Billy's murder. The spirits, too, are drawn to that place, and it is there that you might sense their presence more intensely.

While I have no idea what's in the icehouse, my instincts tell me you should go there. By the time I found out about this link to the spirit, I was unable to go myself due to my health.

I know this is a daunting task, my dear niece, but you are not alone. Your ancestors have always been connected to the supernatural world, and you carry that legacy within you. Embrace your power, trust in your intuition, and you will prevail. I tried to banish the spirits, but alas, I was not strong enough. And now, time is running out.

I believe in you, Amelia. I believe in the strength of our family's bond, and I have faith that you will find the answers you seek. Take your time, be patient with yourself, and remember that you have the love and support of both the living and the departed.

If you ever need guidance, seek out the moonlight —it has a way of illuminating the darkest paths.

With all my love and the hope for a brighter future,

Aunt Shirley

My heart hammered against my ribcage as I re-read the letter. Shirley wasn't joking about any of this. Possibly the most surprising thing of all: I was beginning to believe every single wacky detail about, well, everything.

Demons, hauntings, spirits. Special powers and abilities. Recipes in a cemetery. It all seemed plausible and completely normal here in this hotel and this weird town. The question was, did I want to deal with it? Could I simply walk away at this point?

Probably not, although the idea was still tempting.

"I guess I don't have much choice but to stick around," I muttered, still feeling put out, confused, and overwhelmed. What the heck was an icehouse?

I paced the small apartment, wandering from kitchen to living room to bedroom and back again. On one of my trips into the bedroom, I paused at the bureau. A lumpy, green-and-red piece of glazed pottery caught my eye.

It was in the shape of a bowl. Or an attempt at a bowl. Inside, there were two dainty earrings in the shape of daisies. When I got closer, I spotted the crude letters carved into the clay.

MERRY CHRISTMAS, AUNTIE, it said.

I frowned. Shirley only had one niece (me) and one nephew (Mike). This had to be from one of us. But I didn't recall ever making her pottery.

My hand reached to snatch up the bowl. The minute I touched it, I felt a tingle in my arm, and then a vivid image flooded my mind. I was six, and we were here in the hotel. I got the impression that it was the same visit as when Mike and I ran up the stairs, and when I first saw the demon in the mirror.

Shirley was sitting near a Christmas tree, laughing. Dad was picking up a mountain of wrapping paper, Mike was tearing open his Commodore 64 video game box, and Mom was smoking a Virginia Slims and still wearing her bathrobe. We were in one of the rooms in the hotel — I think the library.

The scent of cigarette smoke and pine trees were heavy in the air, so thick I could feel the scent in my nose. I went to the tree and picked up a badly-wrapped gift.

"This is for you, Aunt Shirley! I made it at camp and Daddy told me to hold onto it until I could give it to you."

She opened it and the wonder on her face was unmatched. Even my parents weren't that excited when I gave them something I'd made.

"How beautiful, my dear! You have a true creative streak. I will treasure it always. Thank you." She folded me into a hug.

I hastily set the bowl down, then sank onto the neatly made bed. The odor of cigarettes and Christmas trees and tropical-scented perfume were still in my nose, the memory was so powerful. I sniffed several times, trying to get rid of it.

Finally, I gave up and buried my face in my hands. Tears sprang to my eyes at the sheer emotion of recalling such a lovely childhood memory. I hadn't recalled anything that vividly ever, in my life. Seeing my family like that, happy and together, was a gift.

Maybe this psychometry wouldn't be too awful. It might allow me to regain some memories.

I sprang up from the bed, eager to test my theory. I began picking things up, carefully at first. I started with a bracelet on the bureau, holding it in both hands, anticipating some major revelation.

Nothing.

I set it down and lifted a necklace. This time I closed my eyes and waited for an epiphany.

Zilch.

I tried again with a small lamp, a pair of reading glasses, and a book on the bedside.

Nothing happened. I even tried slowly flipping through the book, but the only shock that came was when I realized my aunt had been reading an extremely spicy romance novel involving a throuple comprised of a werewolf, a dragon and a human woman.

"That's enough of that," I whispered while closing the book and putting it back on the nightstand.

I randomly walked through the apartment and picked up dozens of other items. None of them elicited any kind of response, with the exception of a pamphlet from the city about conserving water. My arm tingled a little, but no other sensation bloomed.

Hmm. Perhaps my psychometric sixth sense was attuned to saving the environment. I set the little booklet down and rifled through another stack of papers. I paused when I saw an attorney's embossed logo. The date on the letter was two months ago.

Ms. Shirley Hall
Owner, Crescent Moon Inn
Re: Acquisition Proposal for Crescent Moon Inn

> *Dear Ms. Hall,*
>
> *I hope this letter finds you well. I am writing to you on behalf of my client, Mr. Larry Norton, a local businessman and the Mayor of Cypress Grove. Mr. Norton has expressed interest in acquiring your esteemed establishment, the Crescent Moon Inn, and has asked me to reach out to you.*
>
> *Mr. Norton has long been captivated by the charm and allure of the inn and believes it holds significant potential for further development and enhancement. As such, he would like to present an acquisition proposal to you.*
>
> *Our preliminary assessment suggests that the market value of Crescent Moon Inn is noteworthy; however, in light of various extra-ordinary factors and considerations, Mr. Norton is prepared to make a formal offer that reflects a valuation that may be lower than you anticipate. It is essen-*

tial to underscore that Mr. Norton's offer is reflective of his vision for the property's future and the opportunities he envisions.

In the spirit of transparency and collaboration, Mr. Norton's offer is attached herewith for your review. Please bear in mind that this offer is non-binding and serves as a starting point for negotiations. Mr. Norton is open to engaging in a constructive dialogue to reach an agreement that satisfies both parties' interests.

I kindly request that you take some time to consider this proposal and its potential benefits. Mr. Norton is eager to discuss any concerns you may have and is prepared to work towards a mutually beneficial resolution. We are confident that under his stewardship, Crescent Moon Inn can continue to flourish as a beacon of hospitality and charm in Cypress Grove.

Please do not hesitate to reach out to me if you have any questions or would like to arrange a meeting with Mr. Norton. We genuinely look forward to collaborating with you to bring Mr. Norton's vision to life.

Thank you for your time and consideration.

Sincerely,

Jason Jennings Esq.

Attorney at Law

My fingers holding the paper tingled. The sensation spread into my hand, then my arm, then through my entire body. I shut my eyes.

This time, there was no lovely family memory. This time, there was only a raw, visceral emotion.

Desperation. Either Larry Norton or Jason the attorney

were desperate. I could feel it in the words on the page and the paper itself.

I held the letter for a while, sitting with the uncomfortable sensation, hoping it would reveal some crucial detail. But, no. It was wave after wave of desperate desire. My chest felt tight, as if in the grip of some invisible hand. My breathing turned shallow.

"Come on, come on," I urged, shaking the paper. It was unclear who or what I was urging. I clutched the letter tight. But other than the tingles and the emotion, no images came to mind.

Finally, I let go of the paper, and the feeling evaporated. I went to the kitchen and opened the back door. It led to a small wooden porch and a white metal table and chairs. I sank into one, allowing the thick humidity to envelop me. I shut my eyes against the bright sunshine and basked in the rays.

That letter had to be significant. But how? Why did the mayor want to buy the hotel?

In a town that held so many secrets and questions, that might be the least strange of all. Everyone, even the elderly mayor of the Psychic Capital of the World, wanted a bigger bank account.

Chapter Twelve

I spent a few more hours in Aunt Shirley's apartment, mostly trying to sort out the hotel's bookkeeping and records. This was something I could understand. Not that I was great with numbers, but they seemed more concrete and understandable than hauntings and homicides.

Shirley's records were well-organized. They didn't inspire any shocks, memories, or visions. That was the good news.

The bad: the hotel was operating in the red and had been for months. Even before Shirley got sick, the place was a money suck. According to her bank statements, she'd been spending her own savings to keep the hotel afloat. There simply weren't enough guests to pay the bills.

I also found several printed emails and online reviews from guests, all complaining about the hotel. My heart felt heavy as I read the recent feedback, knowing that my aunt had been sick when they were posted. Folks' biggest problems were the spooky, unsettling moaning noises. Oh, and the suddenly slamming doors. One guest said a "restless demon" broke her perfume bottle.

The bed was incredibly comfortable. I know that we stayed because we thought the place was haunted, but we didn't expect to be actually bothered by the spirits. They kept us awake all night! One star. Don't recommend.

"You want haunted, but you can't handle haunted. Stay at a theme park, why don't you? Jeez." I groused, suddenly protective of my aunt and the hotel. It seemed rather rich that guests came here expecting a haunted hotel, but then left terrible reviews because of the spectral activity.

I let out a sigh. My eyes felt dry and scratchy, and I rubbed them until I saw stars. I needed food and maybe a nap. It was already two in the afternoon, and a sudden wave of exhaustion washed over me. I hadn't felt this tired since I was the parent of a toddler. Weird.

Maybe I should knock off for the day. This had been a lot. I carefully put everything back in its place in my aunt's apartment — I wasn't sure why, since I was the legal owner of all this stuff — and went into the lobby.

I called out Jimbo's name, my voice carrying in the quiet, spooky ambiance of the lobby. In response, a subtle movement caught my eye—a faint swaying of the wooden rocker on the porch. I went outside.

Jimbo was seated on the rocking chair, engrossed in the commentary of a ball game blaring from his phone's speaker. His fingers fumbled with the volume control as soon as he spotted me.

"Well, hey there," his words carried a mixture of familiarity and concern. "Everything okay inside? I was gonna send a search party out for you. I wanted to tell you. A bachelorette party booked the entire hotel for a long weekend in October."

"That's promising." Wincing as I kneaded my lower back with my fingers, I attempted to alleviate the knots that had formed during the hours of squatting, stooping, and bending while looking through my aunt's things. "Shirley's paperwork gave me a lot of insight into the hotel's books. Seems like things have been rather sluggish around here for quite some time."

A raspy sound escaped Jimbo's mouth. "Yes, they have."

Leaning against the porch railing, I cast a gaze toward the peeling paint on the side of the house. "Word seems to have spread about the... restless spirit. Or spirits. Not sure which."

I couldn't believe I was uttering those words aloud.

His head moved in a slow, solemn nod. "That's right, ma'am."

With a thoughtful tilt of my head, I lowered my voice to match the air of mystery that hung around us. Could there be more than one spirit? What an unsettling thought. "Tell me, do you ever catch sight of them, or hear their whispers, or feel their presence? Have they ever threatened you?"

Jimbo's little finger probed absentmindedly in his ear, as if seeking an answer from within. Eventually, he withdrew it and met my gaze. "I ain't got no knack for that sort of thing, Miss Amelia. I have other gifts, but seeing spirits isn't one of them."

"What do the guests say when they come face to face with these ghosts, er, apparitions?"

"A fair number of 'em believe the spirits, or whatever they are, mean to do them harm. Also, we don't like to call 'em ghosts around here. Shirley felt that wasn't quite respectful. She used the term spirits."

"That can't be doing much for business," I mused.

He nodded somberly. "Absolutely not. Miss Shirley was

near her wits' end when it all began. Tourists, they only want so much reality."

My lips curled into a pensive scowl. It didn't quite add up. If Billy had passed more than six decades ago, shouldn't his spectral presence have been felt sooner? Then again, I was in uncharted waters. What did I know about the timeline of the undead?

"So, this has only been going on for a few years?"

"That's right. It's like things took a sharp turn a couple years back. Before that, this place was as calm as a summer breeze. And popular, too. We were even featured in Southern Living magazine. That summer, we were slammed with business. Had to hire two other people to work here."

My mind churned with curiosity. "I wonder what could have triggered this sudden shift."

A sense of weight hung between us, as if the answer itself was buried in the very air we breathed. "Miss Shirley tried to unravel that riddle," Jimbo began. "But she never did manage to put all the pieces together. She had hopes, though, that you might be able to. Figured with your gift and all, you could get to the bottom of it."

So, my aunt had told him about my psychometry. She'd also told Liz and Oliver. Who hadn't she told? "I gathered as much from her writings."

Eventually, Jimbo roused himself, his movement a quiet breaking of the silence. "Well, I reckon it's about time I head on. Unless there's something you need?"

My head shook gently, a faint smile tugging at the corner of my lips. "No, I'll be alright. By the way, how did the visit from the air conditioner repairman go?"

A wistful exhale left his lips. "He needs to price a few

parts, should be back tomorrow with an estimate. Said it could get pretty pricey, he wanted to warn us."

If only exorcizing spirits was as straightforward as fixing an air conditioner. As Jimbo bid his farewell and departed, I was left to contemplate whether I should brave the creepy quiet of the hotel in hopes of a spectral encounter. Yet, fatigue weighed heavily upon my bones. Plus, I hadn't seen Freddie in hours, and I needed to check on him.

I raced upstairs to grab my suitcase, mindful of every creak and crackle in the old house. I hauled the thing downstairs and into the car, sweating the entire way.

It was only a seven-minute drive back to Oliver's house. There were no cars in the driveway when I arrived, and no sign of Sage.

Freddie, ever the diligent feline hunter, greeted me with a catnip mouse clutched in his mouth.

"Why, thank you for bringing me this gift." I always liked to praise him for keeping his hunting skills sharp, even though he'd never seen an actual mouse in his life. Someday it might come in handy.

We played for a while, then I drank a glass of water. I collapsed into the comfy bed and texted Oliver.

> Thanks again for letting me stay. I found a lot of information today, I'll tell you about it later. Even had a few visions from objects. I'm going to rest for a while. Very exhausted.

He texted right back.

That's exciting, can't wait to hear! I'll be back by the time the full moon party begins. Also, it's not uncommon to be tired after using your powers. One of the articles I read said you should give yourself plenty of time in between psychometry sessions, so you don't become too physically or mentally depleted.

Depleted. That was exactly how I felt. Now that I was horizontal, I could barely keep my eyes open. I struggled to type the next text.

That makes me feel better. Thanks. I'll see you later.

And with that, I burrowed under the covers and fell instantly asleep.

Chapter Thirteen

I woke to the sound of rock music.

Smacking my dry mouth, I sat up. My head was filled with sleep since I'd napped deep and hard. My eyes adjusted to the low light in the apartment.

How long had I been out?

Freddie was on the windowsill, his tail wagging. Something outside was captivating his attention. I rose to join him.

"What's going on out there, little man?" His purr motor kicked in as I worked my fingers into the fur on his back.

I peered outside. There were about a dozen people, all standing around a fire holding beers and red solo cups. The flames lapped over the cast iron bowl of the fire pit. I heard the soft strains of Tom Petty. A cooler was set on a long table, and I spied a covered tray of what looked like sandwiches.

If I didn't know better, I'd assume this was a suburban cookout. I spotted Liz talking to Sage. A few feet away, Oliver stood in a group of two men, laughing. Everyone appeared to be around my age — forties to early fifties.

It looked inviting, to be honest. Hunger rumbled through

my stomach, and I wondered what kind of sandwiches were on that table. I stroked Freddie's block-shaped head.

"I'm going down. If I come across any shrimp, I'll snag one for you."

He meowed and head-butted my hand in response.

I quickly freshened up and bounced downstairs, trying to ignore the faint butterflies in my stomach. For some reason, I was nervous about seeing Oliver.

When I reached the backyard, I sidled up to Liz. She greeted me with a giant hug.

"You made it!"

"Had to nap first."

She let out a little pleasurable groan. "If I could take a siesta every day, I'd be a happy woman. C'mon, let's get you a drink. Beer?"

"Please." We walked over to the cooler and I grabbed myself a bottle of a local craft brew.

By now, Oliver had joined us. He wore black jeans, black sneakers, and a fetching, button-down shirt. Somehow, he was even more handsome than yesterday, which was slightly disarming.

He looked at me with a serious expression. "Did you get some rest? Feeling better?"

"Much better, thanks. How was your day?" I wanted to have a few minutes of normal adult conversation before launching into a retelling of my weird situation.

"Oh, you know. The usual. Undergraduates who don't read the syllabus, kids who come into class late, students who spend the entirety of the class on their cell. Today I had a new one, though. A student's mother called me, asking if she could sit in with her son."

I almost snorted beer out of my nose. "You're kidding."

"Nope. I'd be accommodating if her son had a learning disability or some known issue. But he was valedictorian at his high school. Now his mother wants to help him in American History 101. So that was a delicate conversation. How about you? What did you find?"

"Well, nothing as hilarious as your story." I launched into a retelling of everything, talking for several minutes. Oliver's eyes grew larger behind his glasses as I talked.

"So, yeah," I said, wrapping up my monologue. "I've got at least one restless and possibly angry spirit in the hotel. Oh, and there's a bachelorette party that has reserved the entire place in a few weeks because they want a weird, haunted weekend somewhere funky. That should bring in some much-needed cash. If the spirit — or spirits — cooperate, that is."

I took a long slug of my beer, acutely aware of both Oliver's stunned gaze and my predicament. I swallowed. "Changing the subject. Can you please explain to me the similarities between a witch and a cowgirl? Because I'm not understanding that at all."

Grinning, I gestured with my beer bottle at Sage, who was holding court around the fire pit. She was wearing a dress tonight, a flowy, ivory-colored thing. She'd also changed her boots to a pair of worn, tan leather ones, and had lost the hat. Her pretty long hair flowed loosely.

A smile spread on Oliver's face, then a laugh bloomed. After a second, he was doubled over, nearly crying he was chuckling so hard. Finally, he rose to his full height — he was about a foot taller than me — and spoke.

"She was obsessed with cowboys and cowgirls when she was a kid. She's younger than me, so when I was ten and she was seven, our parents took us to the Grand Canyon. Sage was beside herself with excitement. One day, we went on a donkey ride and she fell off."

I gasped. "I'm so sorry! I didn't mean to make fun—"

Oliver shook his head and held up his hand. "She was fine. She had a mild concussion that she recovered from quickly. But ever since then, she's been convinced she's a cowgirl. She embraced the whole aesthetic, as you can see. It made no sense, but my parents were pretty easygoing so we all embraced her new identity."

I nodded, and he continued.

"Because we grew up here in this town, she obviously was exposed to New Age concepts from the time she was born. But it was only when she spent a few years in Sedona that she embraced her, ah, witchy side. She only recently returned from the southwest, which is why she's staying with me."

"Okay, that all makes sense. But you still didn't explain the similarities between a witch and a cowgirl?"

"Let's see. She explains it like this: cowgirls are for the daytime, witches are for the night."

"Uh-huh. Go on."

"Both cowgirls and witches wear big hats."

"True."

Oliver bit his bottom lip, which sent a zing of desire through me. "One wears a poncho. The other a robe."

"Okay." He had a point.

"Rides horses, rides brooms."

I snickered.

"Guns vs. wands."

"Okay, maybe you're onto something there."

Right then, the loud, repeated ring of a cowbell filled the air. Oliver and I looked toward the firepit, where Sage was standing nearby.

“Gather round,” she shouted. “We’re going to begin tonight’s full moon ritual with an incantation.”

Oliver and I moved closer and stood shoulder-to-shoulder. He leaned in, so his lips were close to my ear. Little fireworks of possibility erupted in my brain.

“Did I adequately explain the whole cowgirl-witch thing?” Oliver’s voice was low and gravelly. My face felt warm, but not hot-flash warm. This was pent-up desire heat.

“Yeah. You did. Thanks,” I whispered back.

Sage rang the cowbell once more, then walked to the table with the sandwiches. That reminded me how hungry I was, and how I shouldn’t be drinking this beer on an empty stomach. I’d grab a sandwich after Sage was finished.

She set the cowbell down and walked to the makeshift arch. I noted that she’d wound a garland of white flowers into the sticks. It was quite a pretty backyard decoration.

Standing under the arch, she raised her arms up, into a V-shape.

“I’d like to acknowledge this sacred evening with a spell. Please close your eyes while I recite it.”

I shut my eyes tightly and listened to the sound of the fire crackling. Sage began to speak, her voice clear in the night air.

Out on the range, under stars above;
Cowgirl brews her mystic love.
Rattlesnake tail and lizard's scale,
In the cauldron, they shall sail;
Cowgirl chuckles, tips her hat,
Adding owl's feather and a dash of bat,
A howlin' wolf's tooth, a rattlin' bone,
Stirring the pot with a branch of sycamore.

Double, double, cowgirl's in a muddle;
Fire burn and caldron bubble.
With a yeehaw and a yippee ki-yay,
She summons magic in her own cowgirl way;
Eye of newt and toe of frog,
Wool of horse and a mangy dog,
With witch's charm, she aims to rumble,
Creating a spell of trouble.

Well, that was something. There was a pause. Sage clapped her hands. "You may open your eyes."

I did, fully intent on snagging one of those sandwiches. But Sage wasn't finished, because she clapped again.

"We've got pens and paper here. I'd like everyone to come up and grab one of each, then write down what you're going to let go this month. It can be anything. Big or small. We're letting it all go tonight. Come on down, friends."

I noticed Oliver looking at me with an amused reaction.

"What?" I asked playfully.

"I'll bet you do this kind of thing all the time in California, right? Full moon rituals and stuff."

I snorted a laugh. "Hardly. My part of California is all wine snobs and foodies."

"You don't strike me as either."

"I'm not. Well, I like food. Obviously. But I'm not fussy about it." I hesitated for a beat, thinking of the couple my ex and I had been friends with. They would only eat at Michelin-starred restaurants. "This party, it's nice. It feels comfortable and, dare I say, normal. Even with the spells and the cowgirl incantation spell. It feels like a group of friends hanging out. It's not an event."

I used air quotes with my fingers when I said the word *event*.

"I'm glad. C'mon. Let's grab our pen and paper."

Normally I'm not the type to participate in group activities. I'm more of a loner, an introvert. But Oliver's gentle enthusiasm and the overall vibe of the party were relaxing, and I reached for a blue pen and a piece of paper that looked like it had been homemade.

When Oliver and I sat at a nearby picnic table, he spotted me inspecting the unusual paper. It was a light tan, with jagged edges and what looked like flowers pressed into the fibers.

"Sage makes her own paper from foraged plants. I think this one is a hibiscus. Sometimes she drags me along to haul her backpack."

He was obviously a supportive brother. We talked for a bit about our siblings, then turned to our pen and paper.

"How does this work?" I uncapped the pen.

"She does this ritual quarterly. All you have to do is write down what you're letting go of."

"I could fill a notebook with that. What are you writing?" I craned my neck to look at his paper. It was blank.

"We're not supposed to share," he said with a small smile. "This is between you and the fire."

"I see. Well."

I chewed on my cheek, pondering what to write. My ex-husband? I'd like to give him up for good. The pain of the past few years? The feelings of inadequacy, exhaustion, and overwhelm that have settled into my psyche in midlife?

I settled on something more global. *THE PAST*, I wrote in neat cursive. That would cover all my bases, including my ex.

Since everyone was folding their papers in half, I did, as

well. Without a word, I got up from the picnic table and went over to the fire pit.

Sage was there, and she held out an arm. “Glad you could make it tonight, Amelia.”

“Thanks for having me. What should I do with this?” I waved the paper in the air.

“Let the flames take over.” She gestured to the fire pit.

Careful not to burn my fingers, I wedged the paper between two glowing red logs. Sage and I watched. The paper was almost too pretty to burn. Sage extended her hand and I stared, dumbly.

“Hold my hand,” she prodded.

“Oh, uh, okay.” I clasped her hand, worried that mine was sweaty and sticky.

“By the light of Luna's radiant glow,” Sage started, “Amelia releases and surrenders all that no longer serves her soul's flow. As this fire burns, Amelia’s burdens turn to ash, setting her free with the moon's enchanting crash."

She gave my hand a squeeze, and I squeezed back. I wasn’t sure if I should say “amen,” or something else, so I settled on a more universal acknowledgement.

“Thanks.”

Sage dropped my hand. “How do you feel?”

I ran my tongue over my top teeth. “I feel…good. Lighter. Yeah. Lighter.”

Of course, I didn’t feel any different than five minutes ago. But Sage was so pleasant and welcoming that I didn’t want to hurt her feelings.

“That’s what I want to hear. Now let’s do some shots!”

I winced. “I need to grab something to eat before I do that. Otherwise, I’ll be toasty within an hour.”

By now, Liz had joined us. “We don’t want anyone getting

toasty tonight, friend! I brought mini Cuban sandwiches," she said, taking me by the arm. "You've got to try one."

She led me over to the table, where a tray of delicious, meat-and-cheese filled sandwiches beckoned.

"I'll try more than one." I was on the verge of being hangry. Which meant food took precedence over spells, spirits, and murder.

Chapter Fourteen

Four tasty mini Cuban sandwiches, one impromptu sing-along to Rick Astley's "Never Gonna Give You Up," and a second beer later, I was pleasantly full and a teeny bit buzzed.

This was a fun crowd. It made me a bit envious that Liz, Sage, and Oliver could do this every month with a group of friends.

I sat in a folding lawn chair around the fire pit. The party was winding down. One couple, who had moved here recently from Puerto Rico, announced they were leaving. I studied them for a second, trying to remember what Liz had told me about them.

The woman with short dark hair was a clairvoyant and teacher. Her wife was a reiki master…no, an energy healer, and an insurance agent. I couldn't recall their names, probably due to the two beers. I was a total lightweight.

"Had a blast, as always, Sage!" the woman called out. "It's nine-thirty, and we need to get back to the sitter. It's a school night, you know. Plus, we're old."

"Gen X for the win," Sage bellowed. "Or at least for the win until eleven p.m. Then it's bedtime!"

Her wife gave a little wave. "Nice meeting you, Amelia. I hope you stick around town. I think you'll be surprised by the quality of life. No, I know you'll be surprised. Maybe stay for a few months? We love new folks."

"Thanks. We'll see." I still had no intention of staying that long, but the woman was right. The town did seem incredibly open to newcomers.

The couple walked out, leaving only me, Oliver, Sage, and Liz clustered near the fire pit.

"You know," I started. "I'm impressed at how everyone I've met has been incredibly welcoming. Nothing like where I live. I'm also shocked that everyone's so open about their paranormal, er, extranormal, abilities."

A frown marred Sage's pretty face. "I don't understand. What do you mean?"

"I'd have thought people would try to hide their gifts and talents. That they wouldn't be so open to the otherworldly ideas. I figured someone in town would be against witches and clairvoyants and mediums."

Liz's curls bounced as she shook her head. "Those kinds of people don't last long. This town was started as a refuge for people like us. Everyone's welcome here. Regardless of race, religion, creed, color, or ability. Obviously, there are people with gifts and abilities here, like yourself. Then there are the rest of us, like me, Sage, and Oliver."

I blinked. "None of you..."

Liz shook her head. "We've all tried. Well, Sage and I have. We're still trying and hoping to gain powers since we've hit midlife. Oliver's content to be a researcher and writer. Those are his superpowers."

Oliver, who was cracking open a bottle of water, smiled sheepishly.

"Changing the subject," Liz blurted, sadly breaking my gaze with Oliver. "How are things at the inn? Any new info?"

I let out a sad chuckle and launched into the Cliffs Notes version of my day. By the time I was finished, Sage and Liz were sitting close to me, listening intently. Oliver, who had already heard everything, stoked the fire, which was now glowing embers. The darkness of the night surrounded us.

Sage let out a long whistle. "Hoo-ee. That's a lot to absorb."

"You're not kidding."

"I know where that icehouse is that your aunt referred to," Oliver said. "It's only about ten minutes from here."

He and Liz had a brief back-and-forth about whether the icehouse was on Lake Street or Sunset Road. A consult with someone's cell phone revealed it was on Lake.

"We should go over there." Sage stood up.

"It would be helpful if everyone came with me. What are y'all doing tomorrow? Or this weekend?" Why did I keep saying y'all?

"Oh, I meant now," Sage replied.

"Now?" Alarmed, I looked to Liz and Oliver, who blinked.

"Why not?" Liz said. "It's not even ten yet. We might be old but we're not dead."

"I'll go grab some gear." Oliver rose and walked toward the house.

"G-gear?" I squeaked out.

"Flashlights and stuff," Sage said. "We can take my truck."

The next thing I knew, I was in the passenger seat of said

truck, whizzing down the road. Liz and Oliver were in the back.

"Are you sober?" I asked Sage as she drove.

"Stone cold sober. I don't imbibe on full moon nights. Trying hard to cultivate my spell abilities and don't want any substances to interfere. It's not coming easy, though."

I stared out the window as we turned down Lake Street. The clock on the dash said it was nearing ten p.m. This didn't seem like a wise idea at this hour. Or maybe any hour. Why had my aunt told me to come here?

"Who owns this place, anyway?"

Liz's head popped between the driver and passenger seats. "Mayor Larry Norton."

I gasped. "He's popping up everywhere. Was he ever considered a serious suspect in Billy Jenkins' death?"

A chorus of "dunnos" and "not sures" rippled through the truck.

"Way before our time," Liz said.

"From what I read, he was," Oliver added. "But he was cleared quite quickly. I need to refresh my memory about this case, obviously. We can do that tomorrow, if you'd like. I don't have class."

A warm feeling settled in my chest when he said the word "we." I didn't have time to revel in that sensation, though, because Sage slowed the truck and took a right turn into a circular driveway.

"Here we are," she said, pulling to a stop.

I leaned forward, gaping out the windshield. "What the duck is that?"

"I don't see any ducks." Sage looked around wildly.

"Sorry, I say duck instead of the other word. One time I was angry at my husband, and I meant to send the F word but it autocorrected to duck," I explained. "My daughter thought it was funny. So now I use duck instead, all the time. It's much more polite."

"Ducking right," Liz guffawed.

I wasn't paying much attention to the laughter in the car because I was staring at the icehouse. It was a white, stucco building that resembled a pile of melted frosting.

"What are those things hanging down?" I was so confused. As usual.

"They're supposed to be icicles," Oliver said. "This was built in 1930, for people who were going fishing and needed ice for their catch. Folks would drive up and park under the canopy, right by the door. They'd honk and someone would come out and place a block of ice in the trunk of your car. This place lasted until 1960, but it's been untouched since then. Sad since it's falling down."

"My parents remember coming here," Liz chimed in.

"Ours too," Sage said.

"It's an example of roadside commercial architecture. There's a lot of this in Florida. You know, buildings shaped like oranges or dinosaurs or ice cream cones. These were buildings designed to accommodate the automobile."

"I had no idea. Fascinating," I said.

Sage popped her door open. "Let's go explore the inside of this puppy."

"Wait," I cried. "Are we going inside?"

Oliver opened his door. "We're going to try."

We all climbed out of the truck. "Isn't that breaking and entering?" I asked.

Liz marched over to the front door, her pink peasant skirt flapping in the warm breeze. She easily pulled the old wooden door open. "Technically, maybe. But since there's no lock..."

The four of us stood at the open door and gaped at each other. Oliver clicked on his flashlight while Sage handed me and Liz similar torches. I clicked mine on, then off, then on again.

"Ready?" Sage asked.

"Let's do it." I tried to project a bravado that I didn't feel and strutted in first. Two steps were all it took for me to come to a grinding halt.

I was struck by the temperature. While it was still a balmy eighty-something degrees outside, inside this old icehouse, the temperature had dropped at least ten degrees. A shiver rattled down my spine, but that had nothing to do with the air.

"Super creepy," I whispered.

The space was larger than I anticipated, a cavernous chamber with high ceilings that seemed to swallow the dim beams of our flashlights. The walls were brick, which made sense since people had once made ice in here.

"Imagine making ice in Florida, before air conditioning was common. Now that's terrifying," I blurted. The others chuckled.

The floor beneath my sneakers was a mix of ancient concrete and dirt, creating a disconcerting crunch with each step. Oliver stepped into the middle of the room, while I kept close to the door. Liz and Sage stood in a corner, shining their flashlights downward at an old cabinet.

The air carried a musty odor, a blend of old wood and mold, mixed with the lingering scent of earth. Cobwebs hung like curtains. The walls were lined with rusted metal hooks.

"What are those for?" I flashed my light on a hook, which made it look weirdly menacing.

"Storage for tools," Oliver said in a casual tone.

As my eyes adjusted to the dim light, I began to make out

the faint outlines of old wooden shelves, their surfaces worn and splintered. Decades of disuse had left the icehouse in a state of eerie disarray, with abandoned crates and forgotten remnants of a bygone era scattered haphazardly across the floor.

"This is wild," I murmured. "Why hasn't Mayor Norton fixed this place up? It would be a great museum, or restaurant, or something."

No one answered because they were each absorbed in their own exploration. I aimed my flashlight upwards, revealing a lattice of wooden beams that crisscrossed the ceiling. My mouth had gone dry, and I attempted to swallow. It was only then that I realized my heart was pounding.

Liz's flashlight illuminated a corner where a broken chair lay, its backrest leaning against the wall as if waiting for a long-lost visitor that would never arrive.

Sage's light revealed a series of faded, weathered posters that adorned one wall, hinting at events from decades past – community gatherings, ice sales, and a price list.

"A nickel for a block of ice," she read aloud. "That's a bargain."

Oliver's flashlight beam was the most powerful. It pierced the darkness and landed on a weathered, wood-and-steel chest that was pushed against the far wall. He walked across the room and I followed.

"What have we got here?" He flipped the heavy steel latch, grunting as he tugged at the lid of the chest.

Sage and Liz joined us. We clustered around as the top finally gave way. It made a disconcerting creak.

"Dang, that's heavy," Oliver muttered as he leaned the lid against the wall behind it.

We were greeted by a riot of junk, a veritable treasure

trove of meaningless items. We all dove in with our hands, touching and picking up the baubles and knickknacks. I reached for a stack of postcards, bound together with an aging rubber band. I flipped through, hoping they had been written on. But all were blank.

There was a small box of shells, a stack of newspapers dated from the late 1970s, and a rusted coffee can containing dozens of old bottle caps.

"Hope everyone's had their tetanus shot," Liz quipped while lifting the pile of newspapers. "Sure is a lot of crap in here."

"Looks like the junk drawer in your kitchen, Ollie." Sage elbowed her brother.

He rolled his eyes. "I'm sure none of this is valuable. Look, there's even some charging cables from the '90s and early 2000s."

"Hey, did you ever think of this?" Sage said, "In a couple thousand years, archaeologists will unearth tanning beds and think we were torturing people."

We all turned our attention from the contents of the trunk to Sage.

"I'm not sure what brought that on," Oliver deadpanned.

Sage shrugged and we resumed our focus on the trunk.

Underneath the newspapers was a smaller, ornate wooden box. The thing was so polished that it practically reflected our flashlights back at us. It had intricate carvings in celestial patterns in what looked like abalone, or maybe even ivory. It was difficult to tell in this light. The moon and stars seemed to dance across the surface.

Sage let out a soft whoop. "That's something unusual."

Carefully, Oliver lifted the smaller box from within the

chest and placed it on the floor. We gathered in a circle around it.

"It's like Raiders of the Lost Ark," Sage said excitedly.

"Except there's no Harrison Ford," Liz added, and I snickered.

Oliver placed his hand on the lid. "Well, let's hope our faces don't melt off when I open it."

"I don't think we'll melt, since we're not Nazis," I quipped.

Oliver glanced to me and we exchanged flirty grins. Eep. Was that attraction or just a shared love of nerdy fandom?

"You ready?" he asked.

The air seemed to crackle with energy. I held my breath.

Oliver unlatched the little box, revealing a blue velvet-lined interior. And nestled within was one thing: an old, tarnished pocket watch. Its intricate design hinted at a bygone era, its mechanical heart frozen in time. I wondered what had been going on in the world when the thing ticked its last second.

"Check this out." Oliver plucked it from its velvet cocoon. He turned it over in his hands. "It's engraved. Can someone shine a light closer?"

Sage pointed her flashlight about three inches from the watch.

"It says… to our dearest son, William, from your loving parents."

Oliver handed it to Liz, who inspected it. She then passed it to Sage.

"I'm fascinated by the detail on the exterior. The filigree is incredible. Hmm." Sage offered it to me.

I fumbled with my flashlight, eventually handing it to Liz

so I could inspect it with both hands. I took the watch. It felt heavy and cool in my palm.

As I held it, a scorching sensation coursed through me. It was as if a current of white-hot energy flowed from the watch into my palm, sending ripples of darkness through my body. My heart raced, and for a second, I thought I was having a heart attack.

I closed my eyes for a moment, trying to calm myself. Trying to allow myself to sit with the discomfort instead of fighting it. This was my power. I should embrace it.

When I opened my eyes again, I was no longer in the icehouse.

Instead, I found myself standing in a completely different place. A house, I think, one with a sloping, low ceiling. The surroundings were hazy, as if I were looking through a foggy window. An overwhelming stench of mold hit my nose. I felt like I was about to sneeze, but didn't want to call attention to myself, so I held my breath.

Before me, a young man with disheveled hair and wild eyes stood in the dimly lit room. He clutched the pocket watch in his trembling hand, his face a mask of fear. Something was very wrong.

The room seemed to spin and shift. I saw the guy speaking in strained tones with another man, a shadowy figure whose face remained in the dark. The conversation was tense, filled with heated words and gestures. None of the words were audible, but from the tone, I understood that the shadowy guy was furious.

The other man's hands shook. He held the pocket watch like it was a life preserver.

The scene shifted again, and I watched as he tried to leave. The shadowy guy threw a punch, and I screamed. Or tried to. The young man staggered back, then made his way toward the door. The other man, whose back was to me, grabbed the poor guy's shoulders and pulled him into the middle of the room.

The watch was heating up in my hand. It seared my flesh, like a cattle brand. But I couldn't let go. Couldn't scream. I could only watch the unfolding scene with my gut clenched.

Then the obscure man took out a knife. The blade glinted in the light, almost a silver sparkle that captivated me for a beat.

"No," I cried.

With a swift motion, the man sank the blade into the other's torso. "She's mine, Billy," the man yelled. I gasped.

But the mystery man's voice seemed to crack, as if it was higher-pitched. The scene grew hazier.

I gasped and stumbled back, my fingers releasing their grip on the watch. It landed with a tinny *clunk* on the concrete floor.

My vision faded, leaving me standing in the icehouse, surrounded by Oliver, Sage, and Liz.

"She's using her psychometry! Give her room. Stand back," Sage shouted. "Make sure she doesn't swallow her tongue."

"No, that's a seizure, silly," Liz said.

Oliver grabbed my arm. "Amelia? Amelia? What did you see? Are you okay?"

Everyone was staring at me, their expressions a mix of concern and intense curiosity. I shuddered in a breath. Somehow, I was covered in cold sweat even though I hadn't moved an inch.

"The watch. It showed Billy. Billy Jenkins," I croaked.

I forcefully exhaled a breath, then gasped in an inhale. I

did this a few times. Oliver drew me close to his chest. I stayed like that for a few seconds because it felt so safe and pure. The opposite of what I'd witnessed.

If only I could remain in his arms for the rest of the night.

Dimly aware that the others were watching, I pulled away, sniffling.

"I... I saw something. Something terrible," I stammered, my voice barely a whisper. "I saw Billy Jenkins's murder."

No one talked as we drove back to Oliver's. I stared out the window while the radio played *Jesse's Girl* by Rick Springfield. Unlike the ride over, I was in the backseat.

The song was far too bubbly for my mood. I couldn't shake the image of Billy's death from my memory.

I also couldn't ignore the fact that Billy had likely been killed in the hotel's attic, not just found there. At some point, I needed to check out that space for clues, but wasn't eager to do it tonight. Or physically able.

Similar to this afternoon, exhaustion tugged at my eyelids and weariness had invaded my bones. Seeing those visions seemed to deplete me in ways even midlife hadn't.

Just my luck. I had a latent power, but it dovetailed nicely with my perimenopause symptoms. Why couldn't my newfound ability leave me with dewy, moisturized skin, or the ability to vanquish hot flashes with a single thought?

"You okay?" Oliver's fingers touched the top of my hand, then withdrew. "How's your palm?"

The watch had left an angry red blotch on the skin of my

left hand. I turned to him. "It's going to be fine with some ice. I don't know if I'm okay. It was intense. Like watching a 3-D movie."

"Did y'all ever see Jaws 3 in 3D?" Sage asked from the driver's seat.

She and Liz launched into a discussion about it. Turns out it was a popular movie here in town in 1983.

"I'm beyond tired," I murmured to Oliver.

He nodded. "That's to be expected with psychometry. You should take it easy tomorrow. The more intense the vision, the longer it will take you to recover."

"I don't have time to recover. I need to resolve this spirit situation before the bachelorette party." Now, however, there was more than simply my own financial needs. I had to think about Billy. How could I not?

"That poor kid," I said, repeatedly raking my bottom lip through my teeth. "Billy didn't deserve to die that way."

"But you didn't see who killed him?" Oliver asked.

"It was a guy. I think. The voice sounded garbled. Or it changed in pitch. Maybe that's my memory, though. Or the visions aren't completely accurate. Is that possible?"

"It takes time to use the full range of the ability, from what I've read."

"Billy looked so young. About the age of my own daughter, maybe a little younger." I sighed. "I wonder what happened that night. We've got to find out."

Liz turned in her seat. "Sounds like someone wants to investigate a homicide."

I groaned and let my head flop back against the seat. "I don't know. We should probably go to the police and give them all our evidence."

The other three began talking at once, debating whether to

bring our discovery to the cops. Apparently, the local police force was in a transition period and the department didn't have much money or resources. The detective division was one guy who had been on the force for decades.

Liz explained that crime was rare in town, what with all the psychics. "Everyone knows when someone's breaking in or about to steal a car," she added.

"Then there's the issue of the new chief," Sage said.

"Shh," Liz said, waving her hand. It was the first time I'd seen her flustered.

"What?" I piped up. "What's the issue with the new chief?"

Oliver cleared his throat. "There are rumors about him."

"Like what?"

"Supposedly he's a werewolf," Sage said. "But that might be town gossip. Either way, I'm sure he's a fine lawman."

"He's not a werewolf," interjected Liz. "He's got a beard. I think he's Italian."

I pressed my forehead against the window and shut my eyes. "Duck me," I whispered.

A werewolf? Oddly, I could almost believe it here in this place. I shoved that detail aside and focused on the one thought that had burned into my brain, much like the pocket watch's metal had seared into the flesh of my hand.

Billy Jenkins deserved justice.

* * *

The next morning, I woke to the sound of driving rain against the window. Freddie was next to me, but instead of being curled up and velcroed to my side, he was sitting up and looking in the direction of the window.

His whiskers quivered. His tail twitched and thwacked me in the face. A clap of thunder made him stiffen.

"You're not used to the storms, are you? You're a California kitty. It's okay, little dude." I reached out to stroke his back. He'd stayed with me all night, almost as if he instinctively knew I needed his comforting, soft presence.

I'd had a fitful night of sleep, mostly because I couldn't get the vision of Billy's murder out of my head. Also, the intermittent thunder didn't help. I simply wasn't used to dramatic storms like this after years of living in drought-ridden northern California.

As if on cue, a flash of lightning illuminated the room. I hadn't seen weather this wild in years, and mused how it would be romantic under certain conditions. None of which applied at this moment.

For at least fifteen minutes, I lay in bed, replaying the night before. How did Billy's pocket watch end up on a property owned by Mayor Larry Norton? It was too wild to be real. There were too many questions to count, starting with, who killed Billy?

Was Billy the demon in the mirror? Was he the one haunting the hotel? I sure hoped he was the only restless spirit. I wasn't sure if I could deal with one, much less multiple. How did that work in a multi-spirit household, anyway? Did they take shifts to haunt the living? How did they communicate to each other?

I pondered this for a while, feeling ridiculous. My earlier vow to seek justice for Billy seemed quite ambitious in the light of day. Still, what other choice did I have?

Another detail also nagged at me: Mayor Larry Norton. Why did he want to buy the hotel so badly, especially since business had recently been poor? Was he greedy, or did he have an ulterior motive? I knew he was kind of a jerk from our brief exchange at the coffee shop. And he'd found Billy.

Was it all an unfortunate coincidence?

I might not be a business whiz, considering how I hadn't safeguarded my cookie delivery service from my ex-husband. But I was older and wiser now and wasn't about to sell the hotel to someone like Norton. It was definitely worth looking into his background, as well.

What if he'd killed Billy? No, that was way too obvious. He'd been mayor for decades, according to Liz. Wouldn't someone have known that he'd killed someone when he was younger? That sort of detail would be hard to overlook in a small town like this. Especially if so many psychics were wandering around.

"None of it makes sense, Freddie."

He responded with a *brrrrap*.

Finally, I flipped the covers back and climbed out of bed. Moving quickly, I performed my morning routine: coffee, feeding Freddie, showering, dressing. Although I had a plan for the day, I didn't have one key item.

An umbrella.

Surely Oliver or Sage owned one that I could borrow. After kissing Freddie goodbye, I walked down the stairs and stood under an awning. It was really coming down now, pouring in near monsoon levels. Had I somehow missed a hurricane?

I eyed Oliver's side door, which was also covered with an awning. It was maybe ten steps away. I had to make a run for it.

It was difficult not to squeal as I sprinted the short distance. I paused under the awning to catch my breath. When I was about to knock, I realized two things. One, was that the door was open, which meant I could see through the closed screen door. And two, someone was playing guitar inside.

A man's voice soared through the air. Was that Oliver? If so, I was impressed. His singing voice was low and gravelly and… sexy. His guitar playing was also pretty good, in my totally amateur opinion.

After a few lyrics, I realized what he was singing: *Jesse's Girl*, the song from the car last night. I stood there, listening and grinning. When he broke into the guitar solo part of the song like that, I clasped my hands to my damp chest.

For some reason, my heart felt like it was growing three sizes. Even though I knew he wasn't singing that and thinking of me, it was plain fun to hear. And a little romantic, if I thought about it hard enough.

I waited until he finished the song to knock. Oliver answered the door quickly.

"Good morning," he said with a giant smile. He held a guitar in one hand while opening the door for me. "Quite the rainstorm, right?"

"Did I ignore a hurricane alert?" I stepped inside.

He laughed. "No, this is pretty typical weather for September. Hey, did you want coffee? I'm brewing a pot now."

"Sure, I'd love that. Here, let me take off my shoes, they're pretty wet." I toe-heeled off my flats.

Oliver watched. "You're going to need to get some rubber flip-flops if you're staying any longer."

"Oh, is that a requirement for living in Florida?" I asked as I followed him into the kitchen.

"It kinda is. Have a seat. Now, do you want cream or sugar in your coffee?"

"Both, in large quantities, thanks." I sat at the island counter and looked around. "This is a beautiful kitchen."

He opened a cabinet and took out two mugs. I couldn't help but notice that he looked as handsome in gray sweatpants and a hoodie as he did in jeans and T-shirts.

"I got so lucky when I bought the place. The kitchen had been redone like this. It was the only room that had been improved. Everything else, I did."

"Impressive."

Rough-hewn beams crossed the ceiling, while white cabinets and white marble made the space look elegant but not fussy. The stove and oven looked pricey; I'd had a similar model in my California home.

"Here you go." He set a mug in front of me. "How are you doing this morning? I was worried about you after last night. You looked like you had three ounces of energy."

"Hanging in there. I didn't get the greatest night's sleep." I sighed. "But I've come to some conclusions."

"Oh yeah?" He took a sip from his mug.

"I need to know more. Maybe there's a simple explanation for all this. Or perhaps there's an easy way to move the spirit, or spirits, along. I can't sell the place as-is. Can't really rent hotel rooms to folks, either. I've gotta put on my big girl panties and solve the problem."

While he nodded thoughtfully, I slipped both hands around my mug and continued. "It's not what I want to do. It was my aunt's wish for me to handle this, though. I'm the kind of person who likes to see things through. And it's not like I'm doing anything else at the moment."

Oliver tilted his head. "You don't have a job to go back to in California?"

"No." Even if there had been an attraction on his part, it

was about to evaporate. “I haven’t had a job in a year, when I handed over my, well, the business I shared with my husband. As part of the divorce agreement, my husband got our cookie delivery operation. Even though it was originally my idea and my business, the court didn’t agree with me.”

He snorted indignantly. “I hope you got the house or alimony, or something.”

“I got a little alimony and the house, but we didn’t have much equity in it, since we’d taken out a home equity loan. I’ve been living off the alimony and a small settlement from relinquishing control of the company.”

He winced. “That sucks. I’m sorry.”

A sad chuckle slipped out of my mouth. “It’s funny, when I was flying here, I had a brief fantasy that my aunt’s hotel would be adorable and easy, and I’d move here and run the place. You know, a quaint bed and breakfast, decorated all pretty. I imagined baking cinnamon rolls for guests and arranging fresh flowers every morning. Helping folks with directions and outings. Then I got here and whoa. The reality is so much different.”

“I understand how the hotel would be a shock. Honestly, though, you could have all that, if…”

“If I manage to evict the spirit demon thing that’s causing all the problems?”

He nodded. “That.”

Things were too chaotic to even consider what life would be like here. I took a sip. “Tasty coffee.”

“Thanks.” He beamed. “What’s on the agenda for today?”

“My aunt suggested visiting a lady at the library. Martha somebody. I figured I’d start there.”

“Martha Johnstone. She’s been the librarian in town since

I was a kid. She can be a bit frosty. Want some company? I might be able to help."

"Absolutely. I was also hoping you'd have an umbrella." I gestured to the window.

"I can also help with that."

He seemed genuinely thrilled to come with me today and poured our coffee into two travel mugs. Then he grabbed an umbrella and held it over our heads as we dashed to his car in the downpour.

Chapter Sixteen

The Mirror Lake Library was an adorable building a couple of blocks off Main Street.

The little yellow wooden structure was next to a small pond. Palm trees swayed in the wind, and the rain beat down on the sidewalk path that ringed the water.

Even in a storm, it looked so peaceful that I suspected the scene had been — or was currently — featured on a postcard showcasing the town's beauty.

Oliver and I pulled up and he killed the engine. "It used to be a home, built a few years after the town settled. Then the city bought it, expanded the footprint, and turned it into a library," he said. "It's the only building in town with angels as decoration."

He pointed to the door. There were several cherubs etched above the wooden entrance.

We made a run for the front door and he pulled it open. We burst inside, breathing hard and shaking off water. A woman sitting at the nearby reference counter who looked to be about a hundred years old lowered her black-rimmed oval-shaped glasses and studied us with a steely-eyed gaze.

I was wiping my feet on the doormat when Oliver stepped toward her. She was wearing a blue polo shirt with the library's name embroidered on the front.

"Martha! It's been a while," he said.

She adjusted her glasses. "Not long enough. I'm still shelving the microfilm you had me pull. What do you want today?"

Yikes. What kind of customer service was this? I joined him at the counter and raised my hand into a wave. "Hi."

"Who's this? Your girlfriend?"

Oliver laughed. "No. She's a friend. I'm helping her with some research. We're here to look at the microfilm."

We stood watching as she took a long, wheezy inhale, and an equally long, wheezy exhale. "Fine," she finally said.

She rose from her chair slowly. That's when I noticed she was wearing jeans and Converse All-Stars.

We all shuffled past stacks of books, a bank of computers, and several tables until we reached a door. She grunted as she pushed it open.

"Oliver, you know the drill. I don't need to tell you how to work the machine." She scowled in his direction while flipping a light switch.

He grinned, and I wondered how she could be immune to his charms. "Sure do. I'm sure we'll have some questions when we're finished."

She rolled her eyes. "When do you not have questions? You've had questions ever since you were knee-high to a grasshopper." Shaking her head, she ambled away.

I turned to Oliver. "I guess you and Martha go way back?"

Oliver chuckled. "My mom first brought me here when I

was three. By the time I was five, I was researching the history of mummies and pestering Martha for books. At ten, I was looking into the origins of extra sensory perception. Martha's been here for it all. She's a big softie. You'll see."

He paused at the door. "Do you want this open or closed? Are you claustrophobic?"

I glanced around the room. It was small and I appreciated his attention to my comfort. "Maybe leave it open."

"Good plan." He set his messenger bag on the table that took up half the room. In the corner was something I hadn't seen in years: a microfilm machine. It sat on a small desk, with a chair nearby.

Next to that was a bank of tall, gray filing cabinets. Oliver ran his finger down one row. "We're looking for August 1956."

He opened a drawer, studied it for a second, then closed it. He did this twice more, then plucked out a small box, setting it near the machine.

"Let's pull up a chair for you." He flipped a chair around to face the microfilm screen and pushed the larger table toward one wall, giving us more room. "Here we go. All set."

I plunked down and watched as he expertly threaded the microfilm into the machine. Two spools whirred to life. It was obvious he knew his way around the contraption, whereas I hadn't seen once since high school.

The image on the screen flickered to life, then whizzed past as he pressed a button. The motion made me woozy, so I focused on Oliver's face. *Much better.*

"What are we looking at?" I asked.

"This is a local newspaper that's no longer in business. Believe it or not, the town had two papers back then. One that came out in the morning, one in the evening. Eventually they merged and that's the paper we have now. This particular film is from August 1956. We're going to look starting August ninth, the first day after Billy Jenkins was murdered."

"I'm sure his death was front page news."

Oliver nodded. I slid a glance at the screen, which was now still. An old front page took up the entire screen. The date atop the masthead read August 10. The bold, large headline told me we'd hit the jackpot right away.

MYSTERY DEATH AT CRESCENT MOON INN

"Here we go," he murmured, adjusting the focus so we could see the letters more sharply. We both moved closer to the screen.

A sense of shock has engulfed the serene town of Cypress Grove as the lifeless body of 18-year-old William Jenkins was discovered early yesterday in the attic of the famed Crescent Moon Inn. The tragic incident has left the community in a state of bewilderment, and authorities are scrambling to unravel the puzzle surrounding the young bellhop's untimely demise.

Mr. Jenkins, a cheerful and dedicated employee at Crescent Moon Inn, had been working part-time at the hotel for over a year. The shocking discovery was made when another staff member stumbled upon his lifeless body while searching for misplaced items in the attic. Authorities were alerted immediately, and the tranquil hotel transformed into a crime scene.

Jenkins is the son of Mr. and Mrs. Vernon Jenkins of Broad Street. He graduated from Cypress Grove High School in May. He lettered in football.

Preliminary investigations reveal that Mr. Jenkins was murdered, but the circumstances of his death remain shrouded in mystery. Law enforcement officials, led by Detective

Samuel Turner, are tirelessly working to piece together the puzzle, but as of now, no solid leads have emerged. The cause of death remains undetermined, leaving the community in a state of heightened unease.

Local residents are grappling with fear and uncertainty as they wait for answers.

The police department implores anyone with information about William Jenkins or his activities leading up to the tragedy, including details about his evening in Orlando with Ann Baer, to step forward and aid in shedding light on this horrible case.

With hearts heavy with sorrow, the town remains united in the hope that justice will be served and the perpetrator of this chilling crime will soon be apprehended.

Reading this made me perk up. "We've now got two names to investigate. Girlfriend Ann Baer and Detective Samuel Turner."

Oliver shook his head. "Detective Sam died a few years ago. Drowned during a fishing trip on the lake."

"Oh." I wiggled my nose. "What about Ann? Do you know her?"

"I don't, but it's worth looking for her. Although she'll likely be well into her eighties by now. Let's hunt for more articles."

He pressed a button and the machine whirred to life until we reached the next day.

GRIEVING COMMUNITY SEEKS SOLACE, PRAYERS

Cypress Grove remains shrouded in a heavy blanket of grief and bewilderment after the shocking murder of 18-year-old bellhop William Jenkins, whose lifeless body was discovered in the attic of the Crescent Moon Inn. The tight-knit community is grappling with the loss of a young man whose infectious laughter and dedication touched the hearts of many.

The memory of William Jenkins, affectionately known as "Billy" to those who knew him, is vividly etched in the minds of the town's residents. His former high school football coach, Mr. Robert Thompson, recalled, "Will was not only a standout on the field, but also an outstanding young man off of it. His determination and sportsmanship were an inspiration to us all."

Jenkins' close friend, Mark Henderson, a recent Cypress Grove High graduate, said students are stunned. "We had dreams of the future, and now those dreams are shattered. Will was a true friend, always there to lift your spirits with a joke or a listening ear."

The tragedy has taken an even more poignant turn as details emerge about Jenkins' last hours. Prior to his untimely death, Jenkins had attended an electrifying Elvis concert in Orlando, accompanied by his date, Ann Baer. The pair had enjoyed the show. Authorities are diligently probing this key element of Jenkins' final night, hoping that it could offer insights into the sequence of events that led to his demise.

Detective Samuel Turner and his team are focused on piecing together the puzzle of Jenkins' whereabouts in the hours leading up to his death. "We are treating all leads with the utmost seriousness," Detective Turner stated. "Our priority is to bring justice to Jenkins' memory and provide answers to his family and the community."

Cypress Grove residents continue to demonstrate their solidarity as they contribute any information that might aid the investigation. Memorials for Jenkins, adorned with flowers and messages of remembrance, have sprung up in various parts of town, reflecting the deep sense of loss that envelops the community.

The article was disappointing, basically reiterating the same information as the day before.

"At least we can try to track down Mark Henderson," I offered.

"Dead," Oliver said. "He owned the hardware store and died about ten years ago."

"Rats. I don't suppose Robert Thompson is alive?" This was getting frustrating. Had too much time passed?

"Probably not, but we can check."

We scrolled through several more days, then turned to the film from the other newspaper. Each article mentioned solace, prayers, and investigation. No leads were ever disclosed — if there were any. Eventually, the local papers stopped covering the story altogether.

Oliver and I sat in front of the glowing screen, stumped.

"Here's what I don't get." I shifted in my seat. "If this town has so many psychics and mediums and people who can predict the future and see the past, why didn't any of them step into this case?"

A small smile played on Oliver's mouth. Today a sprinkle of stubble dotted his jaw. "I knew you'd ask that."

"It's a logical question, right?"

"Yes, it absolutely is. But things were complicated back then. Different than they are now. Back in the 1950s and '60s, people here didn't embrace the paranormal as they do now. People with abilities were looked down upon. Of course, there weren't as many folks with abilities in town back then. On top of that, it was the beginning of the Civil

Rights era. Most of the few people with special powers lent their support to the Black activists in town, who were fighting segregation. Some of the residents here traveled around the south with the Freedom Riders, and that was covered in detail in the local papers. It doesn't surprise me that Billy's murder was moved to the back burner after a while."

"Interesting. Did you learn all this from books and microfilm, or talking to people?"

"Both. I did my thesis on the history of the paranormal in town."

I had to admit, Oliver seemed knowledgeable. And trustworthy. "What do you think we should do now? Is there any other microfilm to look at? Wait. Let's check the articles about the Elvis concert. Maybe that will yield some clues."

We did but found nothing except for a funny quote from a mom who attended the concert: "Elvis looks just like a hound dog in heat and sounds like a sick cat."

I snorted. "Sounds like me when I took my daughter to a One Direction concert when she was thirteen."

Oliver pressed a button, causing the two spools on the machine to spin at dizzying speed. "We should talk to Martha. After all, she was alive back then and might have even known Billy."

I had my doubts whether Martha would tell us anything, if the way she scowled at me was any indication. But we dutifully put the re-spooled microfilm back into the drawer and turned off the machine, then walked back out into the main part of the library.

We found Martha at the reference desk, dozing.

"Maybe we shouldn't wake her," I whispered to Oliver. There was no evidence of anyone else in the building.

"Oh, it's fine." He waved me off and leaned over the desk and cleared his throat loudly.

Martha's eyes fluttered open. "I'm here," she said crossly. "What do you need-oh, it's you."

Oliver grinned, making my stomach flutter.

"We found what we were looking for in the microfilm."

"Did you put it away?"

"We did," I said. "But we were wondering—"

Oliver quickly interrupted, pressing his shoulder into mine. "We were wondering what you remember about the Billy Jenkins murder."

Martha's flinty-eyed gaze went soft. "Billy Jenkins. That's a name I haven't heard in years. Why are you poking around in that old case?"

We paused. I sensed Oliver wasn't sure what to say, so I piped up. "I'm the new owner of the Crescent Moon Inn. I'm trying to research everything I can about it, and Oliver's helping. I'm Amelia Matthews, by the way."

I stuck my hand out. Martha looked down, then back up at me. Eventually, she clasped my palm with a surprisingly firm grip, given her age.

"Oh, don't be shocked at my strength. I do Crossfit, missy."

I didn't have a response for that. The irascible older woman dropped my hand.

"Billy Jenkins. We were in the same class in high school. He was a good egg. Quiet. Polite. Like kids were back then. Not like these ones today. The other day, I had a kid in here who set up a tripod and was doing a dance. Right in the middle of the non-fiction section. Said he was doing it for Tip Top. That's an app."

"TikTok?" I asked.

She scowled at us. "Whatever. Back to Billy. We weren't friends. He ran with a different crowd, mostly the jocks. He'd dated Ann Baer since they were sophomores. That summer, before everything happened, I'd heard that he was going to propose to her."

Martha shuffled back behind the desk and eased her body into the chair. "Then he was murdered. What more do you want to know?"

"Who was the main suspect at the time?" I blurted, unable to contain my curiosity.

Her lips quivered. "There were many suspects. Ann, for one, but she was cleared. The night he died, they'd gone on a date to the Elvis concert. You probably saw that in the paper. Afterward, they drove back to town and parked by the lake. You know, to make out, like kids do, or did. God knows what they do these days. Eventually Billy drove Ann home. Here's where it got interesting, though."

Oliver and I leaned closer and Martha's voice dipped to barely a whisper.

"I heard that Billy got into a fight with Ann's father, for bringing her home so late. Her father — I can't recall his name right now — was questioned by police. Nothing came of it, though."

"Who else was questioned?"

"Pfft, everyone. The then-owner of the hotel, Armand Mortimer. He died a few years afterward. A boy named Hank was also questioned. He's still alive and in town. Hank Green."

"What about Larry Norton?" Oliver asked.

"Since he found Billy, he was questioned. But not much." Martha shook her head. "Only once, in fact. Probably because his father was a bigshot state representative."

She snorted, and I wondered if she and Norton had a deeper backstory. I sensed from Martha's sour expression that she was almost done with this conversation. I figured I'd try a softer approach.

"Thank you so much for sharing all this with us. It must be rather triggering to talk about. Very traumatic for a young person back then. I'm so sorry." A sympathetic smile spread on my face.

Martha shifted in her seat to look at me. "Triggered? My generation didn't get triggered like you fragile youngsters. We mourned Billy, oh sure, but we didn't dwell on the bad things like you all do now."

Eep. So much for a softer approach.

"Thanks for all your help, Martha. We really appreciate it." Oliver didn't seem at all fazed by her rebuke.

"It's my duty to tell you not to poke around in that case, but I know you, Oliver, and know you'll ignore me." She sighed dramatically and waved her hand toward one wall. "It might be worth looking at our yearbooks. Maybe you'll find something there."

Oliver chuckled. He walked around the desk and kissed Martha on the cheek. She scrunched up her face and waved him away with a wizened hand. "You're such a pain in the butt. Shoo."

We started to walk away, but one more question lingered in my mind. I whirled and Martha looked up.

"What about Ann Baer?" I asked.

"What about her?" Martha responded in an annoyed tone.

"Where is she? Did she move out of town?"

"No." Martha's voice was flat. "She stayed. You can find her at Enchanted Eternity."

My mouth hung open as the truth began to dawn on me. Crap on a cookie. "The cemetery?"

"That's where dead people go, isn't it?" She reached for a book, opened it, and began to read.

Oliver motioned for me to follow him, steering me between two rows of books. Once we were out of earshot of Martha, he leaned closer. "She always acts like that. Today she was pretty helpful."

"Yikes. I'd hate to see her at her *least* helpful," I murmured. "The yearbooks are a smart idea, though."

"They should be right…" Oliver looked over my shoulder. "Here."

I turned to see row after row of large, maroon hardcover books. Each had a year in gold stamped on the spine.

"1956." I eased the book out. "It's too bad Ann is gone."

"Yeah, I'll bet she had some key info. I'll grab nearby years too." He removed five yearbooks from the shelf. "There's a table back here."

We spread out at the large, round table. I held the 1956 yearbook, my hands tingling. My heart thumped fast. It was kind of exciting, poking around like this. Then I remembered that we weren't doing this for kicks and giggles.

Oliver took the seat next to me and pointed at the book in my hands. "Let's start with the year Billy graduated."

I cracked open the book, starting with the first page. There was a black and white photo of a group of kids near a brick building.

"That's the high school." Oliver tapped on the page.

We flipped through a few pages. "It's like taking a peek into an alternative universe," I said.

"In what way?"

"Everyone's so formal. So well put together. When my

daughter went to high school, she and her friends looked like they were going to mow someone's lawn. And I was happy about that, because at least she didn't look as though she was going to a shift at the local strip club."

Oliver stifled a laugh. "It was a different era back then."

"It looks so familiar, yet, so foreign. Check out these beehive hairdos."

We were at the beginning of the 1956 senior class pages. I flipped forward a few pages.

"Here we go," Oliver said.

There were only four photos to a page. All of the girls appeared to wear the identical black top — a slightly off-the-shoulder portrait neckline. The boys all wore ties, suit jackets, and sheepish smiles.

Billy blended in with his slicked-back hair and tilted head. There was a sense of sadness in his eyes, or maybe that was me reading into the photograph. Something about him seemed innocent and dignified, which tugged at my conscience.

How could this young man's death go unsolved? His poor parents. Being a parent, I couldn't even think about it too hard, otherwise I'd dissolve into tears.

"It's the same photo that's in the hallway at the hotel," I said. Underneath the photo was a paragraph of text. Oliver read it aloud.

William Jenkins

"Billy"

Billy will be remembered as one of the most popular, smoothest fellows in the class of '56. We will never forget his performance on the football field and at the homecoming game. Billy plans on working at Crescent Moon Inn after graduation and hopes to eventually attend college for business. He says he'll never forget his chums and plans on marrying his special girl. Smooth sailing, Billy! You deserve it!

Activities: football

"Hmm. This doesn't reveal much." I couldn't help but be disappointed.

"No, it doesn't. Let's look at Ann Baer's photo."

I turned a few pages until I found the Bs. "There she is."

Like the rest of the girls, Ann wore the black V-neck. Unlike the others, she wore a necklace — a delicate chain with a gold locket.

"I wonder what's in the locket," Oliver mused aloud.

"Dunno. She's gorgeous, that's for sure." I started to read aloud.

Ann Baer

"Annie"

With her pleasant disposition and beautiful smile, Annie will be a swell nurse who makes her patients cheerful.

"Oh, she wanted to be a nurse," I said. "She had career ambition. That's sort of surprising for the 1950s, no?"

Oliver continued to read.

Her quick wits make her ready for any emergency, even meeting that nice, young intern doctor.

"Oh. Ew. Well." It wasn't the first time that I was happy to have been born in the 1970s instead of thirty years earlier.

The very best wishes to you, Annie, from the class of 1956

Activities: Yearbook, Cheerleader, Senior Class Treasurer

We sat back in our seats, surveying Ann's pretty photo.

"I wonder why she didn't mention Billy in the yearbook blurb," I said.

"Did she write that, or did the yearbook staff? It seems like these blurbs weren't written by the students themselves."

"True, but if she'd been dating Billy since their sophomore year, everyone would've known. The cheerleader and the football player? Come on. Plus, she was on the yearbook staff. She could've done whatever she wanted. Unless…"

I leaned in, as if trying to extract secrets from the black-and-white image.

"Unless what?" Oliver asked.

"Unless they were sneaking around. Martha said Ann's father and Billy had gotten into a fight the night Billy died. What if she was trying to hide their relationship?"

My question hung in the air. I tapped on the page, then moved my index finger to Ann's photo. I ran the pad of my fingertip in a circular motion over her image.

Tell me your secrets, Annie Baer.

Chapter Seventeen

Warmth spread from my finger to my hand. Then my arm. Like before, my entire body was enveloped in the sensation within seconds.

But unlike my last vision of Billy's death, I didn't feel fear. Or horror. No, today, a long-buried emotion welled inside me. I couldn't pinpoint what it was, but it made my stomach flip-flop and my knees weak.

A millisecond later, and I was in a cavernous building. A high school hallway, with grey-green lockers lining the walls. The warmth I felt turned to tingles.

The entire room seemed to tilt, and then I was standing near a girl. She didn't seem to notice me, and I didn't say a word. She stared into her locker, then shut it, a dreamy smile on her pretty face.

It was Annie Baer.

She wore a tight, cream-colored sweater and a navy skirt that was so flared it almost touched me. The skirt had a poodle on it, a detail that made me love Annie. Brown loafers with white, frilly ankle socks rounded out the adorable outfit.

She looked like an extra in Grease, which had been my favorite movie as a kid.

She whirled around. "Billy," she gushed.

"You look like the bees' knees, Annie."

I watched as he swept her into his arms. They swayed a little, both of them dancing to music only they could hear. He dipped her low. She giggled the entire time and I found myself grinning at their young love.

"How did you get out of class?" she whispered while still in his arms.

"I'm officially running an errand for Mr. Nicholson. I don't have to be back for the rest of the period." He kissed her cheek. "I don't want to keep you from lunch."

"This is better than any lunch." She leaned in and kissed him full on the lips.

For some reason, this shocked me. I looked around, worried that they'd be spotted. There was no one, and I turned my attention back to the couple.

They ended their kiss but stared into each other's eyes for several long beats. A rush of euphoria hit me, and I had to stop myself from sighing and saying, *Awwwww.*

"I have something for you," Billy finally said.

Annie's eyes lit up.

Billy, who was wearing a white, short-sleeve, button-down shirt and black pants, reached into his pocket. He pulled out something that looked suspiciously like a ring box, and my eyes widened.

Was he asking her to marry him right here in the halls of the high school? Weren't they too young? I had to remind myself that I was watching a scene unfold in 1956.

Annie gasped as he opened the box. "A necklace? With a locket?"

"Look inside the locket," he replied.

With shaking hands, she carefully opened the small gold bauble. "It's us," she cried.

Then she wrapped her arms around him. "Thank you, thank you, thank you. I love you so much, Billy Jenkins."

"I love you too, Annie. Don't tell your dad I gave this to you." He put his forehead to hers and I could almost feel her swoon.

"I won't."

The sound of heels on linoleum echoed, and Billy murmured in Annie's ear. "I think someone's coming."

They broke apart, and so did my vision. Suddenly I was back in the library, sitting at a table, staring at Oliver.

"What did you see? Tell me," he asked.

I blinked slowly. "I saw…" My tongue darted out to lick my dry lips. "I saw love. First love. You know, the kind that's silly and all-consuming and wonderful. And I felt it, too. Wow."

For some reason, I was breathing heavily, as if I'd run a few miles. Unlike many of the other visions, this one had left me energized. Happy, even. Probably I looked like an idiot because I was grinning so hard.

"I didn't know I could also feel such deep things from the objects I touch."

Oliver nodded. "As your powers grow stronger, you'll experience vivid emotions and even internal sensations that feel real."

"They are real," I corrected him. "My heart's racing."

His brows drew together in a frown. "Really? I don't think that's supposed to happen."

I held out my hand, palm up. "Feel my pulse."

"I'll do one better. I'll take your pulse." With his left hand, he placed his index and middle finger on the sensitive underside of my wrist. His touch felt electric, and I chewed on my bottom lip. Our eyes met, and the fluttery feeling inside me bloomed again. Oh dear. What was happening to me?

He quickly focused on his watch. A few seconds later, his eyebrows shot up. "Your pulse is 140. Not dangerously high, but high enough considering you haven't moved in a while."

I blew out a breath. No way would I tell him my heart rate might be spiking because of him. "Do I need to be worried about heart attacks?"

He shook his head, still holding on to my wrist. "It's coming down. You should be okay. Do you have a smartwatch?"

"A smart phone, yes. Watch, no."

He nodded and released my arm. I rubbed at where his fingers were. "Oh, I didn't tell you what I saw."

"Right!" Oliver looked flustered for some reason.

I took a fortifying breath and tapped on the photo. Every tap was met with corresponding tingles in my finger. "It was in the high school. Billy and Annie were there, and he gave her this locket."

"Did you see what was in it?"

"Nope. He said it was a photo of the two of them. And, get this: he told her not to tell her dad that he gave her the necklace."

Oliver's face lit up. "Perhaps her father was the killer."

"He seems to be the most likely suspect. Back in the 1950s it wouldn't have been unthinkable for a father to kill her daughter's boyfriend." A heavy feeling settled in my chest, pained that Billy and Annie didn't get their happy-ever-after.

Oliver stroked his stubble. "Where do we go from here?"

He sounded as though he was talking to himself. I shook my head and we sat without speaking. The only sound in the room was the hum of the air conditioner.

"Dunno. What happens if we do find the person who killed Billy? Will they be brought to justice? Will Billy's spirit rest? There are too many questions."

As if she materialized out of thin air, Martha was suddenly next to us. I yelped.

"Oh, goodness, you scared me." I pressed my hand to my chest, suspecting my heart rate had spiked again.

"Sorry." She didn't sound apologetic at all. "I thought of someone who might help you. Here. I just talked to her, and she's waiting for you."

She tossed a torn slip of paper on the table between Oliver and me and shuffled away, muttering something about how she had to do everything around here.

We both stared at the scrawled, blocky handwriting.

Marisol Cross
Medium
99 Oak Street

Chapter Eighteen

"You're quiet," Oliver remarked as we walked up to the door of the pink stucco Mediterranean home.

It was a small place, with a cute archway for a front door and several potted tropical plants nearby. Even the porch was adorned with gorgeous Spanish tile, and near the doorbell, hung a brightly painted tin iguana. The place exuded tropical cheer, not fortune-telling.

"I don't know what a medium even does, much less how she can help us. I'm wondering why I'm here. How I got involved in all this. How—"

I was interrupted by the door opening. On the other side stood a gorgeous woman. She was one of those people who could be forty or seventy. Her glowy, deep bronze skin wasn't giving up any secrets, and I wondered about her skin care routine. She had long, dark hair twisted into a thick bun, and only when I focused could I see the strands of gray.

"I'm so glad you could come over," she gushed. "Martha told me all about your investigation. Oliver, it's been too long since we talked."

They leaned into each other for a hug while I was still reeling from her use of the word "investigation." That's what we were doing, I guess, whether I liked it or not.

"I'm Amelia Matthews." I offered my hand but she held her arms open. I'd have to get used to this hugging thing around here, so I gave her a quick embrace.

"Come on in, I've put on a pot of tea. I hope you like herbal. You know I'm a tea witch in addition to being a medium." She said this while we were walking inside, as if it was the most normal thing in the world.

"What's a tea witch?" I asked.

"I specialize in the realm of magic teas, tinctures, herbal mixtures, that sort of thing."

I nodded, but that didn't make anything clearer. I stifled a sigh. We followed her into a living room that was both cozy and interesting.

It was an eclectic mix of vintage and mystical decor. The walls were painted a warm shade of lavender, giving off a soothing and enchanting vibe. Soft, plush rugs covered the wooden floor. Antique wooden bookshelves lined the walls, filled with tomes on spirituality, herbs, and mysticism. The shelves were interspersed with decorative crystal figurines and small potted plants.

The centerpiece of the room was a large, intricately carved wooden coffee table adorned with an array of crystals, tarot cards, and a few votives. The candles emitted a gentle, flickering light that danced across the walls. Marisol had taken care to create an inviting space, with a plush velvet couch and vintage armchairs arranged in a semi-circle around the coffee table.

Against one wall was a vintage record player, surrounded by shelves of vinyl records. The entire place smelled like patchouli, kind of like a health food store, or a Grateful Dead concert without the body odor.

As I settled into one of the overstuffed armchairs, I couldn't help but feel like I had stepped into a springboard for mystical journeys.

But I wasn't here for an adventure. I was here for answers, the quicker the better. Every hour that I didn't solve this spirit situation meant an hour closer to the bachelorette party that was willing to drop thousands and possibly help save the hotel.

"So," I said to a beaming Marisol, who was standing near the coffee table, "what can you tell us about Billy Jenkins?"

A cryptic smile spread on her face. "We're going to need tea for this."

With that, she casually strolled out of the room.

* * *

Oliver and I spent an awkward ten minutes sitting in the living room, making small talk. When he was explaining about the town's upcoming fall festival and haunted pumpkin patch, Marisol walked in with a tray.

"Here we go. A nice pot of tea. This is a special blend that I created myself. It's perfect for September. Are you familiar with the effect of the harvest moon period?"

"No," I said.

"Well." Marisol set the tray down on the large coffee table, smiling as though she wanted nothing more to explain tea and moons to a total stranger. "The harvest moon is known for letting go and ushering in major life events. Sometimes these events are out of the blue and force us to adapt quickly and trust strangers. A few days before and after this moon is when the energy is at its most potent."

"Whoa," I whispered.

"Yes, quite powerful." She poured the tea carefully into three dainty cups from a teapot that looked like it came straight out of Victorian England. "In case you weren't aware, the full harvest moon was last night."

She handed me a cup and I accepted. I barely knew what day it was, much less the moon cycle. Then again, duh. I'd attended a full moon party.

I raised the cup to my mouth and inhaled deeply. Notes of cinnamon, licorice, ginger, and cloves hit my nostrils. I took a sip and tasted all those flavors, plus orange peel, and a hint of something I couldn't quite put my finger on.

"The tea is delicious, Marisol," Oliver said, and I nodded.

"Thank you. I added a little special something so we'd speak candidly and feel a sense of peace."

I was mid-sip when she said this and reluctantly swallowed. Had she put a spell in the tea? Some sort of truth herb? Was that possible? Legal?

Oh well. This was yet another thing I had to roll with here in this place. Then again, Marisol seemed so kind and friendly, I didn't think she'd add ingredients to the tea to poison us.

"Back to Billy Jenkins. I'm sorry to be so abrupt, but I'm in a real pickle here," I said.

Her eyebrow quirked up. "Oh, really?"

I spent the next few minutes bringing her up to speed on my situation, with Oliver chiming in with details. Marisol sat next to Oliver.

"We were told you could help," he said.

Marisol leaned back, her fingers lightly tapping against

her teacup. Her gaze shifted between me and Oliver. Finally, she settled on me.

"Your aunt was a close friend, and about two years ago, she came to me and asked for help. Much like you are now. When she bought the hotel decades ago, Billy's spirit was calm. He only appeared occasionally and in a very benign manner. You know, things like opening doors or flitting through a room. A flickering light here and there. Normal spirit behavior. The guests who stayed at the hotel loved it, and the place boomed for years."

Normal ghost behavior. I wanted to snicker but couldn't because Marisol looked so serious. And sad.

"Then about two years ago, Billy's ghost began to act up. He made loud noises and scared the guests. He moved things around. At one point, he stole a woman's belongings and brought them to the attic, then arranged them as if it was a store. He left cryptic and vaguely threatening notes. That really concerned people. He escalated his hauntings, and that's always a worry."

"I can imagine," I murmured.

"Then he went overboard. He started to mess with the air conditioner. Kept turning it off. In the summer. Repeatedly. Daily. As you can imagine, the guests were livid and moist."

Moist? I visibly cringed at the word.

Oliver's face turned to horror and he set his teacup down. "Whoa, whoa, whoa. Billy's ghost messed with the A/C in the summer in Florida? That's uncalled for."

It was easy to imagine how uncomfortable that must have been for guests. "Ghosts can do that?"

Marisol shot me a knowing look. "Chica, they can wreak havoc. It was the last straw and, in many ways, the crux of the problems for the hotel. Your aunt had a difficult time after all the mean Yelp reviews."

"That's awful, especially after she'd built such a successful business." My poor aunt. "Did you and my aunt ever figure out why Billy, er, Billy's ghost, changed from Casper friendly to horror movie angry?"

Marisol took a sip. "Did you try the cookies?"

What a time to derail the conversation. She reached for a plate on the tray, passing it to me, first. I reached for a thumbprint cookie that appeared to be filled with a tasty-looking, honey-colored jam. Maybe they were laced with some magic or spell, but they smelled delicious.

Unable to resist baked goods, I bit into one. Flavors of apple and cinnamon exploded in my mouth.

"Mmm," I grunted, then swallowed. "Tasty."

Marisol laughed in response. "Anyway, back to the hotel. Your aunt and I decided to hold a séance to find the exact answer to why Billy's ghost had turned angry."

I nearly choked on my cookie. "You what?"

"We figured the way to reach him was through a séance, and since I conduct them quite often, your aunt felt I was the best person for the job. But I failed." Marisol shook her head and looked into her teacup morosely. "I felt awful."

"No, surely you didn't fail." Oliver's brows drew together.

"I did, unfortunately. It was one of the rare instances that my powers were inadequate. I'm not trying to brag, but I almost always can communicate with the dead. Billy, however, is too unsettled. We did find out why his spirit is angry, though."

She seemed to pause for dramatic effect, and I reached for another cookie. "Well? Why?"

"His true love passed." Seeing the look of confusion on

our faces, she continued. "Annie Baer died. She was eighty-one. From what we gathered, Billy was under the impression that he'd be reunited with her after her death. When she passed on, he remained in limbo and decided to take his anger out on the hotel."

She shook her head. "Toxic masculinity extends into the afterlife."

I sat, stunned, trying to absorb this information. Not only was it disappointing that some men were jerks even after death, but it was disheartening that she and my aunt couldn't crack the case.

"Did Billy happen to say who killed him?" Oliver asked.

"Good question," I piped up.

Marisol shook her head, and a wisp of salt-and-pepper hair broke free from her bun. "My communication with him was extremely spotty. I couldn't connect well with him for some reason. He did mention that we needed a certain potion or spell or tincture, but I wasn't sure which or why. He had a difficult time articulating himself, which occasionally happens with teenage boy ghosts."

Oliver and Marisol launched into a conversation about what would happen if and when the teenage ghost Billy met eightysomething ghost Annie.

I stuffed the rest of the cookie in my mouth, unable to handle the parameters of that conversation. I had bigger fish to fry, or ghosts to banish. Was Marisol another dead end? It didn't seem as though we were getting any closer to fixing this situation. Selling the hotel as-is was beginning to look like a reasonable option.

Marisol hummed as she chewed. "Oh, before I forget. There is one person you should speak with, a man who was questioned in the death all those years ago. He's still alive, one of the few who is. It's worth a conversation at least, since the two of you are leaving no stone unturned."

"Who's that?" Oliver asked eagerly.

"Hank Green. Do you know him? He used to be a mechanic in town, but he's retired now. He owns a junkyard of sorts on the outskirts of town."

"Martha mentioned him," I said. "We'll try him. But what do you think we can do about Billy right now? I have a large bachelorette party coming in a few weeks and I don't want problems. Is there anything? Or is the situation hopeless?" I asked. Inside, I wondered if I could sell the place before the party. Unlikely.

But then Billy's terrified face popped into my mind. No, I had to see this through.

Marisol blew out a breath, her cheeks puffing in the process. "Your aunt and I talked about this for the last two years, right up until her death. It was her hope that you'd solve the problem."

I sank back into my chair, deflated. My record for problem solving wasn't the best, if my marriage was any indication.

"How? Why? Why me?"

"Your aunt told me about your psychometric power. She felt that since you had an early vision of Billy in a mirror when you were six that you could summon him somehow and get the answers. Or glean enough information from objects to figure out how to get Billy to Annie. She was convinced that you were the conduit for Billy and Annie."

"Oh. So that was Billy in the mirror? Is he a demon?" This news didn't make me feel any better. "Well. I don't know if I can reunite a demon."

"Your aunt said you might react this way. That's why she's pointed you to various people in town. That's why your investigation has led you to me. I'm going to help you as much as I can. I intended on coming by to see you this week. I wanted you to settle in first. And Billy's not a demon. He's just a wayward spirit."

I tried to calm myself with deep breathing.

"So, what's next?" By now, Oliver had taken a notebook and pen out of his bag.

Marisol poured herself another cup of tea. "We should start with another séance. Let's see if Billy will communicate directly with Amelia. How would you feel about that, dear?"

I set the teacup and saucer on the coffee table and held up my hands. "Dunno how I feel about it, but I'm willing to try."

Truthfully, I wasn't sure if I was willing, but my options were limited.

She straightened her spine and beamed. "How about tonight?"

I met Oliver's gaze. "Works for me," he said.

"Yeah, okay. Uh, can we invite others? Sage and Liz?" If I was going to delve into the ghostly underworld, I wanted as many familiar faces around as possible.

"Of course, invite whoever you want. We'll do it at the hotel. I think that was one of my mistakes, having the séance here where I normally conduct them. Billy's spirit is strong and forceful at the hotel."

"Is there…anything else I need to know?" I asked slowly. "Any preparations, or items to buy, or I dunno, snacks? Beverages?"

Marisol laughed softly. "I take care of it all. Let's plan on midnight tonight."

"Wait. I have another question."

Marisol and Oliver fixed their attention on me.

"The mirror at the antique store. You really think that was Billy? Or was that another demon, or…?"

Something else entirely? A chill went down my spine at the thought. There was so much I didn't know about the paranormal, but I was certain I didn't want to tangle with more malevolent spirits. Other than Billy, that is.

Marisol tilted her head. "Your aunt thought so. And after hearing your account of what happened yesterday with the watch, I'd have to agree."

As I was absorbing that, Oliver spoke up. "Will we need the mirror to contact Billy tonight at the séance?"

"Good question," I said.

Marisol sipped her tea. "That might be wise."

We then talked about the best way to get the mirror from the antique shop to the hotel.

"I think it was pretty expensive," I added.

"Let me make a call to the owner. We've known each other for decades, I'm certain she'll work with us. Shirley gave her the mirror before she died, I don't think she wanted you to have contact with it because of what you'd seen earlier, although I'm not sure. I'll make sure we get the mirror there by this evening."

I had to say, I was impressed with Marisol's calm, efficient, organizational skills.

The three of us agreed on the details and Oliver texted Liz and Sage. Within seconds, his phone pinged and he looked up.

"They're both in," he said.

"I guess we're really doing this." I turned to Marisol. "We should get going. I'd like to stop by Hank's place first."

"I'd suggest taking it easy and resting up for tonight. You'll want to be alert, so don't eat a heavy meal or drink alcohol beforehand."

"Well, there goes my plan for a margarita-only dinner," I quipped.

We all stood, and an ominous feeling settled in my stomach as we walked to the door. Apparently, the magic infused within the tea and cookies didn't work on me, because I felt like simultaneously screaming and running away.

"See you tonight," Oliver said, kissing Marisol's cheek.

"Oh, and one more thing, Amelia," Marisol added, putting her hand on my shoulder. "Make sure to bring your cat. He will help you tonight."

Chapter Nineteen

"Marisol knew I had a cat. How did she know that? Did you tell her?"

"Nope." Oliver clicked the turn signal.

We were in his car headed to Hank Green's place. Even though I was exhausted, my curiosity won out and I'd insisted we press on.

I squirmed in my seat, slightly freaked out. "Is there cat fur on me? That must be it. Look, here's an orange cat hair on my knee. Freddie sheds. That's how she figured it out. Right?"

I glanced to him and noticed he was biting his lip. As if he was trying not to laugh. "Marisol *is* a medium," he finally said.

"I know, but…"

"You didn't believe in her power?" Now he was smiling. "That's common with newcomers to town."

I let out a breath. "It seems hard to believe. Although I guess it shouldn't, not at this point."

We drove in silence while I became lost in my thoughts.

One thing had become clear: whatever I'd previously thought about psychics, mediums, ghosts, and people with supernatural ability was terribly incorrect. It was making me shift my entire worldview.

I tried to explain to Oliver. "You can't blame me for being skeptical. The sum total of my paranormal experience was that show in the '80s."

"Ghostbusters? I loved that as a kid. Who ya gonna call!" He sang a few lyrics from the song. Oliver had a great voice.

"No, Unsolved Mysteries."

He took his hand off the steering wheel to turn up the air conditioner. "My parents wouldn't let Sage and me watch that. They said it wasn't realistic. They didn't mind comedy, though."

"Hmm. Are your parents…" I waved my hand in the air. "Paranormal people? I don't know the term for it."

Oliver chuckled. "My dad has no abilities. He was the state archaeologist, now he's retired. Not everyone in town is gifted. Mom has a bit of magic ability as a dowser. You know, someone who can locate water with a dowsing rod. It's not much use here in Florida, though, since you hit water if you dig a couple of feet anywhere in the state."

"Interesting. And you have no powers at all?"

Oliver shook his head. "Nope. But lots of people have weak powers and they never develop their abilities. People are running around this earth with only a fraction of their powers."

"Like me, I guess."

My phone buzzed with a call. "Oh, it's the hotel. I should get this."

I answered, and Jimbo's southern drawl greeted me heartily.

"Hey, Miss Amelia, how are you today? Sorry to bother you. I know you're out running around, doin' errands. But the air conditioner man's here and I wanted to tell you what he's saying."

"Thank you, Jimbo. I appreciate that. What's the latest?" My gaze drifted out the window, to what looked like rows of orange trees.

"Well, he returned with the part today, then he discovered that something else was wrong. There's a leak in the coil."

"Okay. Can he fix it?"

"He can, but he wanted me to tell you that it will be about seven grand, and that he thinks the leak came from a hole that was man-made."

Eep. Seven grand? Could a ghost cause that much damage? "What? Who would do that?"

Then it dawned on me. Billy. Billy the ghost would do that.

"I have no idea, ma'am, I mean, Amelia. It's a mystery."

"One of many," I muttered. "Is he fixing it now?"

"He is. I gave him our last thousand dollars in petty cash, but he'll invoice you for the rest. That okay? He'll be back tomorrow to start the repair. Thinks it could take a couple of days."

I did a quick mental calculation of how much I had in savings and what was left on my credit card. It would be tight, but I could swing it — although the bachelorette party was now more important than ever.

"That's fine."

He then informed me that two different people had called to inquire about rooms, and that the town's garbage days had changed from Tuesdays to Thursdays.

"Thank you for taking such good care of the place. I

appreciate you. I'll see you tomorrow, I guess. Please forward the phone to me when you leave."

"Will do, ma'am. See you tomorrow, hopefully."

Hopefully. If I survived the night. I hung up and turned back to Oliver.

"I think Billy tampered with the entire air conditioning system. The repair guy told Jimbo there's a man-made hole in some coil. Can you believe that?"

Oliver shook his head. "For the most part, spirits stay in their realm here. Oh, sure, there's some haunting activity but that's mostly for the tourists. Flickering lights, slamming doors. The usual. But normally spirits don't mess with the creature comforts of the living. At least that's what people have told me, and what I've discovered in my research."

"Do you think his behavior could escalate?"

Oliver was gripping the steering wheel so tight that his knuckles were pale. "That's the worry. I don't think you should stay overnight there anytime soon, if that's what you're asking."

It wasn't, but I appreciated his concern. Freddie and I weren't staying under that roof until Billy's spirit was calm. Or put to rest. Or whatever the term was.

"Okay, here we are," Oliver announced, slowing the car. "That's it up ahead."

An aqua blue, mid-century modern sign came into view. "Clutterville," I read aloud.

We turned right, into a dirt parking lot.

The tires crunched and shifted as we drove in. A place like this wasn't about smooth pavement and polished surfaces. It was about embracing rough edges and unrefined beauty.

Back in California, I loved shopping for treasures at flea markets and junk shops. My ex was constantly annoyed when

I brought something unusual home. Now I was free to acquire all the crap — and all the cats — that I wanted.

Except we weren't here to shop.

As Oliver pulled into a space near a thicket of brush, I couldn't help but be intrigued by the place. There was stuff everywhere, scattered with no rhyme or reason.

Glass garden balls on pedestals. Sculptures made from auto engines. Farm tools that were rusted almost beyond recognition.

We climbed out of the car and waded into the stuff.

"I suspect we'll find Hank over there." Oliver gestured to a tired, pale-yellow building several hundred feet away. It looked like an oversized shed.

We threaded our way through rows of iron sculptures. I stopped in front of one.

"This is, is…" I didn't have words for what I was staring at.

Oliver stood next to me. We stared at the sculpture, which looked like a tin Pac Man with sharp teeth. It was holding a plastic pink flamingo that had been chopped in two.

"Hunh," Oliver said. "Modern art at its finest."

We moved on. The lawn art became better, and more detailed, as we approached the little shack. The sculptures looked to be bird skeletons. Perhaps real ones. I couldn't tell.

"I think whoever did these has a thing for flamingoes," I said.

As we reached the shack, the door flung open. A thin guy with mirrored sunglasses and a shock of pure, white hair, walked out. This had to be Hank, because he didn't look a day younger than eighty.

He was also shirtless.

"Alright now, who've we got here?" He pronounced here

like "he-ah." A cigarette dangled out of the corner of his mouth.

"Hello, sir. We're looking for Hank Green," I said.

"You got 'im." Hank walked up to us and shook Oliver's hand. "Welcome to Clutterville. Now what can I do ya for? Y'all looking for a garden sculpture?"

Because I'm a bit thick at times, it dawned on me that we'd basically rolled up to this man's business to question him like cops. Perhaps I should've focused on that fact in the car and rehearsed some lines instead of worrying about the hotel's air conditioner.

"Well, uh…we, um," I started. Brilliant.

"My name's Oliver Everhart. I'm a historian who's writing a book about the town."

I exhaled. Normally I didn't like being interrupted by men, but Oliver's smooth takeover of the conversation was a blessing.

"Oh yeah?"

"Yes, and this is my research assistant, Amelia Matthews."

"Nice to meet you, ma'am." He eyed my chest and I folded my arms.

"We're here to talk about something that happened a long, long time ago," Oliver said, pointing to a wooden picnic table. "Mind if we go over there and chat?"

"Not at all, son," he said.

We all trooped over and sat down, Oliver and I on one side, Hank on the other.

Hank peeled off his shades and looked at us warily with surprisingly bright blue eyes. The cigarette remained firmly pasted to his bottom lip. "You sure you aren't cops?"

"Absolutely not," I said.

"Yeah, y'all don't give off a cop vibe. Had to check, though."

Oliver leaned in. "We're interested in the death of Billy Jenkins. In 1956. And we were talking to someone who said you were one of the people who's still alive in town who knew him. His is the only unsolved murder in the town's history, and I thought it would be appropriate to include a chapter about him in the book I'm writing."

Kudos for Oliver and his quick thinking.

Hank studied us for a few beats while scratching his bare, wrinkled chest. I tried not to stare.

"What do you want to know?" he eventually said.

"What do you remember about Billy Jenkins?" I asked.

"Billy? Well, hell." He shook his head. "Haven't heard that name in years. Billy was a fine young man. Too good, some would say. He loved Elvis. That's what I remember about him. Kid was crazy about Elvis."

"What about his death?" Oliver asked.

Hank's folksy demeanor evaporated. "Like I told the cops. I didn't kill him. I messed up bad that night, but I didn't kill him. Didn't lay a hand on him."

Prickles raced down my spine. "What do you mean, you messed up bad?"

Hank sighed and looked away. "That was the start of my drinking days. I was seventeen and had recently discovered the wonders of beer."

Oliver, who had taken out a pad of paper, was furiously note-taking.

Hank laughed ruefully and continued. "I was so damned jealous of Billy."

"For what?" I asked.

"Datin' Annie Baer. She was the prettiest girl in town, and

I'd gone on a date with her our sophomore year. I thought I was golden. Even her daddy liked me. Then she started datin' Billy. They were in love, and that burned my biscuit. So that night…" his words trailed off and he shook his head. "I happened to run into them when they were parked at the lake. I spied on them when they were making out."

Under the table, I wrung my hands. He was a teenage pervert. "Okay, and then what happened?"

Hank blinked. "Nothing happened. Being a peeping tom was bad enough. I drank some beer while I watched Billy's car. They left, and I drank some more. The next day, he was found dead at the hotel where he worked."

"Why did the police question you?" I asked. "Was it a situation where they were talking to all of Billy and Annie's friends?"

Hank fixed an unwavering stare on me. "Annie told the officers about parking at the lake, so they investigated there. That's when they found my driver's license, because I'd dropped it. I wasn't real bright back then." He let out a sigh. "That was the start of my drinking days. They're over now, thank the Lord."

"Good for you," Oliver said in a chummy tone. "But listen, who do you think killed Billy? Surely you must remember rumors and gossip."

Hank sucked his teeth. "I don't gossip no more. Stopped that when I stopped drinkin' and runnin' around."

It seemed like Hank was trying to wrap up the conversation. My instinct told me he was harboring more information, but how could we get it out of him? I was also highly skeptical that he'd merely been jealous of Billy. If I had to bet, I suspected he'd also done creepy things to Annie, like stalking her, as well. I shuddered silently at the thought.

"Must've been a real shock back then to have a classmate die." I hoped this would get him to open up.

"Look here now." Hank stood up and the breeze ruffled his white hair. He slid on his sunglasses. "I'm not interested in reliving the past. I'm clean and sober, and I plan on staying that way in the time I have left, the good Lord willing. Thank y'all for coming out, but I need to go now and attend to some business. Good luck with your book and y'all have a nice day."

He started to walk away while we sat there, stunned at how abruptly he'd ended the conversation. That's when Hank turned and shot us a twisted smirk.

"Unless y'all are here to buy a piece of art."

I was desperate to get him to talk more and jumped to my feet. "Oh! I did see something my daughter might like. It's back here."

Oliver trailed behind us. I talked animatedly as we ambled through the maze of junk, telling Hank about my daughter and her love for flamingoes. Jenny had never mentioned the pink birds in her life, but whatever. She was a convenient excuse.

Hank was polite in return, and I stopped, glancing around wildly.

"What're you lookin' for, girl?" he asked.

"It was a Pac-man, er, a monster, with a flamingo in two pieces. Holding it like this." I held my two fists over my head, like I was clutching lightning bolts. It felt silly even saying the words aloud.

"Oh, those are real popular. C'mon."

We walked another ten feet, then we were surrounded by the weird sculptures.

"I make 'em in small, medium, large, and jumbo."

I studied the smallest one. It wasn't as quirky as I'd

initially thought, nor did I want to haul that back to California in my suitcase. Given the sharp edges of the tin teeth, I doubted whether the TSA would allow it in my carry on. It looked like a fairly lethal weapon.

But I also couldn't leave without buying something. This was my last chance to get Hank to talk.

"I'll take the small. You don't ship, do you?"

A low chuckle slipped out of Hank's mouth. "Why would I want to complicate my life with that? That'll be thirty dollars."

I dug around in my purse, came up with two twenties, and handed them to Hank.

"I don't got change," he drawled.

I waved my hand. "No worries. It's worth forty."

It wasn't worth five, I realized as he handed it to me.

"Thanks," I beamed while giving him the cash. "You know, I was thinking. Did you ever talk to Mayor Larry Norton about Billy?"

The fact that Billy's watch was in that old icehouse owned by Norton was a piece of the puzzle that seemingly fit nowhere.

Hank carefully folded the cash in half, then in half again. He hadn't taken his eyes off me. "Now why would I do that?"

"Because he's one of the only other people in town who was alive back then," Oliver piped up. "He might remember something about Billy's death."

"He might. But that's none-a my business. I don't go around trying to reopen cold cases. Nor do I try to raise the dead. No sir, not in this town." He shook his head. "You folks have a good day, you hear."

He did a fast shuffle away from us and I let out a sigh. "Rats."

Oliver looked down at my weird flamingo statue. I was holding the Pac-man monster by his skinny legs.

"Want me to carry that to the car?" He pointed to the sculpture.

He looked so cute in that moment with his curly black hair, his kind brown eyes, and his boyish smile. For the first time, I noticed he had dimples. I've always been a sucker for those, so I handed him the flamingo sculpture and we left.

Chapter Twenty

Hours later, as a near-full moon rose in the night sky, I was back in Oliver's car. Only this time, Freddie was with us, in his carrier on my lap. Sage was with us too, in the backseat, and we were on our way to the hotel. My stomach was in knots.

"This is a really stupid question," I started.

"I tell my students that there are no stupid questions," Oliver replied.

"Okay, maybe not stupid. But uninformed. What happens during a séance, anyway? My only reference is gothic romances set in the Victorian era. You know, people sitting in a circle, candles, maybe a Ouija board. Usually there's a hot duke or prince somewhere."

Sage's head popped in between the front seats. "We don't use Ouija boards these days."

"Good to know."

"I've never attended one of Marisol's, have you, Sage?" Oliver asked.

"Nope. I haven't been to one since I started riding lessons."

"Generally, they're low-key affairs, Amelia. They're nothing like what you see in movies. Sometimes the spirit is quite subtle when communicating with the medium, so don't get your hopes up for something dramatic."

I wondered if this was Oliver's way of preparing me to be disappointed. If tonight didn't yield new clues or answers, we might be out of luck in solving Billy's murder — or giving his spirit a measure of peace.

A lot was riding on this séance. I looked out the car window, lost in my thoughts. It seemed like I'd been in Florida forever. My life in California as a mom and wife felt like decades in the past. I seemed to be in limbo here in Florida, in a world comprised solely of shadows and light and the secrets locked inside my own mind.

Part of me wondered: if I stayed here and mastered my psychometric power, what kind of woman would I become? Someone stronger? Someone more confident? Someone happier?

There was no time to dwell on such things, though. I needed answers… and was relying on a ghost to help me. Goodness. On top of all that, I couldn't shake our earlier conversation with Hank.

He seemed like he was hiding something.

We pulled up to a hotel and parked behind a beat-up, flatbed truck. Jimbo and another man were standing in the bed. Between them was a piece of tall furniture, covered by a dark quilt.

I climbed out of the car while hoisting Freddie's backpack onto my shoulder. He let out a loud meow. "What's going on?" I shouted up to Jimbo.

"This is your stand-up mirror. The one from the antique store. I guess you bought it? We're going to bring it in now for the séance."

Jimbo said this like it was the most normal thing in the world. Like it wasn't nine at night and he wasn't unloading a demon-filled mirror into a haunted hotel for a séance.

"Oh. Right. Okay." I brushed an invisible thread of lint off my sundress.

"Where do you want it inside, ma'am?" Jimbo asked.

Shrugging, I looked to Oliver and Sage.

"Wherever Marisol wants it," Oliver responded.

Jimbo gave a thumbs up and the three of us trooped inside. Well, four, including Freddie.

The hotel was exactly as I'd left it the other day, only the downstairs was pleasantly cool and not humid. Even the mold smell had subsided a little. This seemed to be a fortuitous omen for the séance, and I smiled when I saw Marisol and Liz, chatting on an ornate, red velvet loveseat in the lobby.

"Jimbo let us in," Liz said, giving me a quick hug. "We called him earlier to set up a time for delivery. I think he'd also like to be present at the séance, if that's okay with you."

"Of course." I felt terrible that I hadn't thought to invite him in the first place. Ugh. I'd been so overwhelmed with details since I'd arrived. Where were my manners?

Were there manners when it came to a séance?

"I'm sure you're wondering how we'll do this," Marisol said in a kind tone. "Come."

She threaded her thin arm through mine and walked me into the hotel's dining room, where my aunt had served breakfast, tea, and occasionally, cocktail hour.

When we were inside, I shut the door. "Should I let Freddie out?"

"Yes. That way we can keep this door shut and he can become acquainted with the vibes in the room."

I wasn't sure if Freddie knew or cared about vibes, but I released him from his backpack prison anyway. He jumped out, wrinkled his nose, then darted toward Marisol.

"What a beautiful cat! Oh, yes, you are." To my surprise, Marisol scooped him up. Normally Freddie wasn't a fan of PDA.

While she petted and kissed Freddie — who seemed to eat up the attention — I took the chance to survey the room.

It was a study in faded elegance. A crystal chandelier hung from the ceiling, its once-brilliant surface now dulled with age. Heavy, gold-colored drapes framed large windows, billowing softly in the night breeze. The room was illuminated by a soft, warm glow from antique wall sconces that lined the wood-paneled walls. A long, polished table stretched down the center of the room.

I recalled my aunt telling me about this room in one of her Christmas cards. She said she set out a spread of tasty breakfast offerings for guests. That had been years ago, and she'd been so proud of how pretty it looked — "like something out of Better Homes and Gardens," she'd said.

Now it was covered in a pristine white tablecloth adorned with delicate lace patterns and we were about to chitchat with the undead.

Marisol led me to the head of the table, where a tall, ornate chair awaited.

"First, we'll cleanse the space as a group, prior to starting the session. You'll sit here," she patted the chair. "I'll be next to you. And the mirror, in case we need it, will be behind you. I'm thinking we might need you to physically touch the mirror during the ceremony. I want to give Billy every opportunity to communicate."

Right then, Jimbo and the other man slowly walked into the room, each carrying an end of the mirror. Marisol explained where she wanted it, and we moved to the other side of the room. We watched as they righted the mirror and removed the quilt. Jimbo took a rag out of his back pocket and polished the glass.

I eyed the ornate, free-standing piece of furniture while fear welled inside me. From where I was standing, I could see myself in it. Even though that was a normal thing, something about it made me shiver. What was lurking inside beyond the mirror? Could it see me? Was it like that one-way glass, the kind in police stations?

I guess I'd soon find out.

"How do you feel about possibly speaking with Billy via the mirror?" Marisol asked.

I cleared my throat. "Not great, but this is something I have to do."

To save the hotel. To save the town (even though I didn't quite grasp how). To save myself.

"We're all here for you. If it gets to be too much, tell me. I can stop it immediately. All you need to do is communicate, Amelia."

"Got it. I can communicate. Got my degree in communications." I shot her a wan smile and she squeezed my arm.

We left the room, making sure the door was shut tight so Freddie wouldn't get out. With my hand on the doorknob, I paused.

"Is he okay in there? Alone with the mirror?"

Marisol nodded. "You're the conduit to the mirror, not him. He's probably the safest of us all."

I screwed up my face. "That doesn't inspire confidence."

"We'll be fine, chica. Don't you worry." She smiled and I followed her lead down the long hallway.

Once back in the lobby, I made a beeline to Marisol's food table so I could stress snack. I was an old hand at this.

To my delight, Marisol had laid out quite the spread of cheese, crackers, mini quiches, and cookies, along with lemonade and iced tea. I helped myself to a few cookies and some lemonade. The cookies were homemade, with a hint of coconut. I had to hand it to the townsfolk in Cypress Grove: they sure could bake.

As I snacked, my gaze roamed around the room. Marisol and Oliver were huddled in the corner, talking in hushed tones. Liz, Sage, and Jimbo were on the other side of the room, staring at the creepy oil painting.

This was my team. My crew. My fellow warriors, the ones who would accompany me into metaphoric battle. What was that quote by Winston Churchill and the end of the beginning?

I couldn't think of it, but another quote popped into my head, one from Dolly Parton.

Storms make trees take deeper roots.

It was time to channel my inner Dolly and face the storm.

As I was grazing on my third cookie, Marisol clapped her hands.

"Friends, it is time. Let us move into the sacred space where we'll conduct the séance."

As if on cue, the lights flickered. I whimpered while others chuckled softly.

"Don't you worry, pardner." Sage fell into step next to me as we walked toward the dining room. "We've all been to lots of séances. We've got your back."

"Thanks," I said, and I meant it.

We stepped into the room. The air felt charged, heavy with a sense of anticipation. Freddie ran to me, and I picked him up. Feeling his soft fur against my hands calmed me a little. He brushed his face against my chin.

The scent of old wood and faint traces of incense mingled. As we all took our seats, Marisol carefully lit the candles then extinguished the electric lamps. Soft candlelight cast playful shadows on the walls, as if spirits were already present, engaged in a secret dance.

Freddie squirmed in my arms. I locked eyes with Marisol and I pointed at my cat. “Should I let him roam?” I whispered, and she nodded.

I released him from my grip and he jumped down. Settling into my seat, I felt the cool touch of the chair’s polished arms against my fingertips. It was as if I was hyperaware of all my senses. The hum of the air conditioner was the only noise in the room.

Marisol lit what looked like a bouquet of sticks, but I realized it was probably sage or some other cleansing spice. I took a whiff, and detected notes of wood. Cedar, I think. She carefully waved it in the corners of the room and around the mirror that sat behind me. Tendrils of smoke lingered in the air.

Her voice, calm and unwavering, sliced through the silence. "Ladies and gentlemen, we gather tonight in the spirit of exploration. In the spirit of friendship. In the spirit of truth. Would anyone else like to greet the universe now?"

Sage raised her hand. “I would.”

“You may proceed.” Marisol nodded in her direction.

Sage stood. Tonight, she worc a T-shirt that said HOWDY and a long, denim skirt.

Double, double, toil and trouble;
Fire burn and caldron bubble.
With a hearty laugh and a yeehaw!,
Cowgirl-witch ain't afraid of flaw.
She rides the night, she rides the day,
Makin' magic in her cowgirl way;
For when the Sunshine State meets witch's brew,
There ain't no spell she can't undo.

We all stared at her. I wasn't sure if this was helping or hurting our efforts in communicating with Billy, but Marisol nodded.

"Thank you, sweet sister Sage. Anyone else?" She looked around, but none of us spoke. "Very well. We will proceed. This is a sacred space, one where we feel protected and loved. This is not a confrontation, but a conversation. One between two realms. I invite you to contemplate this as we continue."

Her words seemed to conjure a respectful silence among us, like participants in an ancient rite. I closed my eyes briefly, allowing the weight of the moment to settle over me, before reopening them to the softly illuminated scene. Everything felt serious in a way that it hadn't moments ago.

Beside Marisol, a crystal ball caught the candlelight, its surfaces refracting light. A soft breeze rustled the gauzy curtains by the windows, while the moon's glow filtered in. The room seemed to be holding its breath, straddling the line between the living and the dead.

Marisol's fingers brushed the crystal ball's surface. "Spirits of the past," she intoned, "we invite you to join us in this space. We would like to speak with Billy. Billy, are you there?"

There was a pause, and I studied each face. Jimbo's eyes were closed. So were Sage's. Liz focused on the table, and Oliver eyed Marisol. Freddie was circling the mirror, rubbing his mouth against the metal frame at the bottom.

"There's someone who wants to join us," Marisol said. "But they're having a difficult time getting into the room. Let's all join hands."

I clasped Marisol's fingers on my right and Oliver's on my left. He gave me a little squeeze, and a zing went through me. Now was not the time to harbor lust in my heart. I refocused.

"Someone is trying to tell us something. Reception is spotty," Marisol intoned.

It occurred to me that these were the same things people said during Zoom calls. I stifled a giggle, probably brought on by nerves. My hands began to sweat.

"Billy? Are you there? Can you hear me? I can't hear you." I was impressed that Marisol's tone remained soothing and neutral.

Two things happened in quick succession, and they were so abrupt that I couldn't tell which came first.

Freddie meowed so loud that I dropped Oliver and Marisol's hands and stood, worried he was in pain. Then the air conditioner went out with an echoing *thunk*, leaving behind only hushed, ominous quiet.

"Oh, duck, not the air. Please not the air." I whispered.

That's when I noticed that everyone at the table was staring at me in horror.

"What?" I asked. That's when I realized: they weren't looking at me. They were gaping at something behind me.

"The m-mirror," Jimbo stammered.

I whirled. The mirror no longer reflected the room. Its

smooth surface appeared as though it was covered in swirling clouds or fog.

"What the—"

"Amelia, I think now is the time you should touch the mirror. Billy is near, I can feel it. Use your powers to draw Billy out so we can talk with him. Focus all of your energy on the mirror," Marisol urged.

I froze. Could I do this? The last thing I wanted was to touch that evil hunk of metal and glass. But Marisol nodded and smiled encouragingly.

"We're here for you. Trust us," she said. "You're safe."

First, I glanced to Liz, then Oliver, then Sage. They all nodded. Well, Sage winked and nodded.

I moved around my chair and pushed it into the table to give me more space. Freddie was sitting at the base of the mirror. He looked up at me with round, clear blue eyes, His expression seemed to say, *you can do this, Mom. I got you.*

As I took a step toward the mirror, I tried to calm the shaking in my hands. I was facing it now, with the cat at my feet between me and the mirror's base.

Raking in a huge breath, I extended my hands. Before I touched the iron frame, I decided to try something different. It was time to go big or go home, and going home wasn't an option.

I placed my palm flat on the mirror's cool glass. The fog in the mirror seemed to come alive, surrounding my hand and obscuring it entirely, all the way to my elbow. A low moan came from somewhere, and it was so otherworldly and disturbing that I began to tremble.

Freddie hissed and spat, his back arching like I'd never seen. He swatted at an invisible threat, angrier than I'd ever seen him.

I whispered his name, but he ignored me.

My palm warmed, heated, then quickly felt as though I'd pressed my flesh against a hot stove burner. I swore aloud and snatched it away, afraid of what I'd unleashed.

Chapter Twenty-One

Billy poked his head out of the mirror.

"Excuse me, ma'am." he finally said. "I'm going to have to walk through you, unless you move. The cat's also in the way."

"Oh. Uh. Sorry." I scooped up the hissing Freddie and moved aside.

The atmosphere in the room changed instantly, a mix of surprise and apprehension swirling through the air. The looks on everyone's faces ranged from stunned to rapt attention. Apparently, I was the only one who was wondering if I'd pee my pants from fear.

I wouldn't have believed any of this if I hadn't seen it for myself, and I gaped as more of Billy's body emerged from the mirror. His form wavered like mist, an ethereal figure transitioning from one realm to another. His glowing gray eyes bore into me, a mix of curiosity and a touch of mischief evident in their depths.

I didn't breathe as I watched Billy emerge into the room, his movements flowing seamlessly, as if he was casually stepping out of a car rather than emerging from a supernatural portal.

His appearance was both eerie and mesmerizing, a blend of the past and the present. He wore an outfit straight out of the 1950s, the same as his yearbook portrait with the Brylcreem hair and a shirt that had long since gone out of fashion.

His translucent figure seemed to shimmer in the dim light of the room, and there was a quiet dignity about him that sent shivers through my entire body. He looked around and smiled politely, as teenagers do when they're surrounded by adults.

I didn't notice that Marisol had come to stand next to me and Freddie.

"Amelia, dear, we can all hear and see him, but he can only communicate with you. Remember: you're the conduit, the medium. You must talk with him. We were unsuccessful before because we couldn't converse with him."

I shuddered in a breath while nodding. Freddie was squirming in my arms and I worried he'd shred my skin to ribbons. Part of me wanted to hand him over to Marisol, but another part told me to keep the kitty close by, either to soothe my nerves or for some other, higher, purpose.

"Hi Billy," I started, my voice quavering.

"Ma'am." He nodded. "Nice night, isn't it?"

Well, at least he was a polite ghost. "It sure is. I'm Amelia Matthews, the owner of this hotel. I inherited it from my aunt."

It took a few beats for this to sink in. "Yes, I sensed that Miss Shirley passed. I knew she was sick and was hoping she'd visit me, but I guess she went directly to the other side. My condolences."

"Thank you." Freddie shifted in my arms so I was cradling him like a baby. He'd settled down and had started to purr.

Although this calmed me a little, I wasn't sure exactly what to say next to Billy.

Hey, can you please leave the hotel?

Okay, you can stay but stop messing with the air conditioner. I'm poor.

What's it like on the other side, anyway?

No, none of those would do. As interesting as this was, I was on a mission. We needed answers.

"It's my understanding that you've been haunting this hotel since you passed," I started.

Billy shook his head, which left little streaks of ghostly light behind. "I wouldn't use the word 'haunting.' I prefer the term 'occupying.'"

Nodding, I looked around. The others were also moving their heads up and down. "Okay, fine. Occupying. Is it true that you've been here all these years, waiting for Annie Baer to pass?"

"That's correct, ma'am." He shoved his hands into his pockets.

"She passed a little while ago, so why haven't you reunited?" Maybe I was covering familiar territory as Marisol's previous séance, but I didn't care. I was running this show now.

Billy floated and shimmied toward me. It took everything I had not to step back. Freddie opened his eyes, on full alert even though he resembled a chunky loaf of orange bread in my arms.

"Annie is fully on the other side. I'm in a purgatory here. In limbo. I think she, or someone, needs to make a special potion so it can happen. She was supposed to do it before she died, but, but…"

His voice trailed off and he swallowed hard. He scrubbed

at his face with his hands. Was he crying? Could ghosts cry? This was so above my pay grade it wasn't even funny.

"I'm sorry," I said softly. "How can I help?"

"You need to find the recipe. It's somewhere, I'm sure of it. Maybe in her house? In a book? I don't know. When we were dating, she was learning some things from a witch. She kept that secret back then, and only told me a little. It was a girl thing. One day after school she said she'd created a potion that would allow us to be together forever. I thought it was malarky back then. But since we're not together, I think that's what's keeping us apart. No one's made the potion."

It made as much sense as anything else. Which is to say, it didn't make sense at all. Still, I nodded. "Okay, I can do that. I can look for the potion. Or whatever it is. When I find it, what do I do?"

He shrugged. "I'm not sure. I think it will get me out of this place, though. I hope it will allow me to be with her."

"You didn't discuss this with her before or after you passed? Like, you didn't haunt her house?"

Billy snorted. "I died here. Why would I go to Annie's house? I can't leave this place unless I'm summoned in the mirror by someone with psychometry. Sheesh, lady."

He said this with a dose of teenage contempt, as if I should know all these details. I recognized his attitude immediately from my own daughter's snarky years. I smirked.

"Got it. But listen, in the meantime, can you knock it off with the air conditioner? I don't mind if you do some normal ghost stuff, like turning the lights off or shoving some items of low value off tables. But the air is a bridge too far, dude."

"My name's not dude. It's Billy."

I shut my eyes briefly, summoning patience and courage.

"Sorry. That's a newer term. I would've assumed you've seen television and movies in the past few decades."

He shook his head. "I can't hear or see any of that. Nor do I understand those little devices you all carry around. I don't even know why I can see and talk with you so well."

He pointed to Jimbo's cell, which was sitting on the table.

"Cellular telephone," Jimbo said in a slow, loud voice, as if Billy was hard of hearing and didn't speak English. Apparently he'd forgotten that the ghost couldn't hear or see him.

To Billy, he and I were the only people here. He stared at me expectantly.

"We don't have time to chat about the latest in phone technology," I said. "I'm begging you to please stop with the sabotage of major appliances."

Billy's eyes twinkled, and an impish smile spread on his face. "I can't do that."

"Why not?"

"You haven't seen anything yet. The things I can do would knock your socks off." He rolled his eyes.

This little jerk. He was displaying total teenage insouciance. If I knew anything, it was how to deal with teens.

I tilted my head, ignoring his smirk. "Thank you for letting me know all of this. I appreciate it."

This respect seemed to disarm him. "Okay," he responded.

"I'll make sure you're reunited with Annie. Cool it for a few days, okay?"

"A few days. Fine." He crossed his arms and that's when I noticed that he had a patch of acne on his chin. Just like my daughter had when she was his age. For some reason, that made me want to sob, and I choked back a lump in my throat.

"Thank you," I said, grateful.

“But only a few days. Then all bets are off. This place is Squaresville and I need to lighten it up to entertain myself.”

I stifled a sigh. “I have another question, while you’re here.”

Another eye roll. “Yes?”

“Who killed you?”

His expression grew serious, and the mischievous teen glint in his eyes faded. "Larry Norton.” His voice carried a weight of sorrow and bitterness. "He was a friend, or so I thought. We had a falling out over something stupid, something that shouldn't have ended in violence. But that night... he was drunk, and his anger overtook him."

A heavy silence settled over the room, as everyone absorbed the revelation. Marisol's face turned grim, and even Jimbo's usually jovial demeanor was replaced with a somber expression.

"Why did he do it?" I asked, my voice barely a whisper. “And when?”

Billy's translucent form seemed to tremble, as if reliving the moment. "I think he was jealous. Jealous of the attention Annie was giving me. We were all friends, you know? But jealousy can twist people, turn them into monsters they never thought they could become. That night, Annie and I had the time of our lives at the Elvis concert."

He paused, seemingly overcome with emotion. “Then we went to the lake. To talk.”

It was endearing that he seemed nervous about telling us that he’d gone to make out with Annie at the lake. I reminded myself this happened in the 1950s, not today. If it had happened today, every minute of this saga would have played out on TikTok, only with fewer clothes and a lot of terrible music.

“And then?” I probed gently.

“I dropped Annie off right before her curfew, then came to the hotel. I’d left my jacket here, and I needed my mom to wash it. Larry was here, drunk, and he followed me to the attic where I kept my things. There was no one staying at the hotel that week. That’s when he attacked me. It was…”

His words trailed off, and my body was flooded with his pain, as if I was reliving his murder.

“I’m sorry,” I whispered.

“Thanks, ma’am.”

A mixture of anger and sadness surged within me. If Billy had been in physical form, I would’ve hugged him. A kid so young didn’t deserve any of this. "Why didn’t Larry Norton face any consequences?"

Billy's gaze darkened. "There wasn't enough evidence, or maybe people didn't want to believe he could do such a thing. His dad was pretty rich and powerful, too. I guess he’s lived the rest of his life as if nothing happened. Meanwhile, I was stuck in this limbo, unable to move on."

"I'm so sorry, Billy," I said, my heart aching for the injustice he had endured.

He offered a ghostly smile, his expression tinged with resignation. "Thank you, ma'am. But now, with Annie on the other side and the possibility of this potion, maybe there's a chance for justice and closure."

“I’ll find the potion and the spell. I promise.” How I would do this was a mystery, but I felt like we were at least getting somewhere.

“Now I have a question for you.”

I took a deep breath, wondering what he’d ask.

His image flickered, as if we were watching an old, black and white television.

"Billy? Are you okay?"

"I'm fading," he said, his voice garbled as if we hadn't fully tuned in to a radio station.

"Billy?" I called out.

His form grew brighter.

"Elvis," he said. "What ended up happening to him? I'm not able to see or hear any of your modern electronics. I used to be able to listen to an old radio from the fifties, but the one that was here at the hotel broke decades ago. And of course, I can't ask anyone about Elvis because I can't communicate with anyone outside of a séance. Elvis is my favorite, and I'd give anything to know what he's up to these days. What a cool cat."

He flickered a few more times, then shined strong, enough to see his straight, white teeth. Billy had been a good-looking kid. "Elvis became the biggest singer in the world, right?"

"Absolutely," I said, and the others nodded.

"The King of Rock-n-Roll," Oliver chimed in. Of course, Billy couldn't hear him, so I repeated that.

"And a movie star," Marisol said. I repeated that, too.

Billy's jaw dropped. "That's swell. Wish I could've seen those movies. What about afterward? What did he do? Retire in glory? Maybe run for president? Senator? How cool would that be, an entertainer as president?"

It was impossible not to hide the horror on my face.

Even in his ghostly form, I could see the hope in his expression. I cleared my throat and shot a look at Oliver. He lifted his shoulders into a shrug. The discomfort in the room was palpable.

"Well? What happened to him?" Billy's ghost sure was demanding. Teenagers.

The image of a chubby, drug-addled, perspiring Elvis on a

toilet came to mind. I thought of the 1970s Elvis, with the white jumpsuit and bloated face. I licked my lips. The last thing I wanted was to disappoint or upset Billy, who was already an unstable, wayward soul. My wallet couldn't afford any more big-ticket repairs.

"It's complicated," I finally said.

"Maybe you can tell me more later. I need to hit the road. See you later, alligator. That's a good tune, by the way. Bill Haley and the Comets. You should check it out."

With that, he turned and stepped back into the mirror.

Chapter Twenty-Two

On one hand, the séance exceeded my expectations. We'd solved the mystery of who killed Billy. That was a relief, of sorts, although it was cold comfort because Billy's killer had not only gotten away with the crime, but he'd become the town's mayor.

That frosted my butt.

Liz readjusted the ice pack on my forehead. I groaned. We'd all decamped into my aunt's cheery little apartment on the other side of the house.

"How's the headache?" Liz asked, pressing her fingers to my cheek. "You feel warm."

"The aspirin's kicking in. I'm a little better."

"You gave us a real scare there, pardner." Sage stood over me, a beer in hand.

After Billy had returned to the mirror, my legs had gone rubbery and I nearly collapsed. Fortunately, Oliver was there to catch me. He carried me to the sofa, where everyone fluttered around for several minutes. It felt weird, being tended to like this.

"It was the strangest thing, as if all the energy had drained out of my body. I think I'm good now, though." Holding my hand to the ice pack on my head, I started to sit up.

"Nope. You're resting for a little while longer. No one's going anywhere." Liz's voice had the firm tone of years of parenting.

"Okay, fine," I grumbled, settling back down.

Oliver had dragged a kitchen chair into the living room so he could sit next to me. Liz announced she was making me some tea, while Marisol and Jimbo were talking on the loveseat. Sage went with Liz into the kitchen.

"What do you think?" I asked Oliver. Freddie was tucked next to me, sleeping. His presence wasn't merely comforting, it was reassuring, as if everything was normal and I hadn't just communicated with a ghost.

Oliver sipped in a breath through pursed lips. "I don't know what to think. I've never seen anything like that in my life, and I've been to several séances. Do you think Billy was telling the truth? After talking with Hank today, I've been thinking he was the killer. But now it's all muddled in my mind."

"I thought the same, earlier. But now I don't. I could feel Billy's pain, Oliver. It was raw. Visceral." I shuddered, remembering how Billy's emotions seemed to pour into my very soul as he talked. "What do we do with this information? Go to the police?"

He ran a hand through his messy, dark hair. "What would we say?"

"That's the thing. What are the cops like? I'm sure they're used to psychics and others giving them tips."

"They're open to that sort of stuff, but they have to abide by Florida law. Which means they need evidence to make an arrest. And right now, we're sorely lacking physical evidence. Or even circumstantial evidence. Plus there's the new chief—"

"The werewolf."

Oliver smirked. "I doubt if that's true. Regardless, I'm sure the new chief, who is from out of town, would be highly skeptical of our story."

I wrinkled my nose. He was probably right. "What about the pocket watch and all that stuff in the icehouse? Mayor Norton owns the property."

"I don't think that's enough to convict Norton. Even though it's engraved with Billy's name, it's such a generic name that there's no proving whose it really is." Oliver shook his head. "I don't know what else we can do."

"I know what I won't do: let Larry Norton get his grubby hands on this place."

Oliver raised an eyebrow. "You were seriously thinking about selling the hotel to him?"

"Briefly, because of that letter he'd sent my aunt a few months ago. But now I'm wondering why he wants the place so badly."

"Hmm." Oliver nodded slowly, a far away look in his eyes like he was coming up with a solution. "Maybe it wouldn't hurt to meet with the mayor."

Confused, I tilted my head. "For what purpose, though?"

"To feel him out. To see what he says when we talk about the house, and about Billy. I don't mind a little confrontation, even. How about you?"

Before I came to Florida, I would've said no. Would've run from any sort of conflict. I'd had enough with my ex-husband, and the divorce had sapped my will to fight. But now, after talking with Billy and feeling the injustice of a murder that had been unsolved for decades, I felt my fire returning.

"Yeah. I wouldn't mind that at all. I want to see justice served. And at the very least, Norton might somehow give us a clue to the spell or whatever that Billy needs to reunite with Annie."

"I like that," Oliver nodded.

"What?" I asked. We were now the only ones in the room since everyone else had drifted into the kitchen.

"A woman with a sense of justice." His eyes glittered and the corners of his lips turned up.

I opened my mouth but wasn't sure what to say. "Are you—"

As I was about to ask whether he was flirting with me, Sage burst into the room.

"We found an unopened pack of those Halloween cookies, the kind with the orange filling," she announced, brandishing the cookies in the air. "Who wants some sugar?"

Oliver and I burst out laughing.

"The package says they expired two months ago, but they're probably okay, right?" Sage looked at us hopefully.

"I'm sure all those chemicals keep them fresh," Oliver quipped. "Maybe we should go buy new ones."

With a shrug, Sage grinned. "I'm willing to risk it. They're not perfect, but they'll do. Sometimes ya gotta play the hand you're dealt, not the one you wish for."

That last sentence rolled around in my brain for the rest of the night.

Chapter Twenty-Three

The next morning, Oliver and I marched up the granite steps of City Hall. We'd gone over our plan again this morning on our way here, and I was feeling confident that we would get some kernel of truth out of Mayor Norton.

I wore the one decent dress I'd brought with me, a black wraparound that hopefully gave off professional vibes. And if not professional, then at the very least, *Mom-getting-to-the-bottom-of things-with-a-stern-yet-deadly-calm-expression*. Unfortunately, the pretty dress was comprised of man-made fibers that weren't Florida-friendly.

It was barely nine in the morning and I was sweltering. Oliver and I both wore shades against the white-hot sun.

"We look like we're in a crime-fighting buddy movie," I quipped.

Oliver shot me an adorable lopsided grin as he held the door open. "You think?"

We walked in and I immediately stopped because I wanted to take in the decor. Oliver and I slid off our glasses. I stuck mine in my purse. "Wow, this place is breathtaking."

The City Hall building was in a Mediterranean-revival building, all pink stucco and barrel tile on the exterior. Inside was covered in colorful Spanish tile — similar to Marisol's home — and soaring ceilings. A sweeping marble staircase sat in the middle of the room. It was an impressive example of 1920s architecture in such a small town.

"Upstairs there's a mural of the founding of Florida." Oliver pointed to the stairs. He was giving me a quick history lesson on the place when a thin woman in her twenties walked up to us.

"Excuse me," she said. She wore her long, honey blonde hair loose. Upon further inspection, I realized there were streaks of what looked like silver Christmas tree tinsel woven into her locks.

We stopped talking and turned to her. "Hi," Oliver responded. "How can we help?"

"Are you here for the pet reiki?" She pointed to a far corner of the cavernous lobby, where an oversize pug was lying on a small cot nestled to the left of the stairs. A woman was standing over the dog, holding her hands about an inch above his generous midsection.

I scratched the back of my neck. "Pet…reiki?"

"We do this every week at City Hall. It's donation-based," she burbled. "We don't touch the pets, we transfer energy into them with our hands. Like this."

She hovered her hand over my arm and giggled. "Oooh, you've got some wicked strong energy, ma'am. You should watch out for that."

A snicker slipped out of my mouth because I was imagining someone doing an energy healing on Freddie. Their hands would be shredded to ribbons in seconds. The very last thing he wanted was someone to hover over him.

Then I scowled because I realized she called me "ma'am."

Oliver shook his head. "We're here on business. Do you know where Larry Norton's office is?"

"Oh! I think it's…" the woman whipped her head around, the scent of her patchouli following her movement. "Right there."

She pointed at an ornate wooden door next to the reiki station. Above it was a sign that said, MAYOR AND COUNCIL.

We thanked her and she wandered off. I leaned into Oliver. "Pet reiki?"

"Don't ask. Let's go."

A few seconds later, we were inside the door. A man at a desk and four empty chairs greeted us. Behind him was another door.

"Good morning," Oliver said in a cheery voice. "We're here to see Mayor Norton."

The man's eyes flickered in our direction, then glanced at his computer screen, then back at us. He looked at us like we were something sticky he needed to scrape off his shoe. "I'm the mayor's assistant and don't see that he has anything scheduled. What are your names?"

We told him and he frowned. "I'm sorry, but you're going to have to make an appointment. He has a spot next Tuesday at eight-forty-five."

Oliver and I exchanged glances. We hadn't gone over this scenario. Why had we assumed the mayor's schedule was free and clear? I leaned over the desk a few inches.

"Can you please tell him that I'm the owner of the Crescent Moon Inn?"

The assistant hesitated for a few beats while glaring at me. "Fine."

He rose and disappeared into the door behind the desk. I turned to Oliver with a grimace.

"What do we do if we can't see him today?" I hissed.

"Let's not panic yet."

"Oh, I'm panicking," I muttered. "I've been panicking for days. All panic, all the time. And by the way. What do you think that reiki woman meant when she said I had strong energy?"

Oliver stroked his chin. "Probably a scam. There's a lot of that here, taking advantage of people. Generally, it's preferable to hire energy workers who come recommended by someone."

"I'll file that tidbit away." I tapped the side of my head.

The door flew open and the assistant emerged with a skeptical expression. "Mr. Mayor will see you, but please be mindful of the time. You have ten minutes. He has an appointment at nine-thirty sharp, so you need to be out of here by then."

"You got it," I said.

"No funny business," he warned with a wag of his finger.

Why anyone would think I would be involved in *funny business* when I was wearing my cutest little black dress is beyond me. Jerk.

He led us into the inner sanctum. It was a long corridor with several doors that led to generic offices. We spotted a few bored workers on their computers. The entire place smelled like paper and printer toner, and unlike the rest of the building, there were no pretty Spanish tiles or Mediterranean flourishes.

We came to a door at the end of the hall. The assistant rapped twice then opened it.

"Ten minutes," he warned us as we walked in.

The mayor's office was anything but generic. Every possible surface was covered in mahogany wood: the walls, the desk, the bookcases, even the floorboards. The photos on one wall were also framed in a similar wood. It was like jumping into a vat of chocolate, but not in a good way.

The mayor was the only thing that stood out. He was rail thin and pale, his shock of silver hair practically sparkling against the wood tones. He was talking on a brown phone, a landline with a cord. If he recognized me from the other day at the café, he didn't let on. He seemed every bit of his eighty-something years, possibly because he was dressed in a dung-colored suit that was slightly too big and a blue tie that was a touch too small.

It almost looked comical.

"I will find the troll, Mrs. Trimble. I promise. Yes, I know there's been a rash of troll thefts." The mayor looked at us, rolled his eyes, and pointed at the phone handset. He gestured to the two chairs in front of his desk.

We settled into them and he hung up.

"So sorry," Larry Norton began. "We've had a series of lawn ornament thefts on the north side. As you can imagine, people in town are very attached to things in their gardens. This lady claims her troll has magic properties, and I can't ignore that."

I rubbed my lips together. Between this and the pet reiki, I wanted to laugh. But I was here for a deadly serious matter.

"It's nice to meet you, Mr. Mayor. I'm Amelia Matthews. We don't know each other but I'm the new owner of the Crescent Moon Inn. This is Oliver Everhart, a local friend."

Norton asked where I was from, and I told him. We chatted about California for a minute. As he recounted a wine-tasting trip for his thirtieth anniversary, I grew anxious. We didn't have much time here and I needed answers.

I cleared my throat. "I'm sure you're wondering why we're here, sir. We don't want to take up too much of your time. I wanted you to know that I saw the letter that you and your lawyer sent my aunt a few months back."

Before he could respond, the phone rang. He held up his index finger. "Excuse me," he said, and pressed a button. "Yes?"

The assistant's voice came over the speakerphone. "You have a call. It's a very angry constituent on Lake Drive."

The mayor sighed. "I'm so sorry, but I have to get this. The homeowners on that street are the town's biggest taxpayers."

At least he was honest about who had his ear: the rich. He answered the call on speaker, which I thought was odd.

"Larry?" the man's irritated tone came through loud and clear. "It's happened again."

"What now, Steve? Did the sewer pipes break a second time?" the mayor asked. The two men obviously shared a history.

"No! The UFO sighting. I saw it early this morning, before dark. The thing was hovering over my backyard! Did you get any other reports of it?"

The mayor pinched the bridge of his nose. "I haven't, but I'll check with the police and get back to you. Listen, I have some folks in my office. I'll call you back."

After a few protests from Steve, the mayor hung up. "Apologies," he said.

"UFOs?" Oliver asked.

The mayor waved his hand dismissively, then pointed to his right. "There are a lot of unexplainable phenomena in this town, but UFOs? No. I'm sorry. Cape Canaveral is that way, the extraterrestrials can hightail it there. I've got way too much going on here. Steve's a little loopy, if you know what I mean."

How could he tell "a little loopy" from the average citizen here? I couldn't let Norton derail this conversation with weird happenings in town. We'd be here all day if I allowed that.

"The hotel. We were talking about the hotel." I tried to keep my tone even, but as soon as the words came out, I knew I sounded angry.

"Of course, thank you, Mrs. Matthews. Yes, I'm still interested in purchasing it. I have plans for the property. Multi-family plans."

He smiled, and it struck me that he seemed entirely too slick. Also, I hated being called Mrs. Matthews, and I vowed once again to file the paperwork to return to my maiden name.

"Why?" I blurted.

"Why what?" he said, confused.

"Why do you want the hotel? It's old, it needs a lot of work, and business is terrible. Makes no sense for a man of your age. No offense. The last thing my aunt would've wanted was to turn the property into condos."

He shrugged and glanced toward the mahogany bookcase to his left. "Like I said in the letter from my attorney: it's a good business investment. And you're no spring chicken either, ma'am."

I narrowed my eyes. Under the best of circumstances, it was difficult for me to hide my feelings. He must've picked up on my skepticism and annoyance.

"You doubt my intentions?" The way he said the words was so certain, that I felt the hair on the back of my neck bristle. I imagined I looked like Freddie when he saw dogs.

Mayor Norton, on the other hand, had taken on an expression I knew all too well. One of supreme, total, unabashed arrogance. I'd seen it on my ex-husband's face a million times before, back when I was married to him. I'd been intimidated then.

Now, it only made me rage.

"Here's what I don't doubt: you want the hotel because it's linked to something that happened to you decades ago." Eek. I'd blown through our plan to methodically question the mayor. Oh well.

Oliver shifted nervously. "Well, Amelia, uh, I don't…"

"No," I interrupted sharply. Something about the mayor, from his snarky comment at the café the other day to his arrogant smirk today, got under my skin. My mind flashed to the ghostly Billy, crying dry tears. Then I recalled the horrific vision of his murder.

Billy needed my help. Billy needed justice. I wanted to end this saga, now. Starting with this, this...

Murderer.

"You did it. You're the root of all the problems, Mr. Mayor." I rose, jabbing at the air with my finger, unable to contain my anger.

"Uh-oh," whispered Oliver.

"That's quite the allegation, ma'am." Norton's words came out slow, his southern drawl more pronounced. "Care to explain yourself?"

I swallowed hard, then glanced back at the door to make sure it was still closed. I turned back to Norton and ignored Oliver, who was tugging at my sleeve. I was all in now. To heck with this man who thought he could get away with such an awful crime.

"You killed Billy," I spat. "I saw it in a vision. Billy told me what happened."

After glaring at me for a millisecond, Norton disintegrated into laughter. He tipped his head back, howling. "A vision! You've been in town for five minutes and you're already having visions. So typical of a tourist. Don't tell me—you're planning on opening your own fortune telling shop here in town, too."

I inhaled a deep breath, feeling my nostrils flare. "We found the watch in the icehouse. On your property. We know it's you. We know you stabbed Billy Jenkins in the attic of the hotel that night in August of 1956. I saw everything because I have psychometry."

The mayor blinked as if he didn't know what I was talking about. He laughed a few more seconds.

"It's a, a, superpower," I stammered. "I can touch things and see the past. Or feel emotions. All from the energy in the item."

Now that I said it aloud, it sounded absurd.

He stopped laughing and leaned on his elbows. "I know what psychometry is. I'm quite familiar with it. And whatever happened that night in 1956 is but a horrible memory, sweetheart."

His tone had softened. My feelings had not. My blood felt like it had reached a boil when I heard him call me *sweetheart.*

"I'm not selling to you. Ever." I sank back down in the seat. "I'd rather go bankrupt."

There was an awkward pause while my angry words hung in the air. Finally, the mayor spoke while threading his fingers together. "That's a shame. I'm offering a fair price for the hotel—"

"From what my research has revealed, it's at least a hundred grand below market level," Oliver interrupted.

"A deal's a deal, and I drive a hard bargain," the mayor said, keeping his gray eyes fixed on me. "If you sell, you can leave town without a care in the world. I know you need the money. I've done my research on you, Amelia Matthews. Divorced, lost your little cookie business, the cost of living in California's sky high. I'm sure you can use a couple hundred thousand dollars."

He was correct, but I wasn't going to tell him that. Two hundred grand would go a long way in helping me start a new life somewhere.

He shuffled some papers on his desk while I sat and stewed in my anger. "I don't need your money."

"I don't know the ins and outs of your finances. But more importantly, I fear you won't know how to handle Billy's spirit when it grows stronger. This isn't a situation for amateurs. Billy is going to become more powerful and dangerous as the months go on. Ever since Annie died, he's been beside himself. The place needs to be knocked down."

"Oh, and you know how to deal with an angry ghost?" I scoffed. "You're the only man in town who can handle such a thing. A man has arrived to save the day. Great. Thanks. I'll be over here, the helpless little woman."

Oliver shifted in his seat. "Surely, Mayor, you're not the only person in town who can handle a malevolent spirit. I'm certain we can find a medium to help."

Could we? I gaped at Oliver. Why hadn't he mentioned this option before?

Norton chuckled softly. "I'm afraid not. Don't you think Shirley would've hired that expert if it was that simple? She tried for years to evict Billy."

Oliver's face crumpled into a scowl. Norton had a point, and even my aunt in her letter had said as much.

"Why are *you* so uniquely qualified?" I asked.

The smile that spread on his face was downright evil. "Because you're correct. I killed Billy. And I'm the only one who can free him from the prison of his purgatory."

Oliver and I turned our heads in tandem to stare at each other.

"Is that true?" I whispered.

Oliver mouthed the words I DON'T KNOW.

I focused once again on the mayor. "Why did you kill him? What a stupid, terrible thing to do. Shameful."

The mayor nodded slowly. "It was. It was the biggest regret of my life, and one I've never told anyone until now."

I reared back. This man was either incredibly stupid for unloading his confession to us, or something was deeply, mentally wrong with him. I didn't like either possibility.

"It feels kind of cathartic to talk about it, in fact." He rose and went to the bookcase, running his hand over the leather-bound volumes. "Back then, a lot of people speculated that I killed Billy because I was in love with Annie."

"Were you?" Oliver asked. He looked so eager to hear the answer that I thought he might pull out a notebook and pen.

Norton shook his head. "No. I wasn't. Not at all. Annie was a nice girl and all, but no. There was something more complex between me and Billy."

My stomach sank as a realization hit me. "Oh, no. I'm sorry. I'm sure being gay back then must have been so difficult."

Norton scrunched his nose. "Gay? That wasn't the issue between us. We weren't gay. Billy was blackmailing me."

"What?" Oliver and I yelped at the same time.

"I was a pretty rotten student, so I paid Billy to write a history essay for me. It got an A, of course, because Billy was an excellent student and whip-smart. I thought it was all a big joke, and Billy did it to help me out. We were friends and co-workers at the hotel. We had the best time earlier that summer at the hotel…" his voice faded and he stared into space, as if he were reliving those moments from decades ago.

"How did you go from having a great summer to killing Billy?" Oliver asked.

Norton rubbed his mouth and walked back over to the desk. He picked up a pen, then sat. "Billy threatened to tell the teacher, the principal, and my folks about my cheating on the exam."

I rolled my eyes. "You got away with literal murder. I can't imagine the consequences for cheating on a test would've been that bad."

Norton made a clicking noise with his tongue. "I didn't want to risk it. My dad insisted I go to college, and cheating would've disqualified me. When I saw Billy that night at the hotel, I begged him not to tell anyone. But he said he was going to, the next day. I acted impulsively and stabbed him. Then I cleaned my fingerprints off every surface. Of course, I panicked and fled. I was also a bit drunk."

"You happened to be carrying a knife around." I smirked. "Sure. Totally not premeditated."

Norton hung his head. "I was breaking down cardboard boxes for the owner, it's why I had the knife. Mr. Mortimer had me work late. Back then, the hotel was more of a boarding house, and no one was staying there that evening. The owner had gone out, so I was alone. I didn't even know Billy would be coming by."

"Hmm." His story seemed plausible. Still. "Billy told me you were jealous."

Norton lifted a shoulder. "Ghosts don't always tell the truth, you know."

I huffed in indignation. "Neither do living people."

Then it dawned on me that if ghosts did lie, perhaps Billy wasn't telling the truth about other things, as well. Or maybe Norton was lying. Gah. I couldn't focus on that now.

"Fine. Work your magic on Billy and I'll sell to you. How's that for a deal?" It seemed like a reasonable compromise, one that would at least save the town from… whatever terrible havoc Billy could wreak.

Norton smirked. "No deal. Sell, then I take care of the problem."

"You're a terrible negotiator," I retorted.

Norton shrugged in response. "I'm in no hurry. But you seem like you are."

I looked from him to Oliver, then back to him. "Why would you confess to us? It makes no sense. You confessed to murder. That's pretty dumb."

It was one more wild detail in a place that didn't make sense.

"Yeah, we can walk next door to the police department and ask them to reopen the cold case," Oliver added.

The mayor inhaled and sat up straight. "It's my word against yours. And there's zero evidence. There's nothing tying me to the death, and I was cleared decades ago after extensive questioning. That watch and the icehouse are my property, so you were the ones who were committing a crime by breaking and entering. I'm only telling you so you can make an informed decision about selling the inn."

"So, basically, you're giving me a choice. Sell the hotel to you and there's no justice for Billy's death, or don't sell and deal with Billy on my own?" I folded my arms in front of me. This guy was a piece of work.

"Pretty much. If you choose the latter option, know that you are opening the town up to the possibility of a malevolent spirit growing so powerful that it could take over."

Admittedly, that sounded serious. But I didn't trust Norton, not one bit. I huffed out a breath and stood. "Well, I guess we'll see about all that. I'm not selling because I'd rather take my chances with an angry ghost than an opportunistic, greedy murderer. Oliver, we're done here."

He also stood and followed me to the exit. As I was yanking the door open, Mayor Norton's creaky old voice hit my ears. I turned in time to see him wagging his crooked finger at me.

"You'll find out soon enough, Mrs. Matthews, that communicating with the living is far easier than dealing with the dead."

Chapter Twenty-Four

I began ranting the minute we were on the steps of City Hall and didn't stop until we reached Ice Ice Baby. Oliver had suggested we "sit a spell" to "calm our nerves."

It took a half hour, a cup of iced coffee, and one carrot cake muffin to lower my blood pressure.

"I haven't been this angry with a man since my divorce." I glanced at the pastry case, wondering if this was a valid excuse to eat two muffins. Deciding against it, I turned my attention back to Oliver, who was studying me with a concerned expression. "I'm sorry for taking up your morning. You probably have things to do."

He shook his head. "I do need to head to campus soon. You going to be okay? Would you rather come with me for the day and hang out at the University? Maybe it would get your mind off things? There's a library, and a museum, and several places to eat."

The offer was so sweet and he looked so earnest that I almost wanted to say yes, but I shook my head. "I need to be at the hotel. Need to think about what's next."

"Are you sure? I'm worried about you."

"Now that I have some caffeine in me, I'm good. In fact, I'll walk to the hotel from here, then walk back to your place later. I need the exercise and to clear my head."

After some protests, Oliver left, but not before promising to text each other if we came up with any brilliant ideas about the mayor. I stayed behind to finish my coffee, then bought a few more muffins for the road, figuring that Jimbo would surely eat a couple.

The half-mile stroll to the hotel was pleasant enough, but even the beautiful tropical landscaping and all of the friendly greetings from folks on the street didn't take my mind off my problem.

At the hotel, I said hi to Jimbo, handed him the muffins, and got an update on the hotel. The air conditioner repair guy was scheduled to come again later today to check the system, he said.

"But we all know why it went on the fritz," he added. "That was wild last night."

"Yeah." I sighed. "The air seems to be okay now, thank goodness."

Jimbo nodded. "At least until Billy decides otherwise."

I winced. "Any news on the bachelorette party?"

"Oh, yes ma'am." Jimbo tapped on the computer keyboard. "They've confirmed it will be a party of five, so every room will be taken. Oh, and they want midnight bloody marys on Friday night. That's Friday the 13th, by the way."

I scrubbed my face with my hands. "Did my aunt offer all those extras?"

Jimbo nodded. "It's all on the website, the add-ons, tours, and snacks. Usually, people only pick one or two things, but this group wants the full experience. They're determined to see a ghost or something supernatural, and are equally as bent on getting their drink on."

They would have the full ghost experience if I couldn't figure out a way to get rid of Billy. "Okay, let's organize everything for them. As long as they've paid the deposit, we're good to go. We've still got time to prepare the rooms. In the meantime..."

Jimbo looked up from the computer screen. "Yes, ma'am?"

"I'll be in my aunt's place. I've got a lot of paperwork to catch up on."

"For sure, Miss Amelia. Let me know if you need any help."

I thanked Jimbo profusely — he really was a gem — and went into the library. There, I pulled aside the bookcase, thinking that if I lived here, I'd probably change this setup. It was definitely cool, having a hidden door in a library. But it wasn't practical.

For a few minutes, I paced from room to room in the small apartment, wondering what I should do. Selling was an option. So was running away and leaving all this behind. But neither of those felt right.

I was connected to this place, this hotel, whether I liked it or not. And I wasn't the type to give up. Heck, I even had a difficult time not finishing books that I hated. My need to see things through had resonated through my life. That I'd clung to my terrible marriage was one example of that.

Was this a similar situation? I'd learned during my divorce that sometimes it was better to give up than fight. Better to be happy than right.

This was a different situation than a relationship, though. This was about justice. It was also about carrying on my aunt's legacy and keeping her vision for this quirky old hotel alive. I wanted this place to survive, and I'm certain Shirley did, too.

I stopped in the living room, where the antique mirror had been moved from its spot for the séance. Perhaps if I could chat with Billy alone, I could talk some sense into him. Yes, that seemed logical.

While trembling slightly, I put my flat palm on the cool glass of the mirror, as I did last night. I felt my skin warm, then…

Nothing.

No fog, no feelings, and most importantly, no Billy.

"Hello?" I called out, pressing my hand harder into the glass, tilting my head so my ear was closer to the mirror. "Billy? You in there?"

The warmth in my palm faded. I said Billy's name a few more times, then felt silly. I was talking to a mirror. It felt like I was being gaslighted by a ghost.

"Am I crazy?" I muttered aloud while taking my hand off the glass. "Maybe I am."

I wandered into the bedroom, feeling frustrated and defeated. I changed into more casual clothes that I'd brought in a big tote bag. Why couldn't I conjure Billy? Why had my power worked before, and not now? What was I going to do? Nothing made sense.

Impatiently, I pulled open a nightstand drawer. There was a long, black box embossed with the name of a jeweler, and atop that was a yellow sticky note.

XMAS

Amelia and Freddie

She'd bought us holiday gifts? "Awww," I whispered aloud.

Sitting on the bed, I pulled the box out and opened it, revealing a stunning gold necklace with a giant red pendant, and a matching bracelet. Upon further inspection, the bracelet appeared to be a dog or cat collar.

Both looked expensive and I wondered if they were real rubies.

"So pretty," I whispered, my finger tracing the gemstone. A pang of sadness went through me at the thought of my aunt dying before giving the gift.

I carefully took the jewelry out of its spot and slipped it around my neck. I rose and checked myself out in the mirror over the vanity. It was gorgeous.

But why had she decided to buy me a gift after all these years? Usually she sent only a card, early in the holiday season. I would send one back shortly after. Last year, I'd included a photo of Freddie with a photoshopped Santa hat (because of course he'd never wear a real one).

I took out the other piece of jewelry, and indeed, it was a cat collar. Odd. I touched the red stone around my neck and frowned. Was it slightly warm? Or was that me imagining things?

Then it hit me like a tidal wave: perhaps this was one of my aunt's clues.

I touched the pendant again and it seemed warmer. Maybe this somehow gave me different powers. Or enhanced my own.

I ran into the living room and stopped in front of the mirror. This time I placed both palms flat against the glass.

"Billy?" I shouted in my sharpest, scolding mom voice. "Come on, Billy. Come out of there. Now!"

I waited a second. Then another.

Nothing.

I pushed a little harder and the mirror skidded back a few inches. Swearing aloud, I stepped back. My hands weren't tingling and the pendant was as cool as a stone.

The pendant hadn't been a clue at all. Like everything else, it led me to a dead end.

"I gotta get out of here," I muttered and grabbed my belt bag, strapping it around my waist. I stalked through the exit, into the library. I carefully shut the hidden bookcase door and went into the lobby.

"Jimbo?" I called out.

He looked up from the computer, where he was playing solitaire. "Oh, hey there, ma'am. I mean, Miss Amelia."

"I'm going for a walk. Need to clear my head." I took a few steps toward the door, then whirled around. "Sorry for being so short with you. I'm frustrated."

Pulling open the door, I stomped out. Then I marched down the street, feeling purposeful until I realized that I didn't have any idea or plan of where I was going.

A metaphor for my entire life.

While I walked, I ruminated on my life and problems. The searing Florida sun bored into me, the moisture in the air invading every pore. I glanced at the sky, squinting. There were clouds on the horizon, fast moving, ominous and gray.

I didn't care.

By the time I reached the Enchanted Eternity cemetery, the clouds had overtaken the entire sky. Oppressive humidity caused everything to droop like the Spanish moss in the oak trees.

Normally, I wasn't in the habit of strolling around cemeteries in the middle of the afternoon. But this seemed like as good a place as any to ponder my dismal future, especially since no one was around and I could have a public breakdown alone.

Thunder clapped overhead. I began to chuckle bitterly at the timing of it all. It would be my luck that I'd be stuck in a graveyard in a rainstorm while sweating my tush off in Florida. This wasn't something I'd tell my brother, or my daughter. They'd be alarmed if they saw me now. I could almost feel the mascara running down my face.

Reliable old Amelia, who dresses in mom jeans and owns a fanny pack.

Maybe this was a sign to return home to California. But what would I be returning to?

An empty house? Lots of bills? Fake friends who gossiped behind my back about my divorce? An ex-husband who was running around town, bragging about how he'd taken over my old, profitable business?

I stopped in the middle of a circle of graves and buried my face in my hands. Did I have to solve all of these problems today? Wasn't there something to take my mind off all this stress?

I looked up toward the gray sky as a fat raindrop plopped on my arm. It rarely rained in California, but when it did, I loved to bake.

That's what I needed. Stress baking. Procrasti-baking. Cookies. I imagined myself in Oliver's beautiful kitchen, measuring and stirring my worries away while the sky opened outside.

I could make cookies for all of my new friends. That would be far better than standing here, worrying. But what kind? I could do the chocolate chip chunk, my signature recipe, but I wanted something snazzier, more meaningful…

I recalled the snickerdoodle recipe I'd seen on a grave here the other day when I was with Liz. That was the recipe. Where was it? I started out walking through the rows of graves. Those were the perfect cookies for fall, and I was confident I could make them soft and irresistible.

The place seemed bigger today, now that I was here alone. The granite headstones seemed to stretch forever.

I began to walk faster, a frenzied feeling overtaking my chest. The theme song to that old movie, "The Good, The Bad, and The Ugly" began to play in my mind.

I started to jog, the stones whizzing by. Various things went through my mind as I searched for the grave cookie recipe.

My aunt. Her cryptic letters. Billy, and his sad, ghostly weeping. Annie, who maybe never found true love. How everything in their lives — and my own — was so frustratingly in limbo.

By now tears were streaming down my face and I was running through the columns of graves.

Surely, I looked like a crazy person. Reliable me had given way to a disorganized hot mess.

But I didn't care. Maybe this was my midlife meltdown. Maybe menopause had finally gotten the upper hand. Maybe this was the universe's way of telling me that this was the end and I needed to accept that life was far different now.

Who cared? I was out of ducks.

It began to rain harder, and the toe of my sneaker hit a rock. A swear word slipped out of my mouth. I went sprawling. I had one thought before I hit the ground.

Don't knock your teeth out! Your dental insurance sucks!

I landed on my stomach. Thick, fluffy grass broke my fall. Rain pelted my back and I started to sob for real. My hair was soaked and caked with mud. This was the blackest moment. The lowest point. My personal nadir.

Thunder boomed overhead. Great. Now I'd probably be struck by lightning on top of it all. A strangled cry escaped my mouth.

I raised my head. Before me was a gravestone. The letters carved into the rock swam before my vision. I struggled to rise to my knees. As I did, I noticed the pendant around my neck had grown cold, like a chunk of ice. The cool sensation spread through my body. A corresponding chilly breeze soared through the air, evaporating my sweat.

When I read the name on the grave, I tipped my head back and laughed aloud, knowing that the universe had led me straight to this point.

"Annie Baer, we finally meet."

Chapter Twenty-Five

I climbed to my feet while brushing the mud and grass off my khaki capris and green shirt. There were grass stains on my pants, but that didn't matter because I knew I was onto something.

The universe had led me here. Did I now believe in the universe? In kismet? In serendipity? In fate?

I did. One hundred and ten percent.

For a few seconds, I studied this side of the headstone, looking for clues. Aside from Annie's name, there were only two words underneath.

Blue Moon

I snapped a picture. That had to mean something. Maybe it was a message to Billy. Or to me. Pausing for a second, I tried to recall the words to the song. I couldn't, so I pulled it up on my streaming music app.

Elvis' voice, baritone and ghostly, sounded tinny coming out of my phone speaker. Still, the song provided a melancholic, atmospheric soundtrack for this solemn moment. My face was wet with rain and tears and I wiped the moisture away with my hand. It didn't help much, because the tears kept coming.

The song was evocative, filled with youthful yearning and desire. Exactly what I'd felt when I saw the vision of Billy and Annie.

I moved quickly to the back of the grave, holding onto the phone and listening to the song. As expected, there was a recipe, a long list of ingredients written in small script. Moving closer, I wish I had reading glasses to properly see. Finally, I found the right angle and distance.

Love Potion For My Billy

"This is it," I shouted. "Billy, I can help you!"

My tears evaporated, replaced by excitement.

1 c. red rose petals

½ cup hibiscus flowers

½ cup rose hips

½ cup spearmint

¼ cup orange peel

½ cup fresh squeezed Florida orange juice

¼ cup cinnamon bark chips

Handful of hawthorn leaves

Two shavings catuaba bark

One rose quartz crystal

A fifth of vodka

"Whoa," I said, reading that last one aloud. "Now we're talking."

4 cups sugar syrup

1 tablespoon orange blossom water

I pumped my fist in the air and snapped several photos. This was the recipe, the potion Billy had mentioned. The one that could reunite him with Annie.

Or…was it?

If the recipe was on her grave, and she'd obviously written the instructions, why hadn't she simply made the concoction and gotten back together with Billy on her own time? What was the catch? Or was my aunt right in that I was the key piece of this puzzle?

As the rain tapered off and the song ended, I pondered this question as I circled the grave several times. Perhaps there was a reasonable explanation. Did it matter, though? It was the only chance I had to solve this situation.

Once again, I pulled out my phone. But instead of taking photos, I started a group chat with Liz, Oliver, Sage, Marisol, and Jimbo.

> Hi friends-

> I think I've found the spell or tincture or potion that Billy mentioned. We have to meet tonight at the hotel. Are you all available? Here's what we need:

I typed out all the ingredients. Most seemed like run-of-the mill things one could get at a grocery store. A couple, though, like the cautaba bark, were more esoteric and I said a silent prayer that one of these wacky and wonderful people would have the items lying around.

Within seconds, Liz texted back.

> On it. I've got all of these items in the store and home, but someone will have to stop for the vodka because I drank my stash. Anything else?

I nodded at the screen. "Nice," I whispered.

A record player. And whatever record of Elvis' that came out in 1956 that included the song Blue Moon

I'll bring those things

That was from Oliver.

I've got the perfect bottle of vodka for this ceremony. I have some from a trip to Russia. Oh, this is Sage.

When did you go to Russia, girl? This is Jimbo

Laughing, I glanced up from the phone in time to see a full rainbow in the sky. It was over direction the hotel, or at least where I thought the hotel was. I nodded my approval. Oh yeah. The universe was finally smiling on me.

It was about damn time.

* * *

"Let's move the mirror over there." I pointed to a space in the middle of the room.

Jimbo and Oliver nodded as they carried it to the spot. It hadn't been easy getting the bulky, standalone mirror up the narrow stairs, but they'd done it without damage.

Pressing my hands into my hips, I surveyed the attic. Within a few hours, we'd transformed it from a dusty storage space into… a less dusty storage space, with room for the mirror, two folding card tables covered in batik-print cloth, and six people.

Everyone from the previous séance was here. Marisol was

at one of the tables, stirring the potion. She'd mixed everything carefully while chanting. The rose quartz crystal made a scraping sound against the glass bowl as she moved the wooden spoon in a circle through the liquid.

Oliver, Sage, and Liz were deep in conversation nearby. Jimbo was polishing the mirror with a rag, while Freddie was again rubbing his mouth against the mirror's feet.

I walked over to Marisol while mopping my brow. It was sweltering up here, probably because Billy had tampered with the air again. "Do you think we're ready?"

"I do. How are you feeling?"

I shook out my hands. "Dunno. Nervous."

"You'll be perfect. I'm glad you found the pendant, too."

"Yeah, that was pretty shocking, finding it. Shirley had written my name on a sticky note atop the box. Did you know she'd bought the necklace for me?"

Marisol shook her head. "Had no clue. But from what I can see, it looks like a protection pendant. It's interesting that Shirley bought one for you and your cat. She never mentioned Freddie to me."

"I'd sent a photo of Freddie in my last Christmas card. What is a protection pendant, anyway? Will it keep me from getting killed by a nasty spirit?"

"Not exactly. It's more about protecting yourself with inner strength. It helps clarify thoughts and boosts your faith and powers. Rubies also signify protection. For you and for Freddie."

"Those are things we definitely need tonight." I sipped in a breath. "I hope it helps a little, and I really don't want Freddie caught up in anything dangerous."

"In my experience, spirits won't get involved with animals. Freddie's here for you. Remember that when you need comfort. He'll also feel the protection of the stone, but in a different way than you."

"I've felt the stone changing temperature depending on the circumstance."

She nodded. "Sounds like a protection pendant to me. Okay, do you remember the sequence of the ceremony, or do you want to go over the order of it all again?"

"I remember everything. Let's do this."

Nodding, she lifted the spoon out of the punchbowl. The concoction looked like something I would've drank in college during a Halloween party. Dried flower petals floated among the cinnamon sticks and spearmint leaves. The entire thing smelled like flowers and alcohol. The Russian vodka seemed pretty potent.

"I'll pour the potion into the glasses." Marisol reached for a silver ladle and a wine glass. "I really wish we had those chalices."

We'd spent a solid half-hour looking for a set of chalices that my aunt allegedly owned. Since we were unable to find them — we'd turned Shirley's apartment upside down — we settled on crystal champagne flutes.

I walked over to Liz, Oliver, and Sage, telling them we were about to begin. Then I scooped up Freddie and asked Jimbo to join us at the larger of the card tables.

We gathered around. Marisol placed flutes of the potion in front of everyone. I got something extra, in addition to the drink: a crystal bowl containing some of the concoction.

"May this session begin with an incantation," Marisol said. "Sage, you may speak the opening words."

Sage nodded gravely and removed her pink cowboy hat. None of us had time to change, and I was still in my grass-stained pants.

With a strong, clear voice, she closed her eyes and began.

Underneath the starry skies,
Where the realm of spirit lies,
I call upon the cosmic thread,
To guide our friend Billy who's lost, now undead.
Through the veil of time and space,
Grant us, spirits, your embrace.
With open hearts, we gather here,
To bring two loved ones near and dear.
By the power of earth and sky,
In this place where spirits fly,
Let our voices join as one,
To mend the bond that once was undone.

Sage opened her eyes and glanced to me, nodding. I nodded back.

"That was beautiful," I said, taking the cue that Marisol and I had rehearsed earlier. "Now I'd like to call forth our spirit friend."

I released Freddie, who began to yowl and pace around the mirror. Holding the little crystal bowl firmly in the palm of my left hand, I walked toward the far end of the attic, near the window that overlooked the backyard.

"This is where Billy Jenkins passed." I dipped my fingers into the potion and flicked the drops on the wooden floor. As I repeated this motion three times, I felt the pendant and my fingers grow warm. Freddie stopped his yowls and sat in the middle of the floor. He wore the cat collar that my aunt had bought, and his whiskers twitched.

Something was happening.

I returned to the table and set the bowl down. Then I nodded to Oliver.

He stepped to the other folding table, where an old, suitcase-style turntable sat. The case was open, and a stack of record albums were next to it. Oliver selected a record, slid it out of its sleeve, and placed it on the turntable. He flicked a switch and twisted a knob, then lifted the arm and placed the needle on the vinyl.

The scratchy sound evoked decades past, and the candles illuminating the room flickered. Oliver returned to the table as Elvis' voice singing Blue Moon filled the air. Everyone stood, looking at me. I raised my champagne glass and tried to speak clearly and from the heart.

By the power of love's sweet grace,
In this mystic, sacred space,
I brew this potion, pure and true,
To kindle hearts both old and new.
With herbs and spices, we unite,
To summon spirits into the light.
With this elixir, pure and clear,
May love and longing now draw near.

I took a sip. Not going to lie, it tasted like minty chai with a rose aftertaste. I'd had worse, much worse, so I took another big sip. Peeking out one eye, I saw that Sage, Liz, and Marisol had downed theirs in one gulp. Oliver and Jimbo were taking it slower, with soft grimaces on their faces.

I finished the rest. It was then that I noticed it was pretty warm here in this attic.

"It's now time to summon Billy," Marisol said in a gentle voice.

I turned and walked to the mirror. Instead of reflecting my image, the fog had returned. This was a positive sign.

"Let's do this, Billy Jenkins," I whispered, placing both hands into the fog. This time, I couldn't even feel the glass. It was only eternity beyond my hands.

The lights flickered, went out, then flamed bright again.

"Oh, boy, here we go," Jimbo muttered in his Florida drawl.

A ghostly gray hand extended from the fog. This was my cue to step back.

"Billy? Hello?" I asked. "We've got some news for you about Annie, and we'd like you to come out. We've found the potion."

I took another step back. A thumping noise filled the attic. It almost sounded like footsteps, and we all glanced around. This was not part of the plan.

The sound wasn't coming from the mirror. It seemed to be from…the stairs? We all stared at the door leading to the staircase.

When it flung open, I gasped.

When I saw Mayor Larry Norton's head poke into the room, I pointed. "Get him out of here!"

Oliver began to move in his direction. But we all froze when Billy climbed out of the mirror, grinning. I'd seen him do this before, but it was no less shocking a second time.

"Where is she?" he asked. "Where's Annie?"

Chapter Twenty-Six

I had a few brief seconds to choose what to focus on: Mayor Norton crashing the party, or Billy's ghost.

I chose the ghost. Oliver had the rest under control. He walked toward Norton and leaned into his ear. He pointed to a chair next to a wall, and Norton nodded. The old man's eyes were wide and hadn't moved off Billy since he stepped in the room. He sank into the seat, seemingly stunned.

He rasped Billy's name, and Oliver shushed him. I sent a glare his way and put my index finger to my lips. The mayor nodded but looked terrified.

Whatever. That was his problem. I'd deal with him later. Now, I had to reunite two dead people.

"Hi, Billy. She's on her way. We need to do the spell. We found it on her gravestone." I wondered if I should inform Billy that his killer was in the room. But if Billy could only see and communicate with me, then perhaps there was no need. Yeah. I'd go with that. The last thing I wanted was a fight between a ghost and an elderly murderer.

Or perhaps I should let them settle it between themselves.

It hit me that I was winging this entire thing. I fought back a cringe.

Billy was dressed in the same clothes as before and also sported the same saucy grin. He shrugged. "Fine with me. Let's hope this works."

Liz refilled my champagne glass and handed it to me. I pounded it like a shot, coughed a little, then began.

Spirits of the past, arise, I pray,
In this twilight, guide your way.
May love's embrace your souls ignite,
As we weave our magic here tonight.
As I sip this potion, enchanted and bright,
Let love's warm glow be our guiding light.
With open hearts and spirits aglow,
Let love between Billy and Annie forever flow.

The candles extinguished, plunging everything into pitch blackness. The song had ended, and everything was silent and heavy. It was as if the entire room was holding its collective breath.

That's when the fog in the mirror began to shift and spill onto the floor like that fake smoke at concerts back in the early 90s. Then the smoke began to sparkle. It was the only illumination in the room, and I walked over to it, running my hand through the glittering, cool air.

"Annie?" I whispered. "Are you there?"

The fog began to clear, giving way to a bright, golden light.

"Move back, I think she's coming," Billy said in an excited tone that cracked a little, like it would with a teenager.

I stepped aside in time for a female form to emerge from

the mirror. She was elderly, and like Billy, was a luminescent gray. I noticed that the locket was around her wrinkled neck.

"Annie!" Billy cried.

"Is it you, my love?" Annie said in a creaky voice.

The two embraced, their ghostly bodies merging and blending. My entire body tingled as I watched the pair hug and kiss. It was an entirely private moment, but instead of feeling like I was intruding, it seemed as though I was the most privileged person in the world to witness their love.

It was only after a few seconds that I realized tears were flowing down my cheeks.

The two ghosts broke apart. To my shock, they'd changed.

"You…oh my goodness," I whispered.

Billy had grown older, his nose longer and his brow heavier. Annie had gotten younger, her wrinkles smoothed and her chin firmed. Apparently, some sort of ghostly Botox had helped her, which was impressive.

Universe, I see what you did for Annie, and when I reach that phase in my celestial journey, I'd appreciate the same facial treatment…

It seemed as though both were in their thirties. They were smiling and holding hands as if they'd been a couple for decades. What kind of magic was this?

"You're together," I sniffled. "And you're the same age."

Billy nodded. "Finally. Finally! Look at how beautiful she is."

Annie looked up at him, grinning. She leaned into his ear and whispered something. He chuckled.

"She can't communicate directly with you, but she wants me to thank you."

I nodded, tears getting in my mouth. "Please tell her you're welcome."

She really was a gorgeous person. Er, ghost. She looked like something out of Vogue, if the year was 1976. She wore a pantsuit with flared legs and a large, chunky necklace, while he wore what looked to be a leisure suit with wide lapels, an open shirt, and a chain around his neck. Odd, but apparently everyone didn't look like Victorian-era ghosts in flowing nightgowns.

Someone had to look like they were going disco dancing in the afterlife.

"I'm glad y'all are together," I finally said after watching them nuzzle each other for a few minutes. Billy broke from her lips.

"Amelia, I can't thank you enough. Honestly, I didn't think you were up for the task. But you did it. Now I can get out of this limbo and live with my true love for eternity."

I pressed my hand to my chest, overcome with emotion. "It was an honor to help. I was really thrown off when Mayor Norton told me he killed you because of an argument over a test."

Billy rolled his eyes. "Yeah, I took that test for him. It wasn't a big deal. He killed me because of my relationship with Annie. If he didn't tell you that, he's lying."

He kissed Annie's temple. "But in the end, I won. I guess this is so long, pal."

"Wait," I said, extending my hand in a stop motion. "I have a couple more questions. If the potion recipe was on Annie's grave, why didn't she make it herself and reunite with you decades ago?"

Billy whispered something to Annie, who responded. I couldn't hear her words and waited for Billy to explain.

"She tried," he said. "But after a few attempts, including once with your aunt, she realized she needed someone with the power of psychometry to touch the mirror. Your aunt remembered your experience with me when you were a little kid and that's when she knew she had to get you here somehow. Soon after, she got sick. She decided to leave you the hotel, in hopes you'd help me. You were the conduit, the medium, the key. We needed you, Amelia. Don't ever underestimate your power. The dead and the living need you."

My jaw dropped. This was too much to process in one night. "Th-thanks," I stammered. "So it was you in the mirror when I was six. And when I was at the antique store? Did you see me? Why did you act like an evil demon?"

Billy tipped his head back and laughed. "Yes, it was. I'm sorry for that. That first time, when you were a kid, I was trying to be funny. You got so scared, though, that I stopped. And yes, it was me in the antique store. I was trying to reach out to you and explain, not be scary. You took it the wrong way."

Who wouldn't, I thought, but didn't say that aloud. "So why didn't you come out when it was just me, earlier today?"

He lifted his shoulders into a ghostly shrug. "Didn't feel like it. That was during my teenage phase."

Time must bend and shift in different directions in his dimensions. I pushed a breath out of my nose. "I see. That makes sense, I guess. Thank you."

"Now I have one last question for you," he said. "Can we hear another Elvis song as we leave?"

"Absolutely. Which one?"

He wrapped his arms around Annie. "Surprise me."

I glanced around until I found Oliver. Our eyes locked and I felt another power surge of heat. It was as if I was looking into Oliver's soul, even though the only illumination in the room was coming from Billy and Annie's ghostly bodies. Super weird.

I nodded. Oliver nodded. We'd expected Billy would ask about Elvis and would appreciate a song. Oliver went to the record player. The strains of Elvis crooning *It's Now or Never* filled the attic.

Billy kissed Annie's temple then turned to me. "This is a cool tune. Elvis became president, didn't he?"

This again. I rubbed my neck. "I'm sure Annie will bring you up to speed on the trajectory of Elvis' career."

"Good thinking. I'm sure she will." Billy winked. "Well, see you later, alligator. Thanks again."

"Have a great life. Er, afterlife." I waved.

He guided Annie toward the mirror. As if they were climbing into a luxury car, they stepped into the sparkling fog, flickered, and disappeared. A surge of happiness went through me and I clapped my hands together.

It felt like a party, a wedding, New Year's, Passover, and Christmas all at once.

The room remained dark for a beat, then the candles flickered to life. So did the air conditioner. It blew a strong stream of welcome, cold air out of the two vents in the ceiling, evaporating the sweat on my face.

With my jaw still hanging open in a dazed half-smile, I did a quick check on everyone to make sure they were okay.

Marisol was at the table, smiling beatifically.

Liz was, too.

Sage and Jimbo were helping themselves to another glass of potion.

Oliver was cueing up a record.

Freddie had jumped up onto a trunk and was snoozing.

And Mayor Norton, well, he was still in the chair, slumped

against the wall. His eyes were wide open, as if he was shocked to his core. He looked unnaturally stiff.

"Oh, no!" I ran to him.

With my hands on his shoulders, I shook hard. "Mayor. Mayor! What's going on?"

All the shaking didn't rouse him. It also didn't make him shut his eyes. By now, everyone was clustered around us. The record began to play, and I immediately recognized the tune. I was even more shocked to remember when I'd first heard it: in this very house, when I was six. My aunt had the album.

Dean Martin's *Memories Are Made of This.*

Oliver leaned over me and pressed his fingers to Norton's neck. He held his hand over Norton's nose and mouth while shaking his head.

"He's dead," Oliver murmured.

Well. Maybe there was justice for Billy after all.

Epilogue

Eight days later…

"Hey, pardner! You want a veggie burger or a cow burger?" Sage pointed in my direction with a long spatula.

I held the phone away from my ear. "Cow," I called out. "Medium rare. Thanks."

"You got it." Sage turned back to the grill.

I returned to the call. "Where are you?" my brother Mike asked.

"I'm at the place I'm staying and we're having a cookout. Oliver and Sage. I told you about them. They're brother and sister. It's just the girls here today, though. Me, Sage, Liz, Marisol, and I think even Martha the librarian's coming over."

There was a silence on the line and I thought the call had dropped. "Mike? You there?"

"Yeah, I'm shocked, honestly. I've never known you to make this many friends so quickly. Remember when you moved to California, it took you years to find people to hang out with, and only because you got to know the moms of Jenny's friends."

Figures Mike would be shocked. He was the kind of guy to make lifelong friends while standing in line at the DMV.

I glanced at Liz, who was mixing a pitcher of margaritas, and grinned. "Things have changed."

"Did you go to one of those fortune tellers? Or a tarot card reader?"

As he spoke, the flames in the grill licked up and Sage whooped loudly. I hadn't told him about Billy, or my powers. Right now, I wanted to keep everything close to my heart, here in this town.

They'd find out soon enough.

"No, I didn't. Some things did happen, though. I'll have to tell you and Jenny in person, because you'll never believe me. Hey, she's coming for Thanksgiving. You and our family should, too. I think by that time the hotel lobby refresh should be done."

With the help of one of Liz's friends, who was an interior decorator and a "lightworker," I had plans to redecorate some of the common areas in the hotel, starting with the lobby.

I still wasn't sure what a lightworker was, but I was told I could redecorate and cleanse the energy at the same time. Efficient *and* effective.

"We'll see. I'll talk to the wife. But whatever happened, I think it's for the best. Unless you're having a psychotic break. In that case, I'll come down there."

"I'm one hundred percent sane. Happier than I've been in a while, actually."

"Cool beans, sis. I'll be there to visit soon, okay? Give my love to Jenny."

"Kay. Love you."

We ended our call. I craned my neck to look into the window of the garage apartment. Freddie was sitting up there, watching us. I waved at him and he did a slow blink.

It had been a little over a week since we'd reunited Billy with Annie. Since then, the haunted happenings at the hotel had ceased.

The air conditioner was running like a champ, and Jimbo and I had been busy getting the place ready for the bachelorette party, which was scheduled to arrive in two weeks. Fortunately, that gave us enough time to do a quick redecoration of the lobby.

The very first thing I did for the refresh: buy that Tiffany lamp at the antique shop downtown. It now sits on the front desk and will greet every guest that walks in with a warm, welcoming light. I'd also mailed the weird flamingo lawn sculpture to my daughter, who is proudly displaying it in her dorm room in Arizona.

Meanwhile, Freddie and I stayed at Oliver's. I paid for a full two months here because I needed a stable, safe place to crash while I got everything organized. I'd spent the last few days going through my aunt's things and had found one final letter to me.

In it, she said she was sorry she didn't call or write with her dilemma about Billy. She'd planned on asking me here so she could discuss the matter with me personally.

I figured you'd rather hear about a ghost from me in person, than in a Christmas card.

I'd laughed when I read that. Was there ever a good time to find out about a restless spirit?

But time ran out, as it often does. Use your time wisely, my dear.

Shirley also said I'd need to grow into my powers before I could help Billy, which was why she set up something of a scavenger hunt for me — so I wouldn't take shortcuts or try to buy my way out of the Billy problem.

Or sell the hotel to Mayor Norton.

The Crescent Moon Inn is your legacy, too, Amelia

Eventually, I'd move into my aunt's apartment and embrace the legacy, but I wanted to sell my house in California and bring a few things here first. Oliver needed a tenant, and I needed a place to gather my thoughts, so this setup was perfect for the short-term. He'd even given me the option to extend my lease.

Yes, I'd decided to stay in Florida. Not because of my newfound psychic abilities, or because I'd had a dream of running a hotel.

I stayed because of the people. There was something special about this town, and I hadn't felt so welcome in a place, well, ever. Going back to California held all the appeal of a bowl of oatmeal.

Staying in this weird, wacky, charming Florida town felt *right*.

My phone pinged. It was Oliver.

> This event with the historian is going longer than I anticipated. I probably won't be there for the cookout. I'm sorry.

I clicked my tongue against the roof of my mouth. I'd been looking forward to hanging out with Oliver tonight. We'd barely seen each other since the night Billy was reunited with Annie, mostly because Oliver was coordinating tonight's talk on campus with a well-known historian. Apparently, the school did big events on Fridays.

We'll save you a burger.

No need. I'll grab something here. But...

I waited for him to finish that thought.

Want to have dinner tomorrow?

"Absolutely," I whispered as I typed yes.

What can I bring?

Nothing — I wanted to take you to a new place in town that I've heard about. That is, if you like fondue.

"A date? Hmmm," I murmured.

Who doesn't love melted cheese? What time?

I was still beaming when Liz walked over to me, toting two giant, salt-rimmed margaritas. As if on cue, the wireless speaker started to play Jimmy Buffett.

"Your hard-earned margarita, my friend," she said. "Oh, and I forgot to tell you. As a new Floridian, it's the law that you learn the words to Margaritaville."

"Already know them," I said, touching my glass to hers. "Cheers."

Marisol emerged from the house carrying a gorgeous charcuterie board.

"Oh, yeah," I exclaimed when I saw the mountains of cheese and cold cuts.

We all gravitated to the table, seeking shade under the umbrella. It was six at night on a Wednesday, but it was still plenty sunny. Not oppressive though, and all week, Oliver had reminded me that fall had arrived. It was a tad too subtle for me to detect, but I did notice I was sweating less.

As we dug into the charcuterie and drank our margaritas, we chatted about everything and nothing. Like friends do. It felt easy in a way that it never did in California, and I sat there listening and grinning my face off. In between sips of my delicious drink, that is.

"I can't wait to try Amelia's snickerdoodles," Sage said.

"Is that from a gravestone recipe?" asked Liz, and I nodded.

"They're so good," Marisol chimed in, then clapped her palm over her mouth. "Sorry, I tried one when I was assembling the charcuterie."

We all laughed and changed the subject.

"There's a meeting of the Gen X Coven next weekend," Liz said to the group. "Anyone want to go?"

She leaned into me to explain. "That's the coven in town for people our age, who are starting out with their powers. You're welcome to attend."

"Am I a witch? I know I have this power of psychometry, but does that make me a witch?" I scrunched up my nose.

Everyone started talking at once. The consensus was that

while not technically a witch, I could attend the coven meeting.

"You probably should, so you can learn what's possible with your abilities," Sage said.

"A coven is merely a group of people who come together for spiritual or magical purposes," Marisol added.

"Does this mean we're a coven?" I asked. "Since we gathered to bring Billy and Annie together with the help of séances, a magic mirror, and psychometry?"

Everyone nodded.

"You know why witches have covens?" Sage asked.

"Why?" I asked, assuming Liz already knew the answer because she was smiling.

"Because it allows us to practice the best doggone magic of all: female friendship."

Her words inspired tears to well in my eyes. I'd been weeping a lot lately, it seemed. I wept tears of sadness for the life I left behind, but ones of happiness for all that was to come.

I'd shed more tears about the latter.

For the first time in years, I was excited about the future. I had all sorts of plans for the hotel.

But Sage was right.

Here in Florida, I'd found what I'd been looking for all along.

I recalled Billy's words, about how the dead and the living needed me. Perhaps that was more about friendship than anything else. At least that's how I was interpreting it. People needed me. And I needed them.

"What's wrong, honey?" Liz asked.

I shook my head as everyone reached to give my arms a squeeze.

After wiping my tears, I took another sip of my margarita.

"Nothing. Everything's great. For once, everything is perfect."

— THE END —

* * *

Thank you for reading EAT, PRAY, HEX! Your support means more to me than you know. I WANT YOUR HEX, book two in the Crescent Moon Mystery series, is next! You can find it on Amazon, or request at your local library.

Also, read on for Janice Dover's cookie recipe!

Janice Dover's Snickerdoodles With a Twist

This is the recipe that Amelia found on Janice Dover's gravestone in the Enchanted Eternity Park.

According to Liz, Janice had been a trailblazer in the culinary world long before toffee bits were available pre-packaged in the grocery store. In the early 1960s, when Cypress Grove was much smaller and sleepier, Janice had perfected her cookies with toffee bits recipe.

Janice's snickerdoodle cookies were renowned for their irresistible melt-in-your-mouth quality. They were a closely guarded secret until she crossed into the other realm, and the recipe was made available to all.

Ingredients

- 1 cup butter, softened
- 1 ½ cup sugar
- 1 teaspoon cream of tartar
- 1 teaspoon baking soda
- ¼ teaspoon salt

- 2 eggs
- 1 teaspoon vanilla
- 3 cup all-purpose flour
- ¼ cup sugar
- 2 teaspoon ground cinnamon
- 1 cup toffee bits

Instructions

Butter Conjury: Preheat the oven to 350. In a cauldron — okay, a mixing bowl —blend the softened butter and 1 1/4 cups sugar until it becomes one harmonious mixture. This is your base spell, so make it enchanting.

Cream of Mysteries: Sprinkle in the cream of tartar, the baking soda, and just a dash of salt. Mix it until your concoction is as smooth as a witch's brew.

Egg Alchemy: Add the eggs one by one, as if you're hatching dragon eggs. Stir in the vanilla essence, which is basically the potion of dreams.

Flourish of Flour: Gently introduce the all-purpose flour, a bit at a time. Watch as your dough transforms.

Toffee Treasure Hunt: Carefully fold in the toffee bits, like discovering hidden treasures in a mystical forest. Let the dough embrace these morsels.

Cinnamon Enchantment: In a separate bowl, mix the remaining sugar with the ground cinnamon. This is your enchanting dust.

Shape-shifting Time: Roll the dough into small orbs of delight. These orbs are your magical cookies in the making.

Cinnamon Sugar Sorcery: Roll your dough balls in the cinnamon-sugar mix until they shimmer like a sparkly vampire.

Baking Magic: Place your sugary orbs onto a baking tray and let them bake in the enchanted oven at 350°F (175°C). They'll transform into golden-brown wonders over 10-12 minutes.

Cooling Charm: Let your snickerdoodles cool on a wire rack. They're gathering their magical strength.

Summon the Taste Testers: As you bite into one of these mystical creations, you'll realize you've just unleashed a toffee-infused snickerdoodle spell upon the world. Share the magic!

Acknowledgments

All of my love and thanks go to my husband, Marco. He is my rock, and I couldn't do this fiction thing without him.

As Nora Ephron one said, "Secret to life: marry an Italian."

About the Author

Tara Lush is a Florida-based author and journalist. She's an RWA Rita finalist, an Amtrak writing fellow and the winner of the George C. Polk award for environmental journalism.

Previously, she was a reporter with The Associated Press in Florida, covering crime, alligators, natural disasters and politics.

Tara is a fan of vintage pulp fiction book covers, Sinatra-era jazz, 1980s fashion, tropical chill, kombucha, gin, tonic, seashells, iPhones, Art Deco, telenovelas, street art, coconut anything, strong coffee and newspapers. She lives on the Gulf Coast with her husband and two dogs.

Discover more about Tara at www.taralush.com

Also by Tara Lush

<u>**THE COFFEE LOVER'S MYSTERY SERIES**</u>

Grounds for Murder

Cold Brew Corpse

Live and Let Grind

A Bean to Die For

Give Me Chills

THIS SERIES IS ALSO AVAILABLE IN HARDCOVER AND AUDIO.

Made in the USA
San Bernardino, CA
17 August 2016